By Nina Sadowsky

THE EMPTY BED

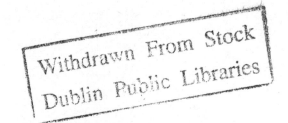
THE EMPTY BED

A Burial Society Novel

Nina Sadowsky

BALLANTINE BOOKS

NEW YORK

Published in the United States by Ballantine Books, an imprint of Random House, a division of Penguin Random House LLC, New York.

BALLANTINE and the HOUSE colophon are registered trademarks of Penguin Random House LLC.

Hardback ISBN 978-0-525-61987-1
Ebook ISBN 978-0-525-61988-8

Printed in Canada on acid-free paper

randomhousebooks.com

2 4 6 8 9 7 5 3 1

FIRST EDITION

Title-page image: © iStockphoto.com

Book design by Dana Leigh Blanchette

*This novel is dedicated with deep thanks to Janet Cooke,
who's believed in my voice since we were students together
at the Bronx High School of Science and whose support
as my "publishing whisperer" has been invaluable
in this chapter of my life.*

*And also to my dad, the Hon. Edward L. Sadowsky, Esq.,
always and still a source of inspiration for his conviction,
intelligence, and principles. Back in high school, Dad,
you thought Janet was trouble. And you were
right in the best possible way.
Love you both.*

THE EMPTY BED

How things begin . . .

I could tell the story differently; of course I could. Every storyteller twists his or her lens to suit an agenda. Or protect the heart.

This impulse to shape the truth is universal, one of the many traits that serve to remind us that we are more alike than we are different.

I find it useful to focus on where we align even as our differences threaten to tear us apart. After all, in order to do what I do, you have to not just learn to see the world through others' eyes, but to live, to breathe, to act, to be another.

Welcome to the Burial Society. Peer into the lens and see what I see.

RISING

——

Catherine,
Phoenix, Arizona

I shut the door of my rental van but don't lock it. It's not only that I don't fear it will be stolen in this exclusive neighborhood; it's that we will need to make a fast exit. The COMPUTER GEEQUE decals I've slapped on its side panels are eye-catching and distinctive (what any witness will remember)—and easily disposable.

The sunbaked asphalt is spongy under the hard soles of my boots. The air is dry as bleached bones, hot and still. The sun, relentless and blinding, hangs directly overhead in a serene blue sky free of any clouds.

I open the passenger door to let Stephanie out and make a mental note to talk to her later about some refinements in her appearance. In her usual uniform of skintight shredded black jeans, rock 'n' roll T-shirt, and leather jacket, bright blue eyes rimmed with kohl, she stands out here in the Arizona suburbs. You can take the girl out of Jersey, but still, she needs to learn to blend in.

I'm also worried she might pass out from the heat in that leather jacket and, purely selfishly, that's the last thing I need right now.

Holding up one hand to signal she should stay put, I pull out a pale pink polo shirt that matches my own and toss it to her.

"Lose the jacket. Put this over your T-shirt."

She complies. It's time to move.

The villa we are targeting sits in a cul-de-sac in a pricey community anchored around a golf course and also featuring a clubhouse, tennis courts, and swimming pools. The monochromatic soft beiges and muted greens of true sunbaked desert should color the landscape here, so the deceptive emerald of the man-made lawns and rolling hills of the golf course give this development a disingenuous feel, temporary, like it could be just a stage set, struck at any moment.

Despite this, the harsh sun reminds us where we really are.

It's why we came at noon; everyone is inside, shades drawn against the blazing sun, air conditioners pumping.

We have a cover story ready if we're stopped, of course, but I'd prefer it if we just slid in and out without anyone noticing. My plan is to get inside her house and then get Leslie Virgenes out of there as quickly and cleanly as possible. If she's there. If not, I'll have to improvise.

We steal across the lawn and past a silver Audi TTS Coupe parked in the driveway of the "Spanish-inspired" villa, a good first sign. We turn the corner and edge along the house to the back door. We did a trial run last night at a sister complex across the road built by the same developer. Under Stephanie's expert tutelage, I picked three kitchen-door locks to get my rhythm down, each one taking progressively less time. Stephanie may need refinements in certain areas, but she has skills and is willing to teach them.

Stephanie joined the Burial Society seventeen months ago. Like most of my recruits, she was a rescue in whom I saw potential. (Her stories, along with those of my other recruits, are tales for another time.)

We snap on latex gloves. I conquer Leslie's lock in less than twenty seconds. As the tumbler clicks over, Stephanie gives me a pleased grin, a teacher proud of her pupil.

We're in. Steph closes the door softly behind us and lifts her shaggy mane of black hair away from her damp neck. The sweat on my skin prickles with chill in a matter of seconds. The powerful hum of the central air system swallows up most sound.

A cup of cold coffee with a congealed ring of cream sits on the gray granite countertop, next to a half-finished piece of toast smeared with peanut butter. A fat fly buzzes lazily over a bowl filled with overripe bananas and a net bag of tangerines. A smaller bowl next to it holds a set of keys. A fob for an Audi is a probable match for the car parked in the driveway.

I extract two loaded syringes of fentanyl from their pouch in the leather satchel strung across my body and hand one to Stephanie. I head through the kitchen into the dining room. Stephanie follows, but then we split paths, she heading toward the front office, den, and main living area, me toward the bedrooms. We've studied the floor plans together, role-played every possible scenario: finding Leslie alone, with her son. Possibly armed. Almost certainly irrational from fear. If Leslie's even still here. My current guess is yes, given the evidence of the car in the driveway and the keys and food in the kitchen.

There will be three bedrooms along this corridor. The first door hangs ajar. The room is tidy and a bit sterile: a guest bedroom. The second door is closed and I push it open. Leslie's son's room, cluttered with sports trophies and posters; the faint aroma of teenage hormones and perspiration discernible even in the chilly air. The room looks like it hasn't been used in a while. A lone striped tube sock sits on the end of the neatly made bed, but otherwise it's tidy, a bit dusty. I'm relieved; the kid is supposed to be away at college (a sophomore playing for the Arizona Wildcats) and it makes my job simpler if he's where he ought to be, someone else dispatched there to ensure he's safe.

The door to the master bedroom is half open, a spill of golden light playing across the russet tile floor of the hallway. I walk toward and then into the light, pushing the door fully open. I enter Leslie Virgenes's private domain, a tastefully and luxuriously appointed master bedroom and bath, the showpiece of the trophy second home she purchased at the pinnacle of her successful career in the pharmaceutical business.

A California king-sized bed with an expensive-looking cream-colored headboard of tufted raw silk dominates the space. The sheets, comforter, and mounds of pillows on the bed coordinate in feminine waves of flowers, all rosy pinks and soft golds except where the stain from her loosened bowels darkens their hue, a foul side result of asphyxiation. A plastic bag is ruthlessly snugged around her head.

My hand flies to my mouth as I fight the sour wash rising up in my throat and the sting in my eyes. We're too late. I back away. They've found her. Killed her. There's no more I can do here. There's no reason to stay.

But it means others I need to protect are in terrible danger.

I swiftly make my way back toward the center of the house. I find Stephanie coming in my direction.

"Nobody," she reports softly. "But the front-door lock was jimmied open. Clean job."

"She's here," I say. "Dead. Poor thing. Didn't think they'd look in her own home?"

The question is rhetorical. I'd tried to help Leslie before she came here, but people don't always listen to reason. Particularly when they're terrified.

"What now?" Stephanie asks.

"We're out of here."

Steph hands me her syringe, and I carefully slip both of them back into their pouch and then into my satchel; we had them ready to drug Leslie only if she wasn't willing to come quietly. We were here to protect her, but she wouldn't have known that.

A framed photograph of Leslie and her son snags my eye. Arms around each other's shoulders. Smiling faces. The same crinkly brown eyes. He was a sperm donor baby; Leslie the only parent in his life. I suppress the rush of empathetic grief I feel for Leslie's teenage boy. We need to get out of here quick and clean.

If they found Leslie, have they found us too?

We slip out of the back of the villa just the way we came, our shoes tapping softly across the Mexican tiles. I pause and scan the empty blandness of the community before we make our move. The heat seems even more oppressive than it did mere minutes ago; perhaps it's the indelible image of Leslie Virgenes's flattened, lifeless face tightly wound in unforgiving plastic. I'm glad I stopped Stephanie before she saw the body. She doesn't need to carry that picture in her head.

I inhale a deep gulp of hot air. The community is quiet as a morgue, except for the angry drone of a lawn mower somewhere in the distance. I nod to Stephanie and we go, slipping quietly across the impossibly green grass, making a beeline for the van. I scan the street, my eyes searching for the telltale flick of a curtain, or a shadow crossing a window, but come up empty.

We climb inside the van and I turn a corner before stopping to quickly strip off the COMPUTER GEEQUE decals. As I hop back behind the wheel, a siren's urgent wail pierces the silence.

I see the flashing cherries of the approaching patrol vehicle. I pull away from the curb slowly and calmly despite my racing heart. I feel in my bones that this is no coincidence. Someone wanted the cops to find us with Leslie's corpse.

Stephanie's eyes are wide; she may not suspect what I do about being set up, but she has enough experience of her own with the police to want to avoid another encounter.

As we pass the squad car, I dare a direct glance at the driver. I see a man, mid-twenties, perhaps, with a slightly doughy face, on which a pair of mirrored aviator sunglasses perch. *A rookie,* I think. *Just a kid.*

I'm glad I can't see his eyes, the "before" picture of innocence that I imagine hides behind his shades. In a matter of moments, those eyes will be altered forever. The sight of the brutally murdered Leslie Virgenes will haunt him for the rest of his days.

In that we are united.

The things we cannot see . . .

These are the things that torment us, even more than the indelible images burned into our mind's eye. The muffled thump on the other side of the wall, the distant scream, the squeal of brakes and crash of metal just outside our view. The things we can't sort and name, evaluate and dissect, make sense of, put to bed.

They loom large, these things we cannot see, even more monstrous for their indistinct forms and blurry edges, for our ability to sketch in the sordid details with the most horrible imaginings.

LEAVINGS

——

Magali Guzman,
New York City

Special Agent Maggie Guzman jogs up the subway stairs and pulls her coat collar a little tighter against the fierce wind whipping through the wind tunnels of downtown Manhattan. She deftly navigates her way through the teeming morning crowds. Makes her way inside a jam-packed corner deli. Luis, the short, stout Puerto Rican guy behind the counter, lifts a bag with her order tucked inside as soon as she enters.

"Toasted sesame bagel butter black coffee," Luis affirms in one breath as he hands her the package and she hands him a five-dollar bill.

"*Gracias,* Luis." Maggie tucks the package under her arm and exits the deli, digging in her briefcase for her badge.

The Federal Building is cold steel, marble, and glass, austere, unwelcoming. But Maggie still feels a thrill every time she enters. She's proud of her work and sometimes still can't believe that the career she's dreamt of since she was a little girl has come to pass.

She greets the security guard manning the employees' side entrance by name and asks after his pregnant wife. As she inserts her SA badge into a turnstile and punches her personal code into the numbered panel, she and the guard chat about due dates and baby names. The glass turnstile slides open. Maggie's sharp eyes take in every detail of the activity surrounding her, despite her friendly conversation with the guard. Her clear-eyed and relentless observation of the world around her is one of the things that make Maggie a good agent. Her supervisor said as much at her last review.

She exits the elevator on the twenty-second floor, flashes her credentials for the FBI cop on duty, and then again inserts her SA card into the security panel and presses the numbers of her personal code. As she makes her way down the hallway—lined with inspirational quotes from former FBI directors—to the squad area, she can hear Ryan Johnson's voice booming.

What is that ass going on about this time?

"No, no, that's not the way I heard it. It went down like this: Yes, she showed up at the bar dressed in a disguise and talked with a bunch of the UC instructors—and only revealed her identity the next morning at the first official day of training. But I also heard"—Ryan's voice drops a notch—"that she flirted with all of them, laid it on really thick, and later blew Connors in the bathroom. That's the real reason they took her."

Maggie burns with a combination of shame, fury, and outrage. *How dare he?* She earned her spot in the undercover training program! Yes, showing up in full makeup, heels, and a sexy dress at the bar where the instructors were known to hang out the night before training began had been a risky stunt, but one that paid off in the end. She'd chatted them up, playing a role all the while. She still thrills to the memory of the slow smile that crawled over Special Agent Connors's face after she morphed into the accent and character she had employed the night before when she'd declined his offer of a drink. She'd showed them she was daring, able to keep her cool, an innovator. But blow him? *Never.*

Maggie reminds herself to breathe. That she is leaving this office to start UC school in just a matter of weeks, while that prick Ryan

Johnson will be staying behind. Twice he'd applied; *rejected twice too.*

Maggie breezes around the corner to see Ryan's broad back and three of her other colleagues facing him. Jim and Bob look like dogs panting for scraps. Karen has a sneer on her face.

"Johnson, you're disgusting," Karen lectures. "A woman can't get ahead without you making up some shit about her?"

"I'm just repeating what I was told."

"About what?" Maggie asks innocently. She decided a long time ago that jerks like Johnson would never see her sweat. It was the first of many lessons her dad taught her over the years, a solemnly sworn vow made when Maggie was just six years old and dealing with her first schoolyard bully.

Ryan spins around.

At least he has the decency to look somewhat embarrassed to see me.

"Oh, nothing. Heard they're changing the cafeteria hours."

"Is that right?" Maggie fixes him with a stare so penetrating it's almost X-ray vision.

"Yeah. Just a rumor, though."

"You might want to watch yourself," Maggie cautions evenly. "Starting rumors is a good way to make enemies."

"Wait, what? Is that? Are you threatening me?" Ryan shifts his bulk from side to side, suddenly uneasy.

Maggie laughs. "What on earth are you talking about, Johnson? Why would I possibly threaten you about *cafeteria hours*? Lighten up, man. By the way, I am truly sorry you didn't make the cut for UC. Better luck next time."

She shoots Ryan a dazzling smile and links an arm through Karen's, pulling her into the maze of baize-covered partitions that take up the center of the floor. More senior agents are the ones granted the windowed offices on the perimeter.

"Thanks for having my back," Maggie says.

"Always, sister. He's such a pig."

"True. But he's not the one starting UC school either, so he can kiss my Latina ass."

"Half-Latina. Why do you deny your Italian heritage?"

"I don't when I'm eating my mother's lasagna. Then I'm a hundred percent Italian."

Both women laugh. "It's just that I know it bothers Johnson that I'm both a spic and a girl. He really thinks that's why I made the cut. That and my supposedly open mouth."

"Well, fuck him."

Maggie recoils in mock horror. "Fuck Ryan? *Dios mio,* what an idea. I bet he can't even get it up."

Jerks like Ryan are part of the reason Maggie wants to go undercover. She loves the Bureau and most of her colleagues. The FBI recruits true Boy Scout types, patriotic, dedicated, honorable, skilled, and *traditional* (which sometimes also means a little sexist or racist). But by and large they are good company men; they play by the rules, and Maggie has always been a bit of a rule breaker. Undercover will be different. Maggie will be more of a lone wolf, coordinating with just one contact agent, not bound (as much) by the rigidities of hierarchy and paperwork. She can't wait for the new chapter of her life to begin. The next forty-seven days will feel endless; of this she is already sure. A head-down deep dive into wrapping up reports and making sure everything is bright and shiny when she hands over her case files. Dull, albeit necessary, transitional work before her life really begins.

Three hours later, Maggie looks up from her computer and leans back for a stretch. Her shoulders are in knots and her neck is tight. She decides to stroll over to the communal kitchen to get a cup of coffee.

As she passes Special Agent in Charge Bates's office she can't help but notice the tall, imposing man sitting in one of the guest chairs.

It's not only his impressive size that makes him stand out. He's clad in a charcoal suit that even Maggie's untutored eye can tell cost thousands. His dark hair is meticulously styled. His shoes seem expensive too, polished black leather that looks as soft as a pair of lambskin gloves. Gold cuff links gleam at his shirt cuffs. A maroon silk tie lies crisply against a creamy white shirt.

Money. Power. Authority. This man reeks of all three. A gray-haired lawyerly looking guy flanks him on one side; Ryan Johnson sits on the other. A smug look passes over Ryan's face when he spots Maggie.

What the fuck is he up to now?

Coffee procured, Maggie settles back in at her desk. Almost immediately her phone buzzes. It's Bates's secretary. Maggie's presence is requested. She takes one quick sip and beats a fast path to his office. The secretary waves her in. Bates is now alone, Ryan and the visitors gone.

"Guzman."

"Sir."

"I'd like you to join Agent Johnson in an interview."

"Of course, sir."

"You know who Roger Elliott is?"

It dawns on Maggie. Roger Elliott is the sleek, powerful-looking man who was just in Bates's office. A wealthy New York developer and businessman, Elliott and his wife, Betsy, had also been fixtures on the charitable social scene. Until Betsy and their six-year-old son, Bear, vanished off the face of the earth thirteen days ago. It was the stuff of headline heaven at first, but as the days went by with no ransom demand and no new information, other more salacious stories have taken center stage.

"Of course I do, sir."

"He's had a ransom demand. No way of knowing if it's legitimate or not yet, could be someone trying to exploit the situation."

"Any evidence this is federal?"

"The demand was postmarked from a town in Pennsylvania and asks that cash be dropped at 30th Street Station in Philly. So if it's legit, that's across state lines." Bates shakes his head. "First, we need to try to determine the legitimacy of the whole thing. They're in the large conference room. You'll interview. Special Agent Johnson will take notes. I'm sure I don't need to say this, but handle Elliott with care."

"Yes, sir." Maggie swallows a comment about being paired with Ryan. *I'm counting the days,* she reminds herself.

Maggie pivots, heads back into the hallway. Finds her way blocked by Ryan Johnson.

"Just coming to join you," Maggie says sweetly.

Ryan steps aside with an exaggerated wave. "After you," he mocks. "Suggesting you lead on this was a favor, you know. You have a reputation for being a bit of a show boater. Kissing some ass will be good for you."

"Thanks so much for looking out for my best interests. I'll be sure to return the favor."

"And, Guzman, Elliott had a reputation as a player before he got married. Be sure you keep it, you know, on the up-and-up."

Maggie feels the flush spreading across her face, angry that he got a rise out of her. She turns so Ryan can't see her reddened cheeks but retorts, "Not my type. I like them poor and single, not rich and married."

Counting the days.

Maggie strides past Ryan and toward the conference room. She pauses to assess Elliott through the glass before she enters. He fiddles with the knot of his tie, pulling it away from his collar. The gesture makes him look unexpectedly vulnerable.

Maggie pulls open the door and enters, trailed by Ryan.

"Mr. Elliott? I'm Special Agent Magali Guzman. Let me begin by saying how very sorry I am. The stress you've been under must be terrible."

Elliott straightens and gives her a quick, easy nod. "Yes, thank you for saying that. It's very true. This is my attorney, Fallon Marks."

Maggie nods a greeting. "Mr. Marks. Special Agent Johnson and I will be conducting this interview. Let's get started, okay? Let's take it from the beginning. From the day your wife and son disappeared."

ONLY FRIEND

———

Eva Lombard,
London, England

Dear Jenny,

I know it's very unusual these days to write an actual letter and I could just email you of course, but something about living in London has inspired me to take an epistolary path. God, don't I sound pretentious? I'm laughing at myself as I write this. Truth is, I got tired of lugging my laptop around and pretending I was working, so I just decided to own my situation. Easier to tote a legal pad instead.

Baxter and I are at my new favorite café, the Sly Fox. We're here every day the weather allows because the owner fell in love with Bax (but really, who doesn't?) and lets us hang on the outside patio all day, bringing me endless cups of tea and Baxter the occasional bone. I do appreciate the British attitude toward dogs. Particularly since Baxter feels like my only friend right now.

Do I sound whiny? Maybe I do. I feel whiny. It's been almost nine months and I'm bored out of my skull. I miss my job (even though I hated it when I had it, as you well know). But I miss the sense of belonging somewhere. Having a purpose. A place to go every day. Plus I'm not getting pregnant. It doesn't help that Pete's always working. And I mean *al-*

ways. We've been reduced to "appointments" ruled by an ovulation kit! So that's sexy, right?

And with each month that goes by, I feel more a failure. And so disconnected from Peter, I'm not even sure I want to get pregnant anymore. And wasn't that the whole idea behind coming to London in the first place?

Jen, honestly, I'm a mess. I don't know what to do with my days. I take Baxter for long walks. I try to think of freelance articles to pitch, but don't know who to pitch to here. And don't tell me that with a little networking I could sort it right out! I don't want to write the same kind of crap I was doing back in New York, and who will take me seriously as a journalist when all I have is a portfolio of articles about celebrity diets and magic healing crystals?

I've gotten into photography again, and that's been good, at least a minor distraction, but the bottom line is I hate my life! And who am I to feel sorry for myself? I'm living in a beautiful townhouse in one of London's most exclusive neighborhoods. Pete makes more money than I can spend. Maybe when I finally do get pregnant this totally empty period of my life will suddenly all make more sense, but it sure as hell doesn't now.

I feel angry all the time. That can't be normal. Or good. Most of my anger is directed toward Peter and I know that's unfair. But why does he work all the time? Surely, if I was a priority he'd make me one. Why does he want to have a fucking baby if he can't even make time for me? Sometimes I'm afraid he's having an affair! I almost wouldn't blame him. I'm a dull girl here in London, unhappy, lonely, and prickly as fuck.

Eva Lombard puts down her pen. Why *had* she given up her job, her family and friends, her entire *life*, for a man who seems to have forgotten she exists? Baxter, her Bernese mountain dog, nuzzles his wet nose into her hand.

"You're right, Bax, I shouldn't send it," Eva says, stroking his head. Why share her misery? Jenny probably wouldn't understand anyway, since *her* chief complaints are about being stuck at home with two kids under the age of three. Eva's cocktail of time, freedom, and money in London must seem an unimaginable paradise to her sister.

Eva rips the lined yellow sheets away from the pad and tears them into strips. She crumples the torn pages. Tucks an errant lock of her brown bob behind one ear.

Eva glances around the café patio. It's a cozy space, a dozen small tables surrounding a massive old yew tree that rises from the center, its gnarled roots upending the ancient cobblestones near its base.

It's midafternoon and the courtyard is sparsely populated. A tired-looking young mother with a pram sits with her toddler on her lap. The child is fussy and the mother's face creases in irritation. A serious-looking young man with thick glasses, maybe a university student, frowns at his open laptop, his hands paused over the keys as if he's waiting for inspiration. Two middle-aged men in business attire, similar charcoal gray suits and rep ties, lean toward each other speaking softly and urgently.

Eva is on her fourth cup of tea and needs to pee. She double-checks that Baxter's leash is tied to the wrought iron leg of the café table, then gathers her bag and camera in order to head for the restroom.

Baxter looks at Eva optimistically, as if to ask if they are going for a walk now. Eva gives him a quick caress.

"Soon, boy."

Baxter obediently settles down onto the cobblestones, his huge tongue lolling. His tail twitches. His eyes begin to close. Eva smiles at him.

"That's why I love you, Bax. You're eminently flexible."

Eva stands, and as she does, a young blond woman enters the

patio with a fluffball of a Pomeranian clutched in her arms. Baxter's eyes flick open with sudden interest.

"What a sweet pup!" Eva croons. She hoists up her Leica and addresses the woman. "Could I take a picture? I'm doing a series on dogs."

The blonde, fashionable in a clingy sweater dress and high-heeled black leather boots, arches a well-manicured eyebrow at Eva.

"Are you a professional?" she asks in a reedy voice.

"Well, no. It's a hobby." Eva gestures toward Baxter. "He inspired it."

"You're American?"

Eva can't read the woman's intonation. Will her nationality work for or against her? It can hardly matter, she decides, she is who she is.

"Yup," Eva confesses. "That's me. An ugly American. Hopefully redeemed by my wonderful Baxter here."

Baxter cocks his head adorably at the sound of his name and Eva shoots him a grateful glance. Peter has repeatedly told her to try to be more outgoing in order to make new friends. This woman's about her age, Eva admires her style, they both like dogs, surely there is a basis for friendship in those handful of commonalities.

"I'm Eva Lombard," she offers hopefully.

"How nice for you," the woman intones in such a pleasant voice that the rudeness of her words is almost obscured. "But it doesn't make you even a bit interesting to me. So, no. Bugger off."

Eva takes a step back as if she's been struck. She tries to form words, but her mouth just gapes open and then closed, like a gasping, newly caught fish. The woman brushes past her and settles down at a table, her Pomeranian on her lap. She pulls out her cellphone and taps at it furiously.

"Time to go, Bax," Eva orders. She shoves her pad and pen into her bag, along with her shredded letter. She unloops Baxter's leash.

She wants nothing more than to head back to the house and un-cork a bottle of wine. Momentarily she reflects that it has been one too many days in a row that she's started drinking in the afternoon, but she pushes that unwelcome thought away. What else is she sup-posed to do? Rattling around that giant place alone all day. No work. No friends. No husband. She fights the burning sting of bit-ter, resentful tears.

Fuck her, Eva thinks. She raises her camera and fires off a series of shots of the blonde and her Pomeranian. *Click. Click. Click.*

The woman looks up from her phone and catches Eva in the act.

"Hey," she shouts. "I said *no,* you stupid twat."

Everyone on the patio stares at Eva: the tired young mom, the student, the gray-suited businessmen. She flees. *Stupid twat.* That's all she is. The girl with the Pomeranian may be a bitch, but she's right.

Baxter has to trot to keep up as Eva races the two blocks back to the townhouse Peter's firm provides for them. Her fingers tremble as she fits the key in the front door. She slams the door behind her and unclips Baxter's leash. He bounds off to his favorite spot: a window seat tucked into the front parlor's bay window that gives him a view of the all the comings and goings on the street below.

Eva is shaking. With no further self-recrimination about day drinking, she hurries into the kitchen and uncorks a bottle of pinot gris.

Once her wineglass is in hand and she's swallowed the first few blessed mouthfuls, Eva starts to relax. She finally pees, in the chilly cream and blue powder room. She wanders back into the kitchen. Tops off her glass.

The kitchen is outfitted with the latest appliances, everything gleaming and pristine. The center island is set with a huge butcher block, which remains unscarred. Nothing has been chopped in this kitchen. The coffeemaker is well used, as is the microwave, but any thoughts Eva may have had of creating romantic dinners *à deux* in their first kitchen roomy enough to actually cook in dissipated rapidly under the relentless pressure of Peter's job. Either he stayed in the office deep into the night or went to boozy business dinners, coming home past midnight reeking of scotch and cigars. Every couple of weeks, they socialized with business associates of Peter's, events where Eva felt tense and insignificant, one step behind the jokes, awkward and gauche. Most nights, Eva ate alone, nuking prepackaged foods or picking up a packet of fish and chips from a little place in the neighborhood. The cod was only average, but the owner knew Eva by name (and order) now, and that gave her a small sense of belonging.

She glances out the glass kitchen door to their private garden. It's a sweet little oasis, well maintained by a gardener paid for by Pete's firm. Eva never sits out there; it just makes her feel lonely.

Eva curls next to Baxter on the window seat. Rubs his head. He gives her a juicy kiss in return. They both turn their attention out the window. A delivery truck parked with its blinkers flashing as the driver delivers a package. A pair of schoolgirls in uniform whispering and giggling behind cupped hands. The blank faces of the stately townhouses crammed in next to one another across the street, uniformly grand old homes that have been gutted and rebuilt to accommodate modern plumbing and central air.

Then Eva sees him: one of the two gray-suited businessmen from the café. He walks down the street slowly, as if searching for an address, his sharp eyes assessing, weighing, missing nothing. Eva watches as he evaluates the schoolgirls, the driver on his route, the quiet row of townhouses. When he draws close to her house, Eva instinctually pulls back and out of view. She watches him, but keeps herself from his sight. He pauses in front of her building. Gazes up at its façade.

Eva shivers. She doesn't know why, but he's giving her the creeps. She shakes it off. *Stupid twat.*

Her cell trills and Eva gets up to fish it out of her bag, grateful for the interruption. It's Peter.

"Hello there," Eva answers. "To what do I owe this unexpected pleasure?" She intends to sound light and jokey, but is painfully aware that her voice sounds strained.

"Put on a dress. I'm taking you out to dinner."

"With?"

"With nobody. Just the two of us. Sound good?"

Eva's heart gives a small involuntary leap. Could he have read her mind? She's excited but also afraid to open herself to disappointment.

"What's the agenda?" she asks, once again aware that she sounds querulous and tense.

To her relief, Pete laughs. "No agenda, honey. Just dinner. Be ready at six forty-five; I'll send a car for you."

"Where are we going?" she asks.

But her husband has already hung up.

Eva glances back out the window. The gray-suited man is gone.

RESERVATIONS

————

Peter Lombard,
London, England

As the maître d' leads him to their table, Peter observes his surroundings with appreciation. The dark wood paneling, pressed white tablecloths, and graciously curved chairs upholstered with plush cranberry-colored velvet all combine to create a warm and intimate feel. The lighting is subdued, a few recessed ceiling lights and an orderly progression of glowing sconces affixed to the moss green walls.

He settles into the tufted velvet banquette the same moss green as the walls, delighted to discover Forrest had come through on his promise to get "the very best table in the very best restaurant in town," for Peter to spring his surprise. He glances at his watch. He's seven minutes early. He knows he's been gone a hell of a lot lately, not only MIA, but frequently late as well when he and Eva had made plans. Tonight, he wanted to be on time.

Peter idly examines the brass peacock that sits in the center of their intimate little table for two, its tail feathers spread in an arching fan. The waiter comes by and takes his drink order. Peter glances at his watch again. When he looks up, Eva is being led to his table. She hasn't spotted him yet and so he's free to observe her unnoticed.

She's wearing that snug, dark blue dress he likes. Her brown chin-length bob is swept away from her face with a couple of glittery clips.

Their eyes meet and Peter rises, walking around to pull out her chair for her before the maître d' has a chance.

"You look beautiful, darling," Peter murmurs in Eva's ear. He inhales the scent of her: citrus and musk, a hint of something spicy. He loves the way she smells.

"How did you ever get us a table here?" Eva inquires. "I thought this place was booked months out."

Peter grins. "Forrest, of course. Who else?"

Eva nods, as if that explains everything. And of course, it does. Forrest Holcomb, the CEO of Peter's investment firm, is a legend in London, not only for his hard-driving business tactics but also because of his wild partying and multiple marriages. A self-made man who rose to great heights after a rough start as a street rat from Hackney, he's now on his fourth wife, Miranda, a beautiful former actress who seems hell-bent on blowing through Forrest's vast fortune.

"Miranda gave up the reservation so they could attend some benefit where she's going to make Forrest fork over a million pounds for, hmm, let me guess, cuddle therapy for war-ravaged porcupines?"

Peter sniggers. It's close enough to the truth of Miranda, and for a moment their eyes meet in collusion, united as they are in genuine fondness for Miranda, while also thinking her a bit of a joke. But part of his reaction is designed to cover his dismay: It's clear Eva was drinking before she joined him; she has that telltale soft slur to her voice. And Peter knows she's been hitting it hard lately, no matter how careful she is to toss the empty wine bottles directly into the outside bin.

Peter's relieved when the waiter deposits his finger of Macallan and asks Eva for her drink order. (It's only much later that he recognizes the inherent irony in the ritual of cocktails forestalling his concerns about her drinking.) Peter takes a healthy swig of scotch. The amber liquid burns pleasantly in his mouth.

"Actually, Forrest knows the chef. Backed him in his first place in Brighton, so he always has a table here if he wants one. And tonight he wanted to give one to us."

Eva looks at him inquiringly. "Okay, Pete, what's up? It's the first time we've had dinner out alone together in months. You snagged a prime table at one of the most exclusive places in town. What's going on? Is something wrong?"

Looking at the furrow between her drawn brows and her nervously twining fingers, Peter realizes Eva is genuinely alarmed. This is not going the way it's supposed to at all.

Peter reaches across the table and captures Eva's small hands in his larger ones. "Nothing's wrong, babe. I just have a surprise for you. For our anniversary next week."

The waiter deposits Eva's glass of Sancerre. Observes the intensity between them and melts away with the prudent grace of the well-trained service employee.

"We're going to Paris! We leave tomorrow! Just the two of us." Peter beams at his wife.

"How did you get the time off?"

"That's your response? How about, 'Darling, thank you, what a great surprise!'"

"Well, of course, I mean . . ." Eva takes a nervous swallow of wine and shoots him a weak smile. "Darling, thank you, what a great surprise!"

"Now, that's more like it."

"What about Baxter?"

"No worries there. I booked him into that kennel you like."

"You're sure you got the right one? Remember what happened last time!"

Her voice is shrill. Peter wonders, and not for the first time, if the devotion Eva shows toward Baxter is deeper than the love she carries for him. He reassures her about the kennel, naming it—"Prince and Princess of Paws"—and reciting the address before she finally relaxes.

They go on to their familiar pre-dinner ritual, debating the menu, eliciting suggestions from the waiter, and waving off the bread. It seems normal, but still Peter can't help but feel a growing apprehension. Eva drinks glass after glass of wine, her soft slur morphing into stumbled words and drifting sentences. She can't quite meet his eyes, at least not for very long. As she orders an after-dinner brandy, Peter considers cautioning her: *Remember, we still need to pack,* but even the unspoken words make him feel more like an admonitory parent than a husband and lover.

Peter is signing the check when Forrest and Miranda Holcomb breeze into the restaurant accompanied by another couple. Forrest, silver-haired and leonine, exuberantly greets the maître d' and asks if they can rustle up an impromptu table. Peter knows despite the self-deprecatory charm with which the request is made that it will not be denied. He's not a bit surprised when Forrest's party is in turn offered the chef's table in the kitchen. The maître d' asks the quartet to wait just a moment. The group is boisterous, dressed in formal wear. Peter guesses they've been to one of the innumerable benefits that clog the Holcombs' calendar. Miranda drips with diamonds, ropes around her neck, chandelier earrings, rings, and bracelets. She throws back her head to laugh and positively shivers with refracted light.

It's awful, but Peter hopes that they pass into the kitchen without spotting them. Eva is drunk; he suspects he will have to hold her upright to get her out to the car without falling on her face.

Still giggling, Miranda spots them and points them out to Forrest. Peter freezes. He casts a look at Eva, who's cradling her brandy. "Look, Forrest and Miranda," he tells her.

Miranda bounds over to their table, tossing her long red hair over her shoulder. "Our little lovebirds," she coos. "Happy anniversary! He tell you all about your surprise?"

Forrest appears behind her. "Miranda, darling," he implores. "What if Lombard hasn't told her yet? You're an impossible gossip."

Miranda's hand flies to her mouth in a gesture of mock horror. "Did I ruin it?"

"Not at all," Peter reassures her. "Eva knows all about Paris."

"See?" Miranda crows to Forrest before giving him a kiss on the cheek and tucking her arm in his. "Now let's go, poppet. I'm starving." She gives Peter a conspiratorial wink.

Forrest gestures to the waiter, who scurries over. "Put their dinner on my tab," he commands, gesturing to Peter and Eva.

"That's not necessary, sir," Peter asserts. "I've already paid—"

"Nonsense. They'll reverse the charge."

"Thank you, then." Peter knows better than to argue.

Miranda and Forrest saunter off to their friends. Eva's eyes follow them as they go.

"I kind of hate them," she slurs.

"Don't be ridiculous," Peter snaps.

Eva drains her glass.

Peter begins to worry the divide between them is bigger than he suspected. He's no dummy; he knows Eva isn't happy here in London. But for the first time he seriously wonders if their marriage is in real trouble.

AGITATION

———

Eva Lombard,
London, England

Peter snores next to her. Baxter's curled underneath the window, his wheezes mingling with Peter's in an all-too-familiar nighttime symphony. Eva slips out of bed.

Peter had pulled out their suitcases the night before and they had both thrown in a few basic necessities before they had tumbled and fumbled into drunken sex. Eva skirts the lumpy mess of packing they'd left behind as she shrugs into a robe and plucks her laptop from the dresser.

She heads downstairs to the kitchen. Pours a glass of cold water and gulps down some aspirin. Refills the glass and then settles at the counter with her laptop, the blue reflection of her screen the only light in the shadowy room. She logs on to the Internet and begins a search: "cooking classes Paris."

Eva hadn't even thought about a present for Peter, so enmeshed was she in her personal spiral of recrimination and misery. And then he springs this extravagant trip! Now she feels embarrassed, petty, self-centered, and guilty. *Terrific.*

Determined to right the scales, she books a French cooking class for them to do together in two days' time, a one-day introduction to classic techniques, something she knows he'll like. She recognizes he'll realize the present was a last-minute inspiration spurred only by his planning the trip to Paris in the first place, but it still feels like a score.

She shuts the laptop, sips some more water, and puts the glass in the sink, ready to go back to bed.

Wait, what's that? Through the glass kitchen door, Eva's eyes catch a flash of movement out in the garden. She strains to see in the darkness. *Is someone out there?*

She takes a couple of steps toward the door, fear prickling her skin. Stops and listens, her breath held, her body taut, her eyes searching.

All seems quiet. *Stupid twat.*

The phrase leaps unbidden into Eva's thoughts once again, dragging her spirits down. She climbs back upstairs with bowed shoulders, praying the aspirin kicks in soon and her head stops pounding.

Peter huddles under the covers with his back to her, his snores dulled to a low roar. But Baxter is on his feet, his head cocked. A low whine emanates from deep in his throat.

"What's up, Bax?" Eva whispers.

Baxter charges past her, nearly knocking her to the ground in his haste. Eva's hip collides with a sharp corner of the dresser.

"Ow! Shit!" Eva yelps.

Peter snaps to a sitting position, blinking, half awake. "What? What's happening?"

From the floor below, Eva hears Baxter's full-throated barking. "I don't know," she manages, her throat tight.

Peter throws on a pair of sweatpants. "Stay here," he admonishes, "while I go check it out."

Eva examines her hip. A bruise is already starting to purple. She hears Peter speaking to Baxter, the familiar squeal of the kitchen door.

"Eva," Pete calls. "You can come on down. Looks like someone might have been trying to break in, but Bax scared him away."

Eva stumbles down the stairs, her heart racing. Baxter barks furiously and she puts a steadying hand on his back. "Good boy," she murmurs. "Good dog."

"Look." Peter points to a long, thin tool lying just outside the kitchen door. "That got left behind. But the door was open when I got here."

"Didn't you turn on the alarm before we went to bed?" Eva's whole body is shaking.

"I do every night."

Eva stares at him. "But did you do it tonight?"

"I don't remember, okay? We both had a lot to drink at dinner." He shrugs. Turns away to rummage in the cabinet for a treat for Baxter.

"We should call the police," she insists, her tone cold.

"I'll call Derrick too."

"Who's that?"

"Forrest's Mr. Fix-it. He'll put in a call so we get top priority."

"You do that," she says, sliding her eyes away from Peter's. "I'm going upstairs to pack. There's no way I'm getting back to sleep now anyway."

Eva turns her back to him and bites her tongue. She knows that if she says one more thing, she will be unable to stem the torrent.

Everything revolves around Holcomb. It's like you've joined a cult, like I don't exist anymore. He's your first thought in the morning and your last thought at night, but for me, to protect me, you can't even remember to put the fucking alarm on.

She hopes she's making a dramatic exit, her cold fury evident in her rigid shoulders and spine of steel, but she hears Peter speaking into his phone and glances back to see he's not even looking in her direction.

Eva snaps her fingers and calls to Baxter, "Come on, Bax. Come with me."

The dog hustles to her side and she strokes his head. *At least Baxter loves me.*

DRUGS AND MONEY

Catherine,
Dallas, Texas

Their bags are already packed when I arrive at their room in the bland airport hotel adjacent to the Dallas/Fort Worth International Airport. Steve Harris, his wife, Lisa, and their autistic ten-year-old son, Finn. The boy circles the room, muttering a repetitive sing-song phrase.

I'm glad to see that my operative, Jake, has the Targets ready to roll; I'm shaken by Leslie Virgenes's murder, as is the watchdog group that hired me to protect both her and the Harris family. We all thought we were further ahead of this curve.

I stumbled into this case. The Burial Society was in the process of helping a battered wife escape her abusive husband when she provided me with an unexpected bonus. It seems her bastard of a husband thought he had her completely cowed, so much so that he spoke freely in front of her about all his business dealings. After all, she'd never have the courage to leave him, as he'd told her many times. But then she did. And brought me his deepest secrets. One of these secrets was that there was a lawsuit burgeoning against Knox Pharmaceuticals, a company in which her husband owned a significant stake, and two potential witnesses were in imminent danger.

I researched. I always do. Confirmed her story. Knox had buried test results, knowingly releasing for sale a drug for the treatment of Alzheimer's with a high percentage of harmful side effects in study participants. Steve Harris and Leslie Virgenes were the lead researchers on the team whose data was buried, as was the subsequent internal complaint they'd filed with the company. The drug's been in the marketplace for a few months now and as the number of deaths among its users mounted, shadowy representatives of Knox reached out to Steve and Leslie, first with bribes, later with threats.

The information I had from the wife was solid, as was my introduction to the chief strategist of the watchdog group mounting the lawsuit. As a matter of principle, I try to leave most people on good terms. You never know when you're going to need a favor, and that philosophy paid off yet again. A story for another time.

The memory of Leslie Virgenes's flattened, bluish face flashes unwelcome in my mind's eye. I feel dangerously exposed by the simple connect-the-dots I've left behind in trying to protect her and have to fight my urge to crawl back into the shadows. Protecting Steve Harris is even more crucial now that Leslie is dead.

The Harrises have been under the watch of one of my operatives, Jake Burrows, currently operating under the alias John Bernake. He's done well since I brought him on board the Burial Society three years ago (a story for another time and perhaps one you already know). He's proven to be smart, malleable, and teachable. Jake's moved the Harrises to three different hotels in the past three days. Good work on his part, but the strain is showing on the family.

"What now?" Steve Harris asks me.

"We've got one more stop. A safe house. Then I'll get you on a flight out of the country."

"What about our daughter?" Lisa Harris's voice is shrill with fear.

"Don't worry," I reassure. "We've got her covered."

I pull Jake aside to give him his next set of instructions. As I do, Finn becomes more and more agitated, circling the room more quickly, slapping at his head with his open palms. "Kota, kota, kota," the boy keens repeatedly.

"Lisa," I hiss at his mother. "You're going to have to calm him down. We need to get out of here as unobtrusively as possible."

Lisa exchanges a look of helpless frustration with her husband before addressing me. "There's not much we can do. We usually have to just wait it out."

"How long does that take?"

"We never know. Could be an hour. Could be two."

I extract my pouch filled with syringes. "I'm going to put him out. Okay with you?"

"What is that?" Steve Harris demands.

"Something that will put him to sleep." I lower my voice. "Look, I found Leslie Virgenes. But not soon enough. She's dead."

Lisa Harris gasps. Her hand flies to her mouth. "Poor Leslie," she whispers.

Steve grasps his son's flailing arms and walks him over to me. "Do what you need to."

I insert the syringe into the boy's neck and depress the plunger. His blue eyes widen momentarily and then he crumples into his father's waiting arms.

I look up to see Jake staring at me with an expression I can't quite figure. *Is that judgment in his eyes? I don't have time for this.*

Jake escorts Lisa Harris in one elevator. I take Steve and his little boy down in another. We meet up in the parking lot. Bundle the family into a minivan with tinted windows. I'll be driving them. I take a final scan of the lot. Clear.

"You did well with them. Ready for part two?"

I take Jake's bearded jaw in my hand and tilt his head so I can look into his eyes. The facial hair is new (it belongs to John Bernake) and it suits him, gives him gravitas.

He shrugs. "Sure."

"Try to inspire a little confidence, will you?"

At that he cracks a smile. "Don't worry. I'm good."

"That I already knew." I smile back at him. My version of a pep talk.

Time to hit the road.

INSTIGATION

—

Eva Lombard,
London, England

TO: Jenny Fitzgerald Mooney
FROM: Eva Fitzgerald Lombard
RE: Paris!

Hey Jen! Just a quick note to let you know Pete and I are going to Paris to celebrate our anniversary! He sprung it on me last night, Mr. Romantic! I'm sure we'll have Wi-Fi in the hotel, but I'm going to try to take advantage of the time with Pete—you know how hard he's been working—so don't be surprised if you don't hear from me. Love to Bill and the kids. *À bientôt, ma petite soeur,* and try not to be too jelly! xo E

Eva hits SEND and drops her cellphone next to the overflowing suitcase sitting open on Peter's and her bed. She zips the suitcase shut, metal teeth snagging on a tender corner of her thumb. Her thumb goes into her mouth and she sucks away the pain.

But why do I feel like I have to lie to Jen that this trip is just one more part of "Eva's Fabulous European Adventures"? God! What if I wrote what I really think to Jen?

Hey sis, Just a quick note to let you know Pete and I are going to Paris for our anniversary! Mr. Romantic sprung it on me last night.

Can you believe it? Months of pecks instead of real kisses, of cold sheets, of "sorry, I've got to work late, work this weekend, work late again," of sex only by appointment, and now suddenly this? What if he's having an affair? What if he's taking me to Paris to end it? I'm not blameless, I know; I've been off my game here, unhappy, resentful. I came to London to have a baby, and all I've gotten is fucked, although unfortunately not literally. We did finally do it last night after a long drought, but it was like fucking a stranger. What the hell has happened to my marriage? I hope this doesn't ruin Paris for me forever.

Shit.

She and Pete loved each other once. Eva's certain of that. Her eyes catch on a copy of their wedding photo on top of their dresser, imprisoned behind glass in its heavy silver frame. In the image, Pete stands behind her with a cocky, crooked grin and his thick dark hair mussed and sexy, his arms circling her from behind. She leans against him, elegant neck twisted, laughing a radiant smile right into his smitten eyes.

She can't remember the last time they made each other laugh.

Eva sinks down on the edge of the bed. She feels a shell of the woman she once was, bright on the outside, but empty and rotting on the inside like a Halloween pumpkin left too long on the stoop.

Peter calls from the hallway. The car to take them to the airport is here.

At least a week in Paris will be a change of pace. And it will be good to be away from this townhouse after last night's excitement. Eva shivers. *Put it behind you,* she admonishes herself. *Try to have a good time.*

After all, Pete is so pleased with all his secret planning for the four-star hotel and reservations at top restaurants, all of which he had explained with delight over dinner last night. Never mind that he's the one with a taste for gourmet; Eva far prefers simpler food. But at least he had remembered to book the right kennel for Baxter.

Try. It appears Pete's trying, I have to give him that.

Baxter trots in and snuffles his wet nose into her palm, his way of asking for a head rub. Eva complies.

"There you go, boy. You're going to have a little vacation yourself, yes, you are. With other doggie friends. At that nice place with the massages."

Eva takes one last look around the bedroom. It's a bright white and airy space, with flowing sheers idling in the breeze. But like the rest of the house, the modern updates supplanting the traditional architecture have left the room feeling spare and a little cold. She closes and locks the window, stilling the curtains.

"Okay, Bax," she croons. "Time to go."

Peter comes in and lifts her bag from the bed. "Got everything?"

"I think so."

"Good. But I can always take you shopping in Paris. In fact, we'll have to plan on it!"

Eva knows he's trying to be expansive, generous, kind, but his words grate on her. He's going to *take* her shopping? If she wants to shop, she can, she doesn't need Peter to take her, for fuck's sake.

With a shiver of shame she recognizes the lie in her own thoughts. They're living off Pete's money now. She stopped being a contributor to this family when they moved to London. Her pitiful little pre-marriage savings account back in a Long Island branch of Chase Bank is the only money that is technically still hers and hers alone. Eva sticks a smile on her face.

"Sure! Shopping sounds like fun." She busies herself corralling Bax, grabbing his favorite toy, settling his bulk in the limo, coaxing him out of the car and into the kennel.

She and Peter are finally alone. The driver sets course for the airport.

Silence sits between them like a third passenger.

Eva eyes the liquor offerings arrayed inside the limo. Individual bottles of wine with twist-off caps. Airplane-sized samples of gin, scotch, vodka, tequila. Her fingers itch to grab the small bottle of white wine, condensation streaking its green glass and pearl-colored label. Will Pete judge her if she goes for it? Probably. She saw the way he looked at her last night at dinner. *Screw it. I'm on vacation.*

Defiantly, she reaches for the bottle and twists it open, fills a crystal tumbler.

"Want some?" she asks.

"A little early for me."

Eva shrugs.

"I have another surprise for you," Peter continues.

Fuck. What now?

"We're not going to Paris!" Peter crows triumphantly.

Oh shit.

"Why not?"

"We're going to Hong Kong!"

"What about all those reservations you made?"

"I have comparable ones in Hong Kong. Michelin stars all the way, baby!"

"Why did you lie to me?" The question bursts from her, angry and harsh.

Peter stares at her, stunned. "Lie? I'd hardly characterize it as a lie; I planned a treat for you. You've been talking about wanting to go back to Hong Kong since we met. I can't believe you. All you do lately is look for things to be upset about."

The wine in Eva's mouth suddenly tastes sour. There is so much about this that just feels wrong. The flip way in which he sprung first one trip on her and then another, like her desires about where to go and what to do when they arrived were meaningless. The shame she feels burning through her as she recognizes her hastily purchased cooking class is money down the drain (not to mention the fact that this change in plans leaves her gift-less). His very *thoughtfulness* about Hong Kong feels like a slap.

And while she's thrilled to be going back, as Hong Kong's a city she's loved since she lived there the summer after she graduated from college, part of her desire had been based in her wanting to show Peter a city that she knew and loved, rather than being dragged along on a trip of his planning.

These thoughts rumble through her like a freight train. She feels monstrous with the weight of her anger. Guilty about the pettiness of it.

"Fuck you, Pete."

"What?"

"You heard me. Fuck you. I'm not your child, I'm your wife, your partner supposedly, but we don't have a life together anymore, not since we got to London. And then we can't even plan a vacation together? For our fucking anniversary?"

Eva gulps the rest of the wine; sour or not, she doesn't give a damn. She's trembling with rage. "And how could you be so deceptive? You've been lying and lying to me."

"Eva, why are you doing this? I know it's been hard, but, babe, I'm working for us, you know that. This job is an investment in our future. Our family."

"That's rich! We're never even going to have a family if you can't ever find the time to sleep with me."

"We made love last night."

"Is that what you call it? Felt more like a pump and dump to me."

The hurt crosses his face, and Eva feels both victorious and shitty at the same time.

Peter drums nervous fingers against his thigh. "Do you want me to tell the driver to turn around?"

"Back to the house where we almost got robbed last night? I don't think so."

"Then just tell me. What is it you want to do, Eva?" Peter barks at her, exasperated.

What she *wants* to do is to pick a fight. She's frayed from lack of sleep, hungover, and cranky. She feels nihilistic, like she'd blow it all up if she could.

What she *does* is douse the flames. A lifelong adherence to convention, a muted sense of hope in her marriage, and a true pull to Hong Kong conspire to make her hold back the poison she aches to expel. Instead she says, "I'm sorry, Pete. I am. I'm just tired. And on edge, you know, from last night. We'll go. We'll have a wonderful time."

Her words sound empty to her own ears; she knows how insincere they must sound to Peter. Nonetheless, he aims a smile at her. "It'll be good, babe, I promise."

Eva gives him the best smile she can muster. They don't exchange another word until they arrive at Heathrow.

Once there, the formality of travel sustains them. They're good together on the road and they click into routine, checking baggage, enduring security, stopping for treats and magazines for the flight.

They settle into the waiting area by their gate. Eva chugs down half a bottle of water. Puts her hand on Peter's thigh.

"Pete, I'm sorry I was such a bitch this morning."

He jerks his leg away from her touch. "Yeah, me too." He drums his fingers briefly then abruptly stands. "I'm getting a coffee."

Fuck me for trying. Eva crosses her arms and legs and stares after Peter with injured defiance. *Didn't even ask me if I wanted anything.*

Peter strides across the terminal, his irritation with her evident in every stomp. He collides with a man, Eva notes, and barely pauses to offer his apologies. The stranger ducks away and continues on his path toward where Eva sits. Her eyes drink him in, caught by a tantalizing hint of something familiar.

Who is he? Why does the mere sight of him cause a tingle of apprehension to run down her spine?

Eva lifts a copy of *OK!* magazine to cover her face and peers out, feeling intrigued and a little silly all at the same time. But a

flush of hot blood sweeps through her system: She has recognized
the man, his square shoulders and sharp eyes. He'd been at the café
yesterday when she was there with Baxter, outside their house later
that afternoon. Apprehension threatens to blossom into something
more severe, paranoia perhaps, but the man sweeps past Eva without a second glance. She exhales. She must be mistaken. *Stupid
twat.*

JET LAG

———

Eva Lombard,
Hong Kong Island

She wakes as the pilot announces their descent into Hong Kong International Airport. Beside her Pete naps, his complimentary-in-first-class eyeshade and earplugs firmly installed. *As much to shut me out as anything else,* Eva fumes. They'd scarcely exchanged a word on the flight. A listless conversation about the (actually quite good) meal served and then they'd burrowed, Eva into her magazines and Peter into work crap on his laptop.

So much for leaving work behind to focus on our relationship.

Eva had pulled on her own eyeshade, snuggled into her pale blue cashmere travel wrap, and turned a cold shoulder to Pete.

They've been in the air for over eleven hours. She's slept on and off for most of it. As she rubs the sleep from her eyes and stretches, she examines what she can see of Peter's face in repose. He's grinding his teeth, a slow, steady circle that gives Eva an ache in her own jaw just watching him.

"Pete," she murmurs as she touches him lightly on the arm. "We're landing."

Peter tugs his eyeshade free and plucks the plugs from his ears. His eyes meet hers for a moment as he focuses on where he is, and in that blissful instant their tensions dissolve. He looks at her like he loves her.

Eva gestures that he should look outside the window. The city sprawls beneath them, partially obscured by swaths of misty clouds. Soaring lumps of mountainous green are crowded with gleaming skyscrapers, and all is surrounded by the enormous glistening spill of aqua-blue water. The airport itself, an island unto its own, looms in the distance.

Eva can't contain the prickle of excitement she feels about returning to Hong Kong.

"Let's make it good, Pete, okay? I'm sorry."

Still looking out the window, Peter reaches for her hand, and Eva exhales a sigh of relief.

"What's that temple you like so much? With the incense spirals?" he asks, finally turning to face her.

"Man Mo," Eva replies. "In honor of the gods of war and literature. Don't you love that combination?"

"We'll have to go."

"I can't wait to show it to you. It's right next to the antiques district too. The shops on Cat Street are high end, but the alley below is great for fun junk."

"We can afford the high-end junk now, babe," Peter says as he gives her hand another squeeze.

Eva departs the plane feeling considerably more upbeat. Once again they kick into gear as successful, competent travel companions, sorting their carry-on belongings and navigating their way through vast white terminal hallways glittering with a seemingly infinite number of tempting offerings from designer boutiques, over through passport control, and then into baggage claim.

As they wait for the luggage carousel to start, Peter stares at his phone, flicking through emails. "I'm going to confiscate that soon," she teases him.

"One small fire I gotta put out. Then I'm all yours."

The overhead warning lights blink, a buzzer sounds, and the

luggage carousel begins its grind. Suitcases tumble onto the belt, belched through plastic flaps. Eva sees her suitcase almost immediately, the polka-dot ribbon tied to its handle a dead giveaway.

She points out her bag to Peter. He tucks his phone away and lifts her bag clear from the belt. They wait until the very last suitcase has been claimed before they accept the harsh fact that Pete's bag hasn't arrived.

Eva feels Peter's irritation mounting as they report the bag missing to the smiling, cheerful, and utterly unhelpful young woman manning the lost luggage office.

"Not a very auspicious start to our trip," he remarks, grumpy, as he folds away his copy of the lost baggage report.

"I guess we'll have to take *you* shopping," Eva offers, hoping to lighten his mood. "You know Hong Kong's a shopper's paradise. Capitalism squared and squared again. Perfect for Peter Peacock."

This comment is rewarded with a smile. A man who grew up wearing hand-me-downs from both of his older brothers, Peter luxuriates in owning beautiful clothes. Eva sometimes teases him about it, affectionately labeling him "Peter Peacock," but delivering the appellation in a seductive tone intended to arouse.

Eva feels the mood lighten as they finally exit the terminal to find a car and driver waiting for them as organized by the concierge at their Hong Kong hotel.

Climbing into the car, Eva spots a flash of pale blue on the ground next to the oversized revolving door that had spit them from the terminal just moments before: her cashmere wrap.

"Pete," she calls. "I dropped my scarf. Be right back."

His eyes follow the line of hers and settle on the lump of blue. "Stay here, babe. I'll get it for you."

Now, this is more like it. Eva smiles, pleased by his solicitude. *Maybe this will be good, after all.*

Her smile disappears when the man, the predatory man, the man who was at the café, then outside their house, then at Heathrow, that improbable man himself, spills out of the revolving door and lands right next to Peter.

The man claps her husband on the shoulder just as Peter rises from his crouch, Eva's scarf in his fist. The two men have a brief exchange that Eva can't hear.

What the hell?

Peter hurries back over to her, the cashmere extended in an outstretched hand.

"Good to go now?"

"Sure. But who's that man?"

"What man?"

"That guy! Just now by the revolving door."

"I have no idea. Kind of an asshole, though, made an elaborate show of telling me to 'watch my step' when I wasn't even in his way."

Eva climbs into the limo and settles in for the ride to the hotel. But her momentary sense of ease has vanished.

Is that man following me? Should I say something to Pete? He'll probably think I'm imagining things. Since they've been in London, he's accused her more than once of being overly dramatic about her problems.

"Eva? Hello! I'm talking to you." Peter's voice penetrates Eva's fog of introspection.

"Right. Sorry. Just tired."

But she isn't just tired. She feels afraid. For reasons she can't pinpoint or name. She looks down and realizes her hands are trembling. Hastily, she folds them together in her lap.

"Pete. That guy? The jerk at the airport? It's not the first time I've seen him."

"What do you mean?" Peter stares at her blankly.

"He was at the Sly Fox. Then I saw him outside our house. And again at Heathrow. You bumped into him there. Don't you remember?"

"Actually I don't."

"When you went to get coffee!"

"I don't think it was the same guy. And even if it was, he was probably just on our flight."

"And outside our house? What if he's the guy who tried to break in last night?"

"Babe, we just got off a marathon flight. We're both exhausted. You'll see things more clearly after a nap."

"Condescending much, Pete?"

"Eva, I'm trying to be nice."

"Then why does it feel so shitty?"

Eva tugs her pale blue wrap tighter around her shoulders and turns her head to look out the window. The towering vertical landscape of high-rises that defines Hong Kong looms before her. *Maybe he's right. Maybe I just need a nap.*

But she knows she's not wrong. She's not safe; she feels the danger in her bones. And her husband doesn't want to hear it.

FRUSTRATION

Peter Lombard,
Hong Kong Island

Peter's working very hard not to be annoyed with Eva, despite the fact that she once again retreated into some kind of impenetrable shell shortly after they left the airport. *But that nonsense about seeing some stranger? Doing what? Stalking her, was that the implication? What the hell was that about?*

Lately they feel less like best friends and more like they're forever fencing. Pete feels increasingly wary of saying the wrong thing.

Which it appears I've done again.

It never used to be difficult between them. It was one of the reasons they got together in the first place. Friends first, introduced by a mutual acquaintance, they'd eased seamlessly into a romantic relationship, followed quickly by living together and then marriage. He would have said he was a happy man in a happy relationship. Except for their time in London.

They pull into the circular driveway in front of the hotel and Peter's pleased to see staff snap to in order to take their luggage and usher them into the lobby. His wealth is new and self-made. Outward manifestations of the powers it brings still thrill him.

The lobby is enormous and serene. Marble tile in shades of beige and cream forms a subtle herringbone pattern on the floor. A white-on-white mural dominates the space. Groupings of dark leather chairs set around glass-and-chrome tables nestle on circular area rugs creating intimate pools of seating amid the grand space. A curving staircase wraps around a massive marble center column backed by floor-to-ceiling windows. The overall atmosphere is one of lavish, welcoming opulence.

"Wow," Eva breathes as she takes in the space.

"Glad something's finally impressing you." Even as the words escape his lips, Peter regrets the snarky tone with which he delivered them.

"For fuck's sake," Eva steams. "Will you give it a rest?"

"Why should I?" he snaps. "I went to a lot of trouble to arrange this, you know. Research. Reservations. Getting the time off at work. And what do you do? Get bent out of shape because I 'lied to you'! It's like you're implying you can't trust me when all I did was try to plan something nice. And then you go on about some random dude in the airport. Paranoid much? Or just looking for attention? Have you thought about me at all? I can't even change my fucking clothes."

Eva takes a step away from him, stunned hurt in her eyes.

Peter realizes the three women and one man standing poised at attention behind the check-in desk are all trying hard not to stare, their eyes resolutely fixed on the middle distance. He squares his shoulders then proffers his ID and credit card.

"Lombard. The reservation is under the name Peter Lombard."

The corner suite on the thirty-second floor is magnificent, but Eva and Peter don't say a word as the polite bellman shows them around. Two full bathrooms, one off the sitting room, one off the bedroom. Normally, they would have joked about it; Eva has often maintained that the key to a happy marriage is separate bathrooms. He waits for her comment and feels a stab as she stays silent.

The sitting room and adjacent bedroom both offer stunning views of a gray-shrouded Victoria Harbour and on the horizon, the towering skyline of Kowloon. Speedboats and ferries streak the steely water in between the two landmasses.

Explanations about the thermostat, spa reservations, television operation, and room service duly given and the complimentary bottle of anniversary champagne and chocolate truffles noticed and acknowledged, the bellman departs with a hefty tip.

Peter wants to start over but doesn't know how. He watches as Eva unpacks, hanging her dresses in the walk-in closet, arranging an array of footwear across its floor.

She crosses into the larger of the two bathrooms, the one off the bedroom, and shuts the door. Peter glances at the champagne. Should he pop it? Should he try the chocolates? He doesn't feel very festive.

He sits down on the cushy king-sized bed, zips open the front pocket of his briefcase, and pulls out a vial of Ambien. His sleep on the plane had been erratic at best. He's exhausted from the flight, from fighting with Eva, from the cumulative pressure of the relentless grind of the past few months at work. He hears the sound of running taps.

She's taking a bath.

The rush of water is followed by the distinct click of a door lock.

And I'm not welcome.

Peter kicks off his shoes. Dry swallows two Ambien. *Screw her.*

His head melts back into the down pillows mounded across the top of the comfortable bed. His eyes flutter. *We should order this mattress.*

Peter's eyes close. He's enfolded in a thick white cloud.

Then deep, blissful nothingness.

NEEDLES AND PINS

———

Catherine,
Wheeless, Oklahoma

The view outside the tattered vinyl window shade is of endless scrub with the occasional ramshackle structure dotted out into the distance, each of them weather-beaten and in various states of collapse. The shack in which we're staying isn't much better than the buildings on the horizon; it consists of three rooms, two narrow bedrooms and an open living/dining/cooking area. There's one bathroom off the kitchen, with a shower that provides only the thinnest of trickles and a toilet that runs incessantly despite how often I jiggle the handle.

The furniture, a generous term at best for the leftovers that fill the dreary place, suits its housing. An ancient, lumpy sofa wheezes dust. It's graced with a remarkably ugly crochet blanket in squares of avocado green and lemon yellow. A scratched block of raw wood serves as a coffee table. An ancient Formica-topped dining table is crowded with six mismatched chairs. The single beds in their cramped rooms are stiff and unyielding, the closets dusty and home to spiders. The power is turned off and I'm keeping it that way. We rely on minimal candles and flashlights at night. There's no luxury here, but it's safe.

We're outside the tiny town of Wheeless, Oklahoma, in the midst of a desolate expanse of the Cimarron Panhandle, one of the least populated areas of the state. We've been able to hole up here with no one the wiser. In every direction there is sheer . . . nothing. I'd filled the joint up with supplies long before we ever arrived here, "just in case"; we've been subsisting on canned food and bottled water for two days.

We're waiting. I'm as edgy and impatient as the people I'm protecting.

I turn away from the window. Stephen and Lisa Harris sit next to each other on the lumpy sofa, shoulders touching, hands clasped. On the floor, Finn nestles against his mother's legs and hums softly as he plays with a Nintendo Game Boy, peaceful for the time being.

The yearning of these parents to be reunited with their daughter is a palpable miasma filling the room.

One of my burner phones trills. Steve and Lisa start anxiously in unison, as if their nervous systems are hardwired together.

I answer. It's Stephanie. She confirms our plane is on its way to our predetermined rendezvous point. She also brings word that the relocated wife who brought us the information on Knox is safely out of the country. This is all fine news. But it's not the news for which the Harrises are hungry.

I ring off. "No word yet," I tell them. "Don't worry. They're on their way."

Disappointment slingshots through both of them; their bodies droop. Lisa strokes Finn's hair, her eyes wet.

I've known fear. I understand loss and have suffered more of it in my life than most. Still, I've never been a parent praying my child is alive. What can I understand about their anxiety?

THE EMPTY BED

———

Peter Lombard,
Hong Kong Island

His mouth is horribly, horribly dry. *Christ, I need some water.*

Peter's gluey eyes peel open. The hotel room is dark and full of hulking shadows. Through the expanse of window across from the bed, he can see the glittering nighttime lights of the Kowloon skyline. The gray shrouds of mist that hugged the shoreline earlier in the day have lifted and the night is sharp and clear. A chunky slice of orange moon hangs boldly in the sky. Stars wink faintly, no competition for the assault of man-made neon lacing the soaring skyscrapers.

The bathroom door is open; the lights are off. Peter stumbles from the bed to the minibar. He winces as the light from the refrigerator hits his eyes. Grabs a bottle of water and chugs it.

Eva's not in the bedroom, that's evident. Nor is she in the bathroom, although damp towels are heaped on the floor and a smear of iridescent bubble bath still rims the edge of the deep tub. Peter crosses to the sitting room. Flips on a light. Empty. The front bathroom? Empty.

Dazed with Ambien and jet lag, he struggles to focus.

The illuminated clock in the sitting room reads 4:18. He checks that against his phone. The same. It's dark outside; logic demands it must be night—4:18 A.M. then. He slept for almost twelve hours. But if it's the middle of the night, where the hell is Eva? He scrolls through his phone, no texts, no calls, no emails.

Peter flips on every light in the suite. He discovers the clothes she wore to travel neatly tucked into a hotel laundry bag. It looks like the clothes she brought for the trip are mostly present, not that he had monitored her packing. Her phone is gone. So are her camera, shoulder bag, and a favorite pair of sneakers. He doesn't see a note anywhere, even though he checks carefully: the desk in the bedroom, the coffee table in the sitting room, the night tables on either side of the bed. He even opens and closes the front door of the suite just in case she had slipped something under the door.

Peter hits her name on the "favorites" list on his phone. The call bounces immediately to voicemail. "Uh, Eva, it's after four in the morning and I . . . anyway, I'm sorry. And, uh, a little worried? Let's start over. Call me back. I promise I'll make it up to you." He doesn't know whether to be anxious or angry with her. He's pissed at himself too. *How did this fight get so stupid?*

He calls five more times, his messages getting increasingly angry as his worry grows. He knows this isn't going to help matters, but he can't stop himself.

The last message is a doozy and he wishes he could take it back even as the words come out of his mouth: "You stupid bitch, I can't believe you're doing this to me. Call me, Eva! Call me now!"

Peter throws his phone down on the bed. Only his side is rumpled; on what should be Eva's side the comforter is smooth, the pillows attractively plumped. He looks out the window as he sinks into the cozy red armchair in the room's corner. He stays there staring blankly as dawn creeps over the water and the lights of nighttime Kowloon glimmer and fade.

When he finally stands, he's stiff; he realizes he's barely moved for hours. He picks up his too-silent phone. It's going on nine A.M. and still nothing from Eva. With a mounting sense of dread, he splashes some cold water on his face and runs a cursory tooth-brush over his teeth. He pulls on his clothes and tugs Eva's brush through his unruly hair.

He stares at his reflection in the mirror hanging over the bath-room vanity. His face is haggard, his brown eyes bloodshot. Should he should try to reach Jenny? Morning here meant what? Late eve-ning yesterday there in New York. Or so he thinks. He pulls up the world clock function on his phone and confirms his guess. But why alarm Jenny? Eva is trying to make some kind of a point. That has to be it. And he'll just feel like a fool if Jenny knows all about their fight and the two of them are laughing at him. He sometimes feels like he and his brother-in-law, Billy, are the unwitting recipients of the sisters' attitude that women are just somehow simply superior, long suffering of their idiot men.

The more he thinks about it, the angrier he gets. *This is bullshit.* He's not going to give her the satisfaction of worry. He's in Hong Kong. He's going to have a good time, with or without his ungrate-ful wife.

For an instant, Peter's thoughts turn to Eva's claims about the man at the airport, but he dismisses them just as quickly. *A plea for attention. Just like her drinking. Just like this stupid stunt.*

Peter tucks his wallet into his jeans pocket. Minutes later, he's defiantly striding from the hotel in search of adventure.

The hotel leads out into a series of elevated walkways. He picks one at random and starts to explore. He's startled by what he sees: scores of women setting up meals on top of flattened cardboard boxes unloaded from hand trolleys with an almost rhythmic preci-sion. The *clack, clack, clack* of their language sounds like chirping birds. He thinks it shocking that such a huge homeless camp exists right outside one of Hong Kong's most luxurious hotels and it's only through eavesdropping on a British couple that he learns these women are not homeless at all. Residential living space is at a pre-mium in pricey Hong Kong, and Peter learns these women are Fili-pina immigrants mostly working as cleaning or kitchen staff in the hotels and office buildings that dominate the city. Their tiny homes are too small to gather in. Instead, every Sunday becomes an impromptu public picnic arranged on the perimeter of the luxury buildings they service. It's half party, half protest.

Peter pushes any thoughts of societal injustice from his mind. He's on vacation, damn it. He can worry about saving the world next week. The humid air is oppressive; breathing is like gulping cotton. He passes an entrance to a massive mall and is lured inside by the blast of chilled air escaping from behind the plate glass sliding door. Prada, Chanel, Louis Vuitton, Michael Kors, Chloé, Celine, Burberry, Dolce & Gabbana. And oh wait, Prada again. Has he gone in a circle? No. It's a second Prada store in this same complex. Eva wasn't lying when she called Hong Kong the city of capitalism squared and squared again.

The thought of his wife irritates him and he strides into the second Prada. Just under six thousand dollars later, he is the proud possessor of a three-quarter-length black coat, a pair of black slim-cut jeans, a lightweight navy cashmere sweater, and two cotton poplin shirts. *I'll peacock all I damn want*, Peter decides as he signs the receipt with a flourish. *I earned it. And who knows when my damn luggage will show up.*

He hits Tumi and picks up a new wallet. Next, he treats himself to a Burberry scarf in the brand's iconic plaid. The salesgirl there is a stunner, waist-length black hair, pale skin, and blood-red lips. Peter engages her in conversation, asking for restaurant recommendations and other insider tips. She's sweet and helpful, and for a brief moment Peter indulges in fantasy: *I'll ask her to go for a drink after her shift. Take her to one of the restaurants she touted.*

Instead he thanks her for her help and exits the store. He's so laden with packages he decides to head back to their hotel. *Surely Eva will be back by now.*

But when he gets to their room and dumps his shopping bags, Eva is still nowhere to be seen. The maids have been in; the bed is made, new towels neatly hung, and the tub scrubbed. A fresh assortment of miniature toiletries graces the vanity. Peter checks the contents of the walk-in closet, but everything seems as he had left it. There are no signs that Eva has been here.

Anger morphs dizzily to worry. Peter heads back down to the lobby. Showing a picture of Eva on his phone, he inquires of the concierge, the desk clerks, the hostesses at both lobby-level restaurants. He takes the elevator up to the sixth floor and asks the two pretty girls working at the desk of the opulent spa. Both shake their heads. Next he steps outside to scan the pool area. The deck chairs are sparsely populated today, as many attendants on duty as there are hotel guests. The two pools look inviting, though, the slate that runs between them striated with rivulets of water. A large bubbling hot tub nestles in a corner of the deck, affording a spectacular view of Kowloon.

No Eva.

Peter heads back up to their room.

The first sweeping wave of real panic hits. Peter checks the time. Eva's been missing almost twenty-four hours. At least that's how long it's been since she ran a bath and locked him out.

Where the hell can she be? What if she was right about that guy in the airport?

Guilt explodes on top of worry. But Peter reassures himself: *She's an unemployed former lifestyle journalist; why would she possibly be in danger from that guy in the airport? Or anyone else for that matter?*

But as he dismisses one concern, another rises with a vengeance. *What if she's injured, the victim of an accident? Or worse, a crime, a mugging or a rape? What if I've been shopping and fantasizing about shopgirls while Eva has been lying in a ditch somewhere?*

Peter's stomach flips. He realizes with a start that he forgot to eat today. On autopilot, he lifts the hotel phone and calls down to room service, ordering a burger with all the extras: cheese, avocado, grilled onions, and arugula. An order of fries and a coffee with milk on the side. He politely acknowledges the estimate on the food: twenty minutes.

He sinks down onto the edge of the bed and stares at nothing.

Where is she? Where is she? Where is she? The refrain runs through his brain on a fevered loop.

He jolts from his tortured reverie when he hears the knock at the door. He rises to answer it, crossing into the sitting room and skirting the jumbled pile of shopping bags. He opens the door to see a young man whose nameplate reads NELSON smiling at him from behind a cloth-draped cart.

"Mr. Lombard? I have your food. May I set it up for you?"

Peter stares at him for a long minute. Nelson shifts uncomfortably.

"Mr. Lombard? Do you want me to bring your meal in?"

When Peter speaks, his voice sounds unnatural to his own ears. It's the voice of a stranger, a man stripped of confidence or purpose or opinion.

"I think my wife is missing," he blurts. To his horror, once he starts he can't stop. "We arrived yesterday. She took a bath. I took a pill and went to sleep. When I woke up in the middle of the night she was gone. And she hasn't been back since."

Nelson maintains his composure. "Perhaps I should get the manager, sir."

"Good idea. Get the manager. Thank you."

"And your food?"

Peter can smell the tantalizing scent of grilled meat and fried potatoes, the heady aroma of coffee.

"I'll take it. Thank you."

He signs the proffered check. Hands it back. "What's the manager's name?"

"Mr. Ho."

"You'll send him right up?"

"Yes, sir."

Peter pulls the room service cart into his room. His stomach unleashes a greedy grumble. *No point in letting good food go to waste. And a man needs to eat in order to think, doesn't he?*

He demolishes the meal, leaving a plate smeared only with ketchup and crumbs. Another pang of guilt hits as he contemplates his careless consumption of a hundred-dollar meal while Eva could be hurt (*or worse*), but he pushes these dreadful thoughts away. *She's fine. She has to be fine.*

A knock and he's on his feet, swiping his greasy hands on a napkin and lunging toward the door.

"Eva?" he asks as he opens it.

No. Nelson again. The bellman smiles apologetically and gestures to the suitcase he's toting on a brass luggage cart. "Mr. Ho will be right up. But good news! The airline delivered your suitcase."

"Thank you," Peter says automatically, reaching in his pocket for a tip. The appearance of his luggage gives him a lurch of hope, as if perhaps the world is settling back correctly on its axis, with Eva's arrival certain to follow.

Before departing, Nelson repeats that the hotel manager will be right up. Peter rolls the bag inside and heaves it up on the bed. Unzips it.

The contents are a total mess, clothes jumbled together, toiletries open and leaking, even the lining split. He feels a little nauseous from the violation and a mounting sense of dread.

This time the knock at the door makes Peter flinch. He puts the bolt on and opens the door the inch the bolt allows. Peers outside.

The hotel manager, Liam Ho, introduces himself and presents an embossed card with his name and title.

Peter closes the door and releases the latch in order to admit Ho, then gestures him inside and toward a seat. Peter describes the timeline of his and Eva's arrival at the hotel, his last sighting of his wife.

Mr. Ho eyes the shopping bags scattered across the plush carpet and Peter leaps in defensively. "I thought she'd be back. I wasn't worried yet. It was . . ." He trails off. *I don't need to explain myself to this man.*

Mr. Ho looks at Peter, expressionless. "Is this your wife's first visit to Hong Kong, Mr. Lombard?"

"No. She was here for two months after she graduated college."

"How long ago was that?"

"Almost ten years."

"Does your wife have friends in the city?"

"A few. Nobody that I've ever met, but I know she keeps up with a couple of people. Facebook mostly."

"Is it possible she went to see one of them?"

"In theory. But she didn't take a change of clothes or anything. Her toiletries are still here."

"Then she probably will be back later today."

"But why hasn't she answered any of my calls or texts?"

Mr. Ho steeples his hands together and places them on top of his crossed legs. Shrugs his narrow shoulders. "You tell me."

Peter meets his hooded, judging eyes and instantly knows that Mr. Ho is well informed about his argument with Eva at the check-in desk yesterday. He decides to take it head-on. "I see you've heard about our little squabble at the front desk yesterday. Look, we had a long flight, and we were tired . . . are you married? Surely you understand?"

"Of course, Mr. Lombard."

Somewhat relieved, Peter continues. "Can you at least see if your security footage can pinpoint what time she left the hotel?" He stands and consciously adjusts his tone to one with more authority as he looms over the much smaller man. "I'd also like to speak with the local police. And I'll contact the embassy myself."

He shows the manager the screen saver on his phone: Eva smiling and radiant, her brown hair a little longer than she's wearing it now, the love and delight in her eyes unmistakable.

"That's my wife, Eva Lombard. We're here celebrating our seventh anniversary, Mr. Ho. . . ." Peter coughs to cover the wobble in his voice. "And I don't think this is about the argument Eva and I had yesterday." He continues, "She told me someone was following her. I dismissed it. But someone did try to break into our house in London right before we left for Hong Kong. And my luggage was taken and gone through. I don't know what's going on, but I'm worried. Genuinely scared. I need your help, sir."

Mr. Ho stands. "I'll call an inspector I know at Central, Mr. Lombard." He extends a hand for Peter to shake. "But I'm quite certain your wife is fine. Hong Kong is an extremely safe city." His words are firm and Peter is sure Ho believes them even though he can't.

"Thank you for your reassurances. Please let me know what your policeman friend says."

But as the hotel manager offers to roll away the room service cart and promises he will get right on the phone to the police, Peter feels anything but reassured.

WHILE PETER WAS SLEEPING . . .

——

Eva Lombard,
Hong Kong Island

The hotel bath is glorious, deep and wide, and Eva soaks comfortably in the hot water, her head tilted back to rest on a rolled washcloth. There's a sliver of window over the tub from which she can see a slice of Hong Kong skyline. She stabs at some bubbles with her big toe, enjoying their satisfying pops. The water is fragrant with the hotel's bath gel, a heady mixture of sandalwood, lemongrass, and vanilla.

As soon as she's out of the tub, she'll slip in next to Peter in bed. Cuddle up to him from behind the way he always likes and get them back on the right foot. She pushes her body up slightly so her pink nipples peek above the soapsuds, hardening as they meet the cool air of the bathroom. Eva splashes warm water over them, then sinks back down into the heat, stroking her body, warming herself up for Pete.

Rising from the soapy water, she wraps herself in a plush bath sheet, briskly drying her body, toweling her damp hair. She drops the towel to the floor and contemplates her naked body in the steamy mirror. It's a strong body, sexy by most modern standards, a body that should be able to produce a baby with no difficulty. Eva takes a deep breath, then unlocks and opens the bathroom door.

She sees Peter, lying on his side, his back to her, still in the clothes he wore to travel. Eva slips in behind him and curls her damp, warm, naked body around his. She nuzzles his neck, breathes softly into his ear. Peter snorts, shifts onto his back, and commences raucous snoring. She lies there for a few moments, watching his face, feeling the rise and fall of his breath underneath the palm she's placed on his chest. She begins to feel chilly. She draws her hand down from his chest to his cock. Lets it linger there. Peter sleeps on.

Eva rises and steps into the bedroom's walk-in closet. She quickly pulls on some clothes: a bra and panties, a pair of black jeans, and a long-sleeved, poppy-colored T-shirt, all topped by a black leather jacket. She laces on a pair of high-top sneakers and winds a rose-colored scarf around her neck. Checks her shoulder bag: wallet, sunglasses, cellphone, lip balm, sunscreen. She pulls the bag on cross-body style and strings her Leica around her neck.

She steps out of the closet and pauses a moment to look at Pete again. He's on his back, mouth open, snoring, dead to the world.

Ambien. I recognize the snore. He'll be out for hours.

Eva pads softly into the suite's sitting room. The plastic key cards sit in their cardboard sleeve next to the champagne and truffles. The ice has melted in the bucket; the champagne bottle looks sweaty and forlorn. It appears Pete got to the chocolate, though; there's only one left.

Definitely Ambien. He doesn't even really like chocolate.

Eva pops the last cocoa-dusted morsel in her mouth and extracts one of the two key cards. There's a map of the city on the desk and she tucks it into her bag.

I'll take a walk. He'll take a nap. Maybe later we'll make a baby.

She plants a light kiss on Peter's forehead and steals out of the suite, careful to close the door softly behind her. She exits the hotel and orients herself. Pleased to discover she's within walking distance of Hong Kong Park, Eva tucks the map in the back pocket of her jeans and sets out.

It feels good to stretch her limbs after their long flight. And it's intoxicating to be back in Hong Kong. She wonders if she dare call

Alex while they're there. Would it be awkward? It shouldn't be. Water under the proverbial bridge, right? Their thing had been years ago; she's married now, Alex's been married and divorced. They'd been just kids back then. It would be weirder not to call him. She's trying to remember how much she's told Peter about her relationship with Alex when something primal clicks: a warning signal, screaming for her attention.

She stops as if to fix a shoelace and peers back behind her. THAT MAN. The one from the Sly Fox, outside her house, in both airports. Now here. Again.

It's definitely not coincidence. Or paranoia. Or even if I am paranoid, it doesn't mean they're not out to get me. Isn't that the old joke?

Except this does not appear to be a joke. There is something about the man. . . .

Her heart quickens, a pulse flutters in her throat. She's conscious of simultaneously feeling afraid, and curious, and also curiously vindicated. Annoyed at Pete for dismissing her so thoroughly. *How can I be thinking all of these things at once?*

Not to mention the part of her mind that is tactically spinning wheels: *Which way should I go? Who can I ask for help?*

Eva bolts into motion; her body overrules her paralyzed mind. She swiftly weaves through the crowded afternoon streets, fueled by fear but also by a cold, furious resentment at this stranger for making her afraid.

Where will I be safe?

She enters the familiar terrain of Hong Kong Park. She knows it well, the koi pond and the aviary, the playground and the Tai Chi Garden, the market stalls and the teaware museum. As well as many lesser known byways and hideaways that Alex had shown her. It may be years since Eva's been here, but even so she feels like Hong Kong Park is home turf, an oasis of greenery and peace surrounded by congested steel and glass.

She darts into the park, fear driving her swift steps down one pathway and onto another. Belatedly, she realizes this second path is nearly deserted; a sole couple wanders hand in hand off in the distance. It dawns on Eva that breaking off into the park was a mistake. *I need to go back to where there are crowds.*

The thought is no sooner in her head than she feels a fierce tug on the strap of her Leica that yanks her back into a broad chest. Eva tilts her shocked face up to confront her assailant. "Get the fuck off me!" she spits, clutching at her belongings.

In reply he merely grimaces. Then he tightens his grip on Eva's camera strap with one hand and slices at it with the switchblade that suddenly appears in his other hand. Eva instinctively swats at the knife and the blade finds the soft pad of her palm. She yelps in pain as blood streams.

He jabs at the straps of her camera and her purse. Cold fury grips Eva. *Fuck you, asshole! Not today!*

She locks her arms around her possessions and jams an elbow up into her attacker's nose. As he recoils, she pivots and slams a knee up into his groin. He releases her as he howls and dances in pain. Eva gives him one last kick that sends him sprawling face-down onto the pavement.

"Asshole," Eva snaps with a force she doesn't really feel. On the inside she feels soupy, as if she might puddle away like the Wicked Witch of the West. Turning on her heel, she runs as fast as she can, grateful for the self-defense class she and Jenny had taken together last year back in New York.

"I'll catch you later!" her attacker yells after her with a snigger.

Eva finds the jeer more chilling than a threat.

She pounds her way past the koi pond with its wide, bench-lined, manicured walkways, out past the market stalls selling kites and flutes and lanterns, and into the flow of pedestrian traffic on crowded Cotton Tree Drive.

It's only then that she finally stops, gasping for breath, still clutching her camera and purse to her chest. She turns and scans the crowd behind her. No sign of him. Her palm is slick with blood. She sets her belongings down and winds her scarf around her hand, applying pressure to stop the flow.

Shit. Now what?

Twenty minutes later, Eva's sipping a steaming cup of green tea and nibbling on a custard bun in a dimly lit tea shop. *What was he after?*

Propelled by instinct, she scrolls backward through the photographs stored on the digital card of her Leica. The shot she took of the view from their hotel room. A couple of snaps in the Hong Kong airport. That bitch with the Pomeranian at the Sly Fox.

And, fuck. There he is. In the background of the shot of the woman and her dog is the man Eva just left bleeding in Hong Kong Park.

Heart pounding, Eva zooms in on him and his companion, both in gray suits, rep ties. The camera has captured their shared look of outraged surprise, as if her taking the pictures was a personal affront to them as well as to the angry blonde and her dandelion of a dog.

Maybe it was an affront. Maybe these are two men who shouldn't be seen together. Is that why he tried to grab her camera? Frowning, Eva zooms in closer on the second guy's face. It's vaguely familiar to her; not like someone she knows, but like someone she *ought* to know. His identification dances tantalizingly on the edges of her consciousness. Still, she can't quite place him.

But the other man in the picture has been following her; of that much she's certain. She adds up the pieces: He trailed her to her home after she inadvertently took his photograph at the Sly Fox. Possibly tried to break into their house later that night. Followed her to Hong Kong. Attacked her with a knife. *Why?*

And is Pete involved? Why did he deny knowing her attacker, especially since she saw them interact *twice*? Is this why he was so condescending and dismissive?

Eva looks down at her bloody hand tightly wound in the soft cotton of her scarf. She peels away the fabric. Blood bubbles up, still fresh and urgent. Fighting nausea, she reapplies pressure.

Why did Peter leave the burglar alarm off last night? Was that Plan A, foiled by Baxter? Is Plan B Hong Kong? Is it easier to dispose of a body here? Because right about now, it looks like her husband might be trying to have her killed.

Eva checks herself. Is she being overly dramatic? Maybe she should just go back to the hotel, wake up Pete, file a police report? Or even better yet, just forget about the whole encounter?

No. There's no way she's returning to the hotel until she has a better idea of what the hell is going on. And how Peter's involved, if he is.

Why the surprise trip? And then the Paris/Hong Kong fake out? It's all plain weird.

Eva realizes there's not a living soul who knows where on earth she is and she feels lonelier than ever. As well as ashamed of the false front she's been putting up for her sister and her friends back home. Not to mention disgusted with herself for day drinking and self-pity.

Eva tucks those unpleasant feelings away in favor of the more delicious tingle that quickens her. Because there's no denying it. She feels *energized* as she finishes her tea and contemplates her next steps. Yes, she's scared. Yes, she's full of questions and doubts. But there is a feeling of *rightness* about this too, as if life had finally handed over the perfect lead she always somehow knew was coming to her as a part of her destiny in investigative journalism. She just never suspected the story she'd write would be her own.

A shiver passes through her as she remembers the mocking laugh of her assailant in the park. No. She's definitely not going back to the hotel. She's going to see the best ally she has in Hong Kong.

How do we choose the paths we follow?

Or is it that they choose us? We embrace the notion of free will as a defining human trait, but how often does any of us really have an opportunity to create the life we desire?

Even more perplexing, how often do we destroy our own chances when that rare opportunity arrives?

RICH PEOPLE PROBLEMS

———

Magali Guzman,
New York City

Roger Elliott had surprised Maggie. Not that she could say exactly what she'd expected. Arrogance maybe? Entitlement certainly. But she'd walked into their interview expecting her hackles to rise, as she knew *just enough* about Elliott beyond, of course, the sensational details about his recently missing wife and child. The son of a wealthy real estate investor who'd become even wealthier, his life was limos to her subway cars, prime steaks to her ground chuck. Maggie's earned everything she has, and paid her own way through college too; Elliott's silver spoon is diamond encrusted.

She hadn't expected to genuinely *like* the guy. But she did. And she felt his concern about his wife and young son pulse over her like a wave, drawing her into the ocean of his anxiety. She found herself wanting to fix things for him, make it all better.

Maggie began their interview by reminding Elliott that they would need to start from the beginning. Apologized for asking him to repeat information he'd no doubt already shared with the police. Told him that while this process might be difficult, she and Special Agent Johnson would be fresh eyes and that sometimes fresh eyes see new things. Then she dove in, confirming times and dates and details, while Ryan took notes.

———

Now, reviewing the notes from the intake, Elliott's magnetic spell dispersing like a cloud of steam, she tries to parse exactly what he did to cast his magic. If she can harness that kind of charisma, she'll *slay* as a UC. He listened attentively, made eye contact, was commanding but also revealed an intriguing strain of vulnerability. She anticipates speaking to him further with an excited clinical eye; what can she harvest from this man to use for her own purposes?

A little ashamed of her naked self-interest in the wake of a missing woman and child, Maggie turns her attention back to her notes. Elizabeth "Betsy" Baer Elliott. Thirty-four years old. Wife of seven years to businessman/philanthropist Roger Deacon Elliott, forty-two. Last seen at their Park Avenue apartment just before seven P.M. thirteen days ago. Last seen wearing jeans, a pink cashmere sweater, and a sheer white scarf threaded with gold. Five feet, six inches. Approximately 138 pounds. Brown eyes, brown hair. Scar from a C-section, three small moles arranged "like a constellation" near the right side of her bottom lip, no other distinguishing marks.

Maggie thinks about the tremor of longing in Roger Elliott's voice as he used that phrase, "like a constellation." She suddenly envisions him declaring it as such to his new bride on their honeymoon, imagines the way in which it became part of their marital code.

What the hell is up with me? Like I'm some kind of romantic all of a sudden? This is ridiculous.

Squaring her shoulders, Maggie shakes off her fancies. Elliott had last seen Betsy with their son, Bear Elliott, age six (42 inches tall and 48.5 pounds as of his last checkup), brown eyes, brown hair, wearing Star Wars pajamas.

According to Roger Elliott, Betsy had been reading Bear a bedtime story when he stopped in on the way from the office in order to pick up a fresh shirt. This wasn't usual, but he'd dripped tomato sauce on his shirt at lunch and he used the need to change as an excuse to take the opportunity to kiss his young son good night. When he returned home after his dinner, Betsy and Bear were gone.

How did Betsy seem when he last saw her? *Fine. The same as always. Happy.*

Was anything bothering Betsy? *Not that he knew of.*

Did anything unusual happen the day she and Bear disappeared? *Not that he knew of.*

Did the family have private security? *Yes, but dismissed after Betsy and Bear were home for the evening.*

Was their building staffed with doormen? *Yes.*

Had the staff on duty seen Betsy or Bear leave the building that night? *No.*

Did he know who the doorman on duty was that night? *Yes. Juan Perez. He gave a statement to the police.*

Are there security cameras in and around the building? *Yes.*

Had Elliott seen any of the footage? *Personally? No.*

Had the police? *Yes, but if that provided any leads they haven't shared them.*

Did Betsy have her cellphone? *No. It was left in the apartment. Along with her purse.*

Did she only have the one cellphone? *As far as he knew.*

Had there been any threats against the family? *No. Nor any communications at all about or from Betsy and Bear since they vanished, except for false attempts by crackpots that had been easily discredited. Until today.*

The demand letter had come via old-fashioned snail mail to Elliott's apartment and is now with forensics. The ask was simple: three million dollars in unmarked bills to be left in a locker at 30th Street Station in Philadelphia. The reward was vague: Betsy and Bear to be delivered safely at a time and place to be determined. The missive concluded by instructing Elliott to wait for further details.

Did Elliott have any idea who might have sent the demand? *No.*

What did he think of the rumors that Betsy had taken Bear and left voluntarily? Was that still a possibility to be considered?

Fallon Marks bristled, interjecting before his client could respond. "Look here, we are presenting you with *evidence* of a *crime.* . . ."

Ryan raised an admonitory eyebrow at Maggie, pen poised in the air, a cocky smile playing about his lips.

But to Maggie's surprise, Elliott raised a hand to shush his lawyer. "I never believed that Betsy left me. I still don't. I don't know where my wife and son are and I'm worried sick, but I don't know any more than you do if this ransom demand is real. That's what I'm here to find out."

Maggie reassured him their goal was the same. Ryan's eyebrow settled. The lawyer huffed and puffed but backed down. Maggie dove back into her questions.

Did the three-million-dollar amount have any significance that Elliott was aware of? *No.*

Did anything about either the envelope or the style of the letter itself ring any bells for him? Anything familiar about them? *No.*

Did he have any enemies?

The look he'd given her in response to that question was rueful, guilty yet slyly proud. "Can't succeed without making some, right? That must be true even in the FBI."

All too true. She'd shot a quick look at Ryan from underneath her lashes and cracked a hint of a smile back at Elliott.

Maggie had eased into asking Elliott about his marriage, but he'd seemed both genuinely affectionate about his wife and firm in his conviction that their relationship was solid. He denied any acrimony or serious quarrels, admitting only to the usual kind of marital squabbles with offhand candor. "Sure, we fight. Who doesn't? But lately our biggest argument was over whether we should do northern or southern Italy this year."

Maggie couldn't hate him even then, although a trip to Italy is the number one item on her wish list, as he'd quickly followed the comment with a self-deprecatory laugh and an engaging smile. "Rich people problems, I know."

Maggie pulls her thoughts away from the conundrum that is Roger Elliott and dives into Betsy Elliott's social media presence.

Hours later, after following threads, looking at links, posts and re-posts, friend profiles, comments, and comments on comments, Maggie has an initial profile. Betsy Elliott's an attractive woman with the well-cared-for gloss of a rich man's wife. Her once curly hair has been tamed in recent years into a sleek, shiny waterfall. She plays tennis and takes Pilates. They keep horses at their East Hampton estate and Betsy rode competitively when she was younger (a number of "Throwback Thursday" posts feature her jumping astride her black mare or collecting ribbons at horse shows). She got her BA from Sarah Lawrence, where she studied literature and art history, attended the University of Chicago Law School, and worked as an intellectual property lawyer until she gave birth to Bear. The little boy is the subject of Betsy's most frequent and adoring posts. She volunteers in his school library and chaperones field trips.

Quotes by famous women authors are frequent in her feeds, as are pictures of a radiant Betsy both solo and flanked by her husband and/or child, with beaming groups of friends. Luncheons, charity events, restaurant openings, the Central Park Zoo, birthday parties, the Met Gala, the opera, the theater, vacations abroad. A glittering life of privilege and pleasure parades before Maggie's dazzled eyes.

The woman's wardrobe alone! Maggie doesn't think Betsy Elliott appears in the same outfit twice. From casual chic to gorgeous couture, she has it all.

Maggie assembles an initial list of people to interview including Betsy's parents and two sisters (one living in Nashville, Tennessee, the other in Portland, Oregon), and several friends here in Manhattan who appear frequently in Betsy's social media.

She'd asked Elliott about family members, of course. He'd told her that the day after the disappearance, he'd called both of Betsy's sisters and her folks, "just saying hello," as he didn't want to panic them unless it was necessary. No one had heard from Betsy. That's still true as far as he knew, but they hadn't spoken in about a week. There had been some disagreement about the $250,000 reward Roger had offered for information about Betsy and Bear's whereabouts. Crazies had flocked to the extended family; Betsy's parents and sisters had since shut him out.

All that needs to be confirmed. Roger Elliott may have charmed her, but there is no way Maggie will allow him to manipulate her.

She checks one last time to see if forensics has delivered a report on the ransom demand. Nada. She clocks out, intending to head home to her cozy little apartment in Hoboken.

Forty-seven minutes and two subways later, Maggie introduces herself to Juan Perez, doorman at the Elliott apartment building on Park Avenue. His dark eyes flicker attraction that fades fast when she produces her badge. Nonetheless, slipping into Spanish paves the way for easy conversation.

Perez has worked at the building for five years. The Elliotts live in the penthouse; Mr. Elliott owns the building. Mrs. Elliott was very nice, very good on tips, very devoted to her son. Mr. Elliott was pleasant enough, not a talker, though, traveled a lot. The only time Perez ever saw Mrs. Elliott lose her shit was when a nanny left little Bear alone in the lobby in his stroller while she ran back upstairs to get something she'd forgotten. Even though a doorman (not Perez) had been on duty and in the lobby the whole time (which had maybe been ten minutes), Mrs. Elliott had come in the front door, found the boy unattended, and gone ballistic. With the nanny departing in tears, the episode had become legend in the building.

Perez shrugs. In his job he's seen it all, things she wouldn't believe. Ten minutes later, Maggie cuts him off. She'll never unhear this shit. Rich people. Crazy. And none of his stories about mysterious "doctor" visits or high-priced transvestite prostitutes seem relevant to the disappearance of Betsy and Bear Elliott.

Driving the topic back around to her quarry, Maggie presses further about the night Betsy and Bear vanished. Juan's shift started at four P.M. Mrs. Elliott and Bear had come in around five-thirty. She'd joked about having to give Bear a speed bath in order to make his bedtime, something about the day being so beautiful, she couldn't bring herself to come inside.

That doesn't sound like the comment of an anxious woman.

Maggie asks the doorman to think carefully. Had there been anything strange? Any kind of a change or unusual event leading up to Betsy and Bear's disappearance?

"Well," Perez volunteers, "there was the new nanny, but even without a scene, the turnover of nannies for the Elliotts is pretty high."

Maggie takes down all the information Perez can offer: The new nanny started about three weeks before the disappearance, but the Elliotts always have a rotating trio. He can't help but offer his opinion about a woman who needs three nannies to raise a child; after all, his single mother raised six kids on her own. "Mrs. E may be nice enough, but come on. No disrespect. I hope she and the kid are all right, but why even have kids if other people are going to bring them up?"

Maggie doesn't comment. It strikes her as odd too. By all appearances Betsy Elliott is a loving, involved mother, one who gave her career up for her child. What *is* with all the nannies?

"What do you know about the new one?" Maggie pushes. "What's her name? She still around?"

"None of them have been around, since, you know. I can't remember her name. Like I said, lot of turnover. Maybe Mr. Elliott knows? She wasn't like the other girls, though."

"Why's that?"

The nannies the Elliotts hired tended to be British, with "*pegas por el culo"* (sticks up their asses). The new nanny is American; Juan guesses local. She didn't seem educated or polished like the others. She had dark hair, kind of skinny. Late twenties, he guesses, when Maggie presses him.

She thanks him for his time. Asks to speak to whoever is currently in the building from the security office. Juan buzzes through on the intercom.

As she waits, Maggie examines every detail of the lobby. Fresh flowers in fancy vases, highly polished marble floors, gilt-edged mirrors.

A flotilla of young women and their stroller-bound charges help one another navigate the glass door leading into the building. Maggie does a quick scan and deduces the women are nannies, rather than mothers, based on a number of factors including ethnicities (varied), wardrobe (more Century 21 than Saks Fifth Avenue), and shoes (Payless not Prada). Both women and children are having a boisterously good time. Cheeks are pink with laughter; happy chatter flows.

Maggie adds another fragment to the picture she's assembling: this community of women raising other women's children. Surely there are secrets buried there? If there are, she will find them.

DIESEL FUMES

——

Jake Burrows, aka John Bernake,
New Orleans, Louisiana

He hears the Target before he sees her. That nervous giggle that punctuates the end of almost every sentence. But if she's giggling, it means she didn't come alone as instructed. *Damn it.*

The humidity in the air makes Jake feel like he's breathing literal clouds. Sweat pools and drips, down his back, into his tube socks, at the waist of his khaki flat-front shorts. He keeps his hands shoved deep in his pockets; he's afraid of what their tremor might reveal.

With studied casualness, Jake leans against an iron lamppost on a rise, a vantage point from which he can survey the streets rimming the campus and the bustle of students and other football faithfuls pouring toward the university's stadium. In the distance, he can hear the blare of the marching band. He reassures himself that he comfortably fits in, dressed as he is. He runs a hand through his newly grown facial hair; it's remarkable how much the Vandyke changes his appearance. He tugs his baseball cap lower over his eyes. Adjusts his Ray-Bans.

Grateful for the training that led up to this moment, Jake still wrestles to calm the nervous anxiety coursing through him. He knows *what* to do. The question is, will he pull it off?

The girls are in front of him before he has another second to doubt. Dakota Harris, long tanned legs sprouting from jean cutoffs pulled over a black one-piece bathing suit. Her sandy hair is pulled on top of her head in a messy knot. The girl next to her wears an almost identical outfit, right down to the pair's matching flip-flops.

"Heya," Dakota greets him. "This is my roommate, Val."

"I told you to come alone." Jake lets the statement hang in the thick air for just a moment. Then he shrugs, turns his back, and strides away.

"Wait!"

Jake hears Dakota call out after him, but he doesn't so much as turn his head. He hears Dakota say, "Val, wait here. I'll be right back," and then shush her friend's anxious protests. Jake allows himself a small smile. Behavior as predicted.

He turns the corner and slows his steps a little to give her time to catch up. He feels her fingers plucking at his elbow. He keeps walking.

"Wait! Stop. I'm sorry. I have the money right here."

Jake finally turns to face her and sees her frantically waving a stack of bills.

This girl's an idiot. "Put that away," he hisses. "And keep your voice down." He takes a quick scan of the street, but it doesn't seem like anyone is paying them any mind. Too much other revelry and game day nonsense compete for attention.

Dakota twirls a lock of hair and provocatively juts out a hip. "But you'll still sell to me, right?" she coos softly, confident of her charm.

"Only if you follow directions." Jake ladles a dollop of flirtation into his response, a hint of smile. *Let her think she's ahead of this game.*

Dakota smiles back. "Yes, sir!" She flashes a peace sign with her fingers. "Scout's honor."

"Okay. Come with me."

"Don't you have them on you?"

"In my car. It's just down here."

The rambunctious music of the marching band cascades through the air. Brass and drums below, the shrill piccolo rising and falling above.

On the distant edge of the deep blue sky, thick dark clouds mass together, the first threat of a storm. Jake turns into a dead-end street and Dakota trails after him without a backward glance, confirming his impression of her idiocy.

"How many do you have?" Dakota babbles. "Because a couple of other kids on our hall were maybe interested; I pooled our cash."

When he turns back, she looks at him eagerly. He realizes her skin in this game; how badly she wants to be the badass rebel turning the whole dorm on to X.

"I have everything you need," Jake replies. He pops open the trunk and leans forward to pull a black canvas bag from its recesses. Zips it open and throws back the top flap.

"Take a look," he says.

Dakota glances at him, her eyes bright with delighted daring. She turns her attention to the canvas bag, leaning over, and as she does, Jake strikes. One hand covers her mouth. The needle filled with fentanyl pricks her neck. Her eyes flare briefly in alarm before she crumples.

Jake bundles her into the trunk. Extracts her cellphone from her front pocket and then slams the trunk lid shut. His heaving breath roars in his ears. He feels dizzy, queasy. He practices mindful breathing as he's been taught: slow long inhales through his nose released through his mouth. He looks around. The narrow dead-end street is deserted. He'd disabled the CCTV cameras the night before. A handful of drunken frat boys stumble past at the far end, laughing and hollering. They pay him no mind. Jake's hammering heart slows.

He climbs into the driver's seat of the Ford Fusion he rented in Baton Rouge and drove to New Orleans. He's changed the plates, of course; destroyed the agreement between Thrifty rental cars and one John Bernake of Salt Lake City, Utah. Jake feels comfortable in

John's persona. He'll be sorry to have to retire him, when it comes to that.

He pulls smoothly out of the alley and into congested traffic, navigating away from the snarl. As he pulls onto the freeway, he drops Dakota's phone out the window of his car.

Damn, the things Jake would like to say to that girl!

Stupid enough to buy ecstasy from some strange dude she met at a party, even dumber to take on the role of supplier to her cohort. Idiotic enough to follow said strange dude into an alley, even dopier to let herself get stuck in the neck and shoved in a trunk.

Smart enough to get into a top school, though, Jake muses.

He drives the speed limit. He keeps a wary eye open for police. He watches the other cars and trucks that flow around him to be sure no one seems interested, on his tail. He resolves himself to the patience needed for a long road trip. Fiddles with the radio until he finds some Johnny Cash. Begins to compose his report to Catherine in his head.

REPORT

As per orders, contact was initiated with the Target the night before extraction. After reconnaissance revealing the Target's weekend plans, "Diesel" arranged to encounter her at an off-campus party held in a cottage on nearby Freret Street. This location was chosen after the premises were duly checked for security cameras, and those as well as the cameras on Freret Street disabled.

Diesel established confidence in his persona and a consequent request for a drug purchase the next day was achieved within forty-one minutes.

All went according to plan with the minor exception of the Target arriving at the rendezvous point with a Collateral, despite explicit instructions to come alone. As instructed, Diesel walked away. The Target followed as predicted.

Jake tends to keep his reports factual and minimal. Catherine uses every single phrase as a point from which to start an interrogation under the guise of expanding his training. *What was it about playing a drug dealer that appealed to you? Why did it come so easy? Did your relationship with your sister impede or assist your ability to create rapport with a teenage girl?*

Jake accepts the personal probing that is a pivotal part of his tutelage. Catherine unapologetically warned him she was going to break him down psychologically in order to build him back up before they began working together and then did just that. He's strong of mind now, stronger than he's ever been. Stronger of body too, buffed and polished. He appreciates the elements of his transformation while also wondering where it will take him.

Does anyone ever feel finished? Jake feels *unfinished,* as well as wary. He's uncomfortably *in process.* Like one of the famous Michelangelo bondage statues, exquisite marble figures wresting themselves from solid rock, half human, half stone, totally tortured.

Unease grips Jake's belly like a claw as he recalls sticking that needle in Dakota Harris's neck. Feeling her crumple in his arms took him back to Paris, where Catherine had neutralized him in just the same manner a few short years before.

For a brief flash, Jake smells the acrid, rusty scent of blood in his nostrils.

He wipes a palm across his suddenly sweaty brow as he thinks of his sister, Natalie. Not much older than Dakota, Natalie is in her junior year at RISD. She'd had a show of her glass sculptures at the end of her last semester that had created a bit of a sensation. At the opening reception, Jake couldn't help but gloomily wonder if the feverish buzz was as much about their tortured and public family history as it was about the tableau of monsters menacing fairies she'd crafted from blown glass. He'd thought her technique impressive but the art's obvious metaphors shamelessly exploitive.

They've been on the road for about an hour. Dakota's roommate might be concerned by now, but probably not enough so that she'll have sounded an alarm. Maybe she'll think she misunderstood and was to meet Dakota back at the dorm, or at the game. By the time the roommate's asking mutual friends or possibly taking the next step of alerting the girls' RA, Jake will be miles gone. When and if they really start searching for Dakota Harris, the only leads left behind will point to a mythical drug dealer nicknamed Diesel.

Misinformation is an essential part of their campaign to keep this idiot girl safe.

The sky finally splits and fat drops of rain plummet from thick clouds. Jake switches on the windshield wipers. He peers uneasily through the coursing water at the suddenly darkened road ahead.

As he takes a sharpish turn his wheels spin out, the Fusion hydroplaning on suddenly slick asphalt. A sickening *thud* booms from the trunk.

Jake leans into the skid and brings the sedan back under control. Weak with relief over righting the car, he panics anew as he questions the meaning of that *thud*. *What if Dakota rolled over and she suffocates? What if she hit her head and she's already dead? What if I've killed her?*

Fear adds lead to his foot. Jake accelerates, crossing two lanes of traffic to take an exit. He pulls off the ramp and turns into a gas station, pulling around to the back of the building near a pair of restrooms. A vehicle is parked, a battered Dodge pickup truck. Jake glances inside the truck as he pulls up alongside. Empty.

Jake pulls on a hoodie to shield himself from the rain and bounds to the back of his car. He glances around to make sure he's unobserved. Pops the trunk.

Dakota Harris is as he left her. Somnambulant. Still. Jake stares at her for a long moment, water coursing down his back. A drop of rain hits the girl's cheek and she stirs slightly, moans.

The ladies' room door swings open, and a leathery cowgirl in her forties sashays out in red cowboy boots and a denim minidress. She pops open a red umbrella. Jake slams his trunk shut.

"Whooee, this rain is something, isn't it?" The cowgirl grins at him as she hustles back to the pickup.

Ducking deeper into his hoodie, Jake climbs back into his car as fast as he can and hightails it out of there.

Dakota looks so young, so vulnerable lying there in the recesses of his trunk.

He understands Catherine has her methods; she's trained him well in both technique and theory. *But is her way always the right way?* He lifts one hand from the wheel and to his neck, his fingers seeking the spot where Catherine had injected him back on rue Saint-Honoré. It feels like a lifetime ago.

Several hours of mind-numbing driving later, Jake pulls over on a swampy stretch of pitch-black backcountry. They came through the worst of the rain a while ago, although the very air itself is misty and wet. The headlights of the Fusion cut deep golden circles into trees weeping with hanging moss and quivering with droplets.

Dakota Harris should be waking up by now.

Jake takes a long satisfying leak off the side of the road, letting his eyes adjust to the darkness. As Catherine had promised, this stopping point is spectacularly isolated. Rustles, coos, and hoots float from every shadowy direction but his flashlight and the Ford's headlights are the only illumination.

Jake pops the trunk, flashlight in hand. Dakota's still curled in a fetal position. Her eyes blink as the beam from the flashlight penetrates her fentanyl fog.

She gasps. Pushes herself up on an unsteady elbow. Attempts a scream, but is too dazed and drug sick, so a sickly yowl like an injured dog's whimper is all that emerges from her throat.

But fear blazes in her eyes. And revulsion. Jake hopes the beam of the flashlight blinds her to his sudden recoil. *I don't want anyone, ever, to look at me that way again.*

When did he become a man who drugs teenagers and bundles them into car trunks? He guesses the day he said yes to Catherine. *The ends justify, right?*

"My name is John. Your parents sent me to get you," he tells Dakota sternly. "And there's no point in yelling. We're in the middle of nowhere." *Two truths and a lie.*

"Why should I believe you?" the girl snarls. "You're a fucking *drug dealer*! You kidnapped me!"

"Believe your parents then," Jake retorts, hitting a preprogrammed number on a burner phone. "This was the best way to get you out of New Orleans. For your own protection."

The cell connects and Jake hands it over to Dakota, taking a step away from the trunk. He can hear the tinny electronic wash of her parents' voices through the phone's speaker, rising, falling, overlapping, beseeching, promising, reassuring.

"Okay," Dakota says into the mouthpiece. "Okay, okay. Right. Okay."

The girl hangs up the phone. "Fuck my life."

Jake holds out a bottle of water. "If it's any consolation, this is the safest way."

Dakota grabs the bottle and cracks it, draining it in three greedy swallows.

He offers her an arm and she climbs unsteadily out of the trunk.

"If you need to, you know, go, you should do it now on the side of the road. First, give me that phone back."

Her fingers tighten around the burner. "Where's my phone?"

"Long gone. Also for your own protection."

"I don't believe this shit! I have friends who will be looking for me, you know."

"Exactly." Jake wrests the burner from her hand.

"Here. Take the flashlight." He holds it out to her, along with a box of tissues.

He feels her fingers tighten around the heft of the flashlight as he passes it over, so admonishes her, "Don't do anything stupid. Just take care of business."

Dakota grabs the flashlight and tissues, moving around to the far side of the car, cursing under her breath all the while.

Jake turns in order to give Dakota privacy. "When you're done, lie down in the backseat. I'll cover you with a blanket. Best if you stay under it. There's more water, crackers, and fruit back there too."

"Are you waiting for a thank-you?" the girl calls back. "So not happening."

Jake drops the burner cell on the ground. Stamps down on it hard. Repeatedly.

"Is that the fucking phone?"

"Yes."

"Is there another one?"

"No."

"What if I need to speak to my parents again?"

"You'll be with them in about seven hours."

"Okay. Get this. I am keeping my shit together," she tells him, "but barely. We are *not* friends. Don't talk to me. Don't look at me funny. Don't say one word. I've had all I'm gonna take."

Jake turns to see Dakota zipping up her cutoffs and striding back to the car. She crawls into the backseat and allows him to cover her as she releases a dramatic sigh and a well-aimed eye roll. Jake gets back behind the wheel.

Next Steps and Risk Assessment: All of Target's previously owned electronic devices have been seized and destroyed, known social media accounts and other Internet histories need to be deleted and scrubbed. The Target will require monitoring, as although she is certainly bright enough to understand the dangers inherent in contact with any of her former friends and associates, she is still a teenager and suffers from limited impulse control.

Jake runs the phone over with the Fusion for good measure before they leave this little piece of nowhere.

It's as much to make an impression on Dakota as anything. Catherine has taught him much about the value of the well-timed point.

REUNIONS AND INTRODUCTIONS

Catherine,
Wheeless, Oklahoma

A relentless drone of chattering bugs vibrates through the open windows. Lisa Harris's soft, anxious voice barely rises above the scrum of noise. "Have you heard anything yet?"

Turning away from the window and the barren landscape it frames, I glance at my burner phone. "No."

Stephanie arrived three hours ago with the Harrises' pristine false papers, but Jake and his precious cargo are late. Nineteen minutes ago, I sent Stephanie out as an advance woman to keep watch for Jake on the long, empty road that leads to this shack. It's really only a ploy to get the Harrises to calm the fuck down. Jake's not terribly beyond schedule and I understand the extraction went seamlessly.

As soon as Jake arrives with Dakota Harris, I'll escort the family to our planned rendezvous with Dex, a pilot friend of mine from Texas who's arranged to meet us at the nearby Boise City Airport. (My history with Dex is a story for another time.) Dex will fly us to Mexico City. I have a safe house there.

"What's taking so long?" Lisa's fraying from the stress. Her normally soft voice is strident, her face pinched.

My burner phone lights up with a text. "She's spotted them. They're almost here."

"Thank god." The words burst from Steve. "Thank god. Dakota. Our little girl."

I realize these are the first words he's said in hours.

Finn peers up from underneath a sandy fringe of bangs. "Kota coming?"

His mother strokes his hair. "Yes, baby. Dakota's coming." Finn smiles and recommences humming.

The door bursts open, but it's just Stephanie, black shaggy hair tousled, binoculars strung around her neck. "They'll be ten to fifteen," she estimates, waving the lenses. "Saw them as they turned down by that big old dogwood."

"Let's get ready then," I command. "Pack up. We'll drive down and meet them on the road. Go right to the airport."

Steve and Lisa exchange a glance, the deadly reality of their situation hitting them in a fresh, sickening wave. When they were waiting for Dakota, that simple act occupied the entirety of their hearts and minds.

This is the moment of action, the moment of no return. Now Steve and Lisa Harris will accept fake passports, flee the country, live undercover. Before my eyes these two people are slamming up against the terrifying consequences of "doing the right thing," haunted by the recognition that this choice is also requiring actions on their part that they would previously have found morally repugnant (not to mention ridiculously far-fetched). All complicated by their quite legitimate fears about the impact this will have on their lives and those of their teenage daughter and autistic son.

"Right now?" Steve's face is white. "We haven't even seen Dakota yet. And with Finn . . . you know, we sometimes have to ease into things."

"I respect that," I answer. "But in that case, I suggest you start preparing Finn to go now. The faster we're out of here and you're all on that plane the better. I always have my kit, if you prefer that option."

"I'm sorry," Steve says to his wife for the hundredth time in my hearing.

"You did the right thing. You're doing the right thing." Lisa's reply is automatic; she's given it as many times as he's offered the apology. She stoops to her son's eye level. "Finn, baby, we're going to go meet Dakota now."

The boy hums on, fixated on his game. "Come on, Finn," Lisa croons. "Let's get ready to see Dakota."

Steve watches his wife coax his son up from the floor. The man's hands hang limply by his sides; a defeated look softens the contours of his face.

"Go pack up," I repeat to Steve. He startles to attention and nods at me abruptly before walking into the bedroom he's been sharing with Lisa and Finn.

I turn to Stephanie. "Get in the car. We'll be out as soon as."

"Yes, boss."

The reunion, when it happens twenty minutes later on a dusty shoulder off an empty stretch of sunbaked road, is epic. Finn Harris clamps his thin body around his older sister and whimpers with joy. Lisa and Steve encircle their two children with their own loving bodies. All four stand in a huddled cocoon of familial relief as I pull Stephanie and Jake over to the side.

I introduce my two operatives to each other by first names only, John and Stevie (although their exchange of sly glances reveals both probably and correctly expect that the names given are false). I explain I will drive the Harrises to meet their plane. The two of them will follow me to the airport. After the family and I are safely out, they will coordinate in order to dispose of the three vehicles we've used thus far in this operation. Then they are to disperse and wait for further instructions.

Stephanie gives Jake a direct, appraising glance. He looks back, awkward at first, but then he straightens his hunched shoulders and meets her stare head-on. She snaps a grin at him. "Okay, dude," she says. "Let's hit it." She jerks a thumb in my direction. "If the boss says go, I go."

I'm pairing them as a test of sorts and I suspect they know that too. So far, both Stephanie and Jake have worked solo or with me, but I've mentioned to each of them that I want to experiment with some other partnerships within the organization. I seem to have more cries for help than ever and I've had to contend with unanticipated growth. A wry smile crosses my lips as I think, *I'm management.*

"I don't know what you're so happy about, boss." Stephanie is as outspoken as always. "Still have to get them out of the country."

"*Bonne chance,*" I murmur to Jake and Stephanie. "Play nice, you two."

I approach the Harris family and lay a hand on Steve's back. "Okay, guys. Back in the car. We have a plane to catch."

An hour later, the Harrises and I are strapped into Dex's Citation VII, taxiing for departure. I'm heaving a sigh of relief as my phone rings. Not a burner. Not a disposable phone assigned to a specific case and never to be seen again. No, the one reserved for my few true friends, the one number on which they know they can reach me if they are ever in trouble.

With the roar of the engines flooding my ears, I hit the button to connect.

"Hello," I say. "Long time."

The voice on the other line is both refined and boisterous, deeply grave yet speckled with laughter.

"Hello, darling," says Forrest Holcomb. "You have no idea how sorry I am to ask. But I need you. By any chance are you anywhere near Hong Kong?"

A HARD ASK

—

Catherine,
Mexico City, Mexico

Toluca airport is located thirty-six miles from the dense heart of downtown Mexico City. Smaller than Mexico City International, it's for private planes like the old Cessna we're coming in on, and also where I've greased a few palms in advance of our arrival. We touch down and I quickly corral the Harris family together and hustle them off the plane.

Gabriela waits in a *fruta* delivery van, motor purring. She's as striking as when I first met her years ago: thick black hair, now with one silver streak, intense brown eyes under thick, arched brows. She's beautiful, yes, but more than that, her essence lets you know immediately this woman is strong, this woman is proud.

I open the back of the van and gesture the family inside. They clamber in, Steve hovering protectively around his wife and kids. I slam the door and lock it. Climb in next to Gabi.

"Thank you, my friend," I say in Spanish. *"Good to see you."*

She snorts with laughter. "Your accent is worse than ever," she retorts. "Speak English."

"Kill me for trying," I shoot back, pleased that we've folded so neatly into our old camaraderie.

"Anything I need to know?" she asks.

"I'll want to keep the family here at least until I arrange a safe deposition for Harris. Get everything on the record. Then we'll assess."

Gabi nods as we pull out of the airport and onto the crowded highway, heading for her townhouse in Roma Norte.

We pass airport hotels, parking structures, warehouses, gas stations, and fast-food joints without speaking. It's been a long time since I've been in Mexico City and as happy as I am to see my old friend Gabi, she also represents a line of harsh demarcation. Gabi is the reason I live off the grid, do what I do; she's the first person I helped escape an abusive relationship, the impromptu reason the Burial Society was formed, how I found my peculiar calling.

I'm dedicated to what I do, but it has its personal costs. One of them is the ungainly sack of bitter memories that always sits heavily, forever a weight on my shoulders.

I turn the conversation to Gabi's daughter, Mia; she's the future, not the past. Mia's twenty now, away at college studying environmental science. I ask Gabi how she's faring with her empty nest. She's happy, I'm pleased to hear. She likes living alone; she may go back to school herself. We don't talk about her husband. We never do. Not since the day I spirited her out of Aspen, Colorado, a sobbing, frightened Mia in her arms, both of them bloodied by that bastard's quick fists.

I confirm logistics. We can enter Gabi's place through the alley. Drive directly into the garage and from there, enter the house. She's gifted her longtime housekeeper (along with the housekeeper's entire family) a three-week vacation at the villa Gabi maintains in Acapulco. It's not the first time the Ruiz family has so benefited from my operations.

While it appears traditional on the exterior, the interior of Gabi's home has been transformed into a strikingly modern, yet still warm, showpiece.

Sustainable bamboo floors run throughout, except for the bathrooms, kitchen, and expansive pantry, where heated tiles powered by solar panels warm your feet. Spotless modern appliances in an unusual copper color blend beautifully with the honey onyx countertops in the open kitchen. Skylights flood the space with light. In addition to the kitchen, with its long oak table capable of seating twelve, there is a comfortable sitting area with a wide-screen television, and a second grouping clustered around a vast fireplace faced in the same warm onyx.

It's almost impossible to feel frightened here; the house is like a hug. Once inside, the Harris family relaxes visibly.

Gabi offers a platter of *tortas* and bottles of water. I show the Harrises upstairs to the rooms we've allocated them: Steve and Lisa in Mia's room, along with a cot for Finn, Dakota in Gabi's studio down the hall. Gabi has been thoughtful, made the beds, laid out towels and sweet scented soaps. She's also removed any and all electronic devices from every room in the house and swept for listening devices (usual precautions), but the Harrises don't need to know any of that. Even the TV downstairs will only play DVDs because, after all, we have to allow them some entertainment.

I need them to eat, sleep, and regroup before I begin to brief Steve on next steps. They are all frightened but will need bravery and resolve to see this through. I leave the family alone together, lingering at the top curve of the stairway. I hear some tears, some murmured words of comfort, what might be a yelp of pain? Or frustration? I can't tell.

It's only when I hear a shower running and the rhythmic lilt of Lisa reading aloud to Finn that I walk back down the stairs. Gabi waits for me with a shot of tequila.

"Give me a minute."

She raises an eyebrow in surprise. I cross to the sliding glass doors leading out to a terrace garden, pull them open, and welcome the gust of bold air that greets me. My spot (as I like to think of it) is as welcoming as ever: a cushioned armchair set deep under an eave in a location that provides a sweeping view of the entire street; a chair equally committed to comfort and to providing a perch where one can see without being seen.

Forrest Holcomb, or Holly, as I call him, is an anomaly in my life: a genuine intimate connection. We met when I first came to Paris. In the aftermath of the destruction of the closest thing I'd had to a childhood home and the disappearance of Mallory Burrows, I was reeling and reckless. Holly picked me up in a club. Or was it the other way around?

I knew who Holly was, although I pretended I didn't. I pretended a lot of things. Like my name, age, occupation, and nationality, just for starters. Our affair was explosive; we fevered for each other, couldn't stay away. Holly found me maddeningly elusive. I was uncharacteristically vulnerable, even so. Particularly to a man my father's age. I've read Freud.

Holly would have married me; after all, he marries freely. But after a while, he became suspicious of the time alone I insisted upon, my mysterious disappearances for days or weeks at a time. He thought I was cheating and had me followed. I surprised, disarmed, and debriefed his investigator. Afterward, I made the decision to expose myself to Holly, at least a little bit.

He learned that I was faithful to him. But also that I was not remotely the woman I'd pretended to be, that even my stories of loss had been just that—*stories*. I'd never tell him that the emotions had all been true; I only smudged the gritty details to protect him as much as myself. To this day he knows little about me, except that he loves me in his way, and I him, in mine. He's also sent me money, no questions asked, on more than one occasion. I always pay him back with interest. If that's not friendship, what is? I punch a number on my phone.

"Holly," I breathe into the mouthpiece.

"Hello, darling. May I ask where in the world you might be?"

"Sorry."

"I suspected as much, but I needed to ask. I'm not just being nosy. As I said, I have a situation in Hong Kong. One of my best and brightest, an American I scooped up and moved to London, is there on vacation with his wife. Big anniversary trip he planned as a surprise. Only she's gone missing."

"How long has it been?"

"Two days. My chap, Peter Lombard, says he woke up after taking a sleeping pill and discovered her gone from their hotel room."

"Is there any reason to doubt his story?"

"I don't. But some of his behavior is reading a little odd. And it seems the local police think he might be good for it."

"Watching cop shows again, Holly?"

"We all have our guilty pleasures."

I smile, loving our easy rhythm. "I don't see how a grand romantic gesture is pointing suspicion, though."

"Hotel staff heard them fighting when they checked in. As did the driver who brought them from the airport. Then Lombard was kind of an ass. He didn't alert anyone she was gone until hours after he realized she wasn't in the hotel. He bloody went shopping instead. Then came back to the hotel and ordered room service. Stupid git."

Holly knows enough about what I do that I don't ask why he thinks this might be a problem for the Burial Society. He must have his reasons. I wait for him to continue.

"Look," he goes on, "Lombard's a good man. His wife seems like a sweetheart. Two days. We all know what that means. If she hasn't taken off on her own, she's probably dead. But there's no way Lombard did it: I'd stake my reputation on it."

"When have you ever cared about your reputation?" I tease.

"I care what you think," Holly replies, suddenly grave.

An image flashes into my mind's eye. Holly and I at the Mandarin Oriental hotel, Paris, all tangled limbs and heated breath. The fiery intensity in his eyes.

"How's your wife?" I ask.

Holly doesn't rise to the bait. He'd asked me to marry him. I said no. Instead he now details the events that have plagued the

Lombards for the last few days: mysterious men, an attempted break-in, rifled luggage, all on top of Eva Lombard going missing.

"Will you look into it? Lombard thought she was imagining things at first, but now of course he's beating himself up over not taking her more seriously."

"For you, I will."

When I hang up the phone fifteen minutes of questions and answers later, I'm scheming. I need to stay here with the Harrises, but this could be the perfect time to test out a pairing of recruits. I walk back into the house and crush the burner phone I just used under the heel of my boot. Take the shot of tequila Gabi has on offer and shoot it back.

Jake and Stephanie are going to Hong Kong.

ANNUAL NUMBER OF DEATHS

———

Stephanie Regaldo, aka Stevie Nichols, Hong Kong Island

Hong Kong is *madness*.

Buckled into the backseat of a taxi zipping its way through a confusing tangle of jammed roadways, Stephanie grips an armrest in terror. Her bright blue eyes take in the extraordinarily crowded vertical skyline rife with cranes signaling even more structures to come. The entire city is hung with mist, gray swaths that float and twist and twine like wraiths around the skyscrapers.

Signs flash by in Chinese and English. Stephanie notes some British spellings and terms: *colour* instead of *color,* GIVE WAY on a triangular sign instead of YIELD. It's the first time she's been out of the United States and she can't deny she's thrilled. Catherine had promised her this: a life of purpose and adventure, even if she'd also warned there would be dangers.

But what life isn't dangerous? Stephanie knows all too well how fragile our ties are to this earth. To have come from where Catherine found her to being here is an impossible dream realized.

She pulls out the passport and studies it again. She still can't believe how real it looks, along with the Massachusetts driver's license and credit cards to which it conforms. She mouths her cover name: *Stevie Nichols.* Stephanie had picked this name as a small nod to her mother living back on the northern tip of the island of

Kauai, raising organic vegetables and keeping chickens; Stevie Nicks is Mom's favorite singer. Stephanie knew she'd keep *Stevie Nichols* straight in her head.

A rush of excitement and, yes, a tremor of fear race through her. *Control your breath. Control your mind.*

Her orders are clear. Proceed to the apartment Catherine's arranged and wait for the arrival of the man identified and introduced to her as John at the Oklahoma reunion of the Harris family. Together, they are to interview Peter Lombard with the questions Catherine's provided for them. After their interview, they are each to send an independent report of their impressions, about which they are not to speak to each other. Catherine wants their individual gut observations and thoughts untainted by comparison. After receipt of both of their reports, they will be given further instructions.

Stephanie figures Catherine is employing this methodology as a kind of control. The discrepancies in their respective reports will reveal more to her than the similarities. Impressive. That's what the boss is. Fucking impressive.

Stephanie wonders about John. She guesses they're pretty close in age; he might be a few years younger. Or he might just be soft. He had that look about him; the one she'd seen on the spoiled rich kids who came to Hawaii for vacations replete with Jet Ski and catamaran rentals and shopping sprees for authentic "Hawaiiana." The kids who believed every closed door they encountered would graciously sweep open, welcoming them inside. And fuck her if those doors didn't actually sweep open after all for them; she'd seen it time and again, just as often as they were slamming in her face.

On the other hand, Stephanie knows enough about the other people who work for Catherine to know they are usually survivors of something painful, if not gruesome. Their stories may not be the same, but their scars are aligned. John might be more like her than she knows, hardened in ways not visible to her eye.

She reviews her brief on their assignment: There's a missing woman. Eva Fitzgerald Lombard, thirty-two, a graduate of Barnard College, with a master's in journalism from Columbia University, raised on Long Island, recently of London, England. Married, seven years this week, to Peter Lombard, BA, Columbia University, Wharton MBA, currently employed by Holcomb Investments, a London-based hedge fund.

A lot of pricey education going on in that marriage.

Stephanie scowls. She'd graduated high school, just barely; college had never been an option. But, as she defensively reminds herself, Catherine has shown her just how smart she really is. She may not have degrees, but she's learned to both code computers and to hack them, drive as if she was behind the wheel of a race car, and correctly interpret the body language of most liars and scoundrels and then ply that knowledge with skill. *We all have our strengths.*

As her taxi whips past an absurdly tall cluster of apartment buildings from which endless rows of air conditioners hang perilously suspended, Stephanie pulls back from the window. She resolves to do an Internet search later for "the annual number of deaths by falling air conditioners in Hong Kong." Maybe that's what happened to Eva Lombard. She went out for a walk and got herself knocked on the head by a plummeting AC unit.

The apartment in the skyscraper in Kennedy Town is on the fifty-second floor. The space is tiny, barely five hundred square feet, Stephanie guesses. She drops her bag in the center of the single room and explores. No kitchen, just a toaster oven, a hot plate, and a microwave crowded on a shelf over a dwarf refrigerator nestled next to a washing machine, no dryer.

Behind a sliding pocket door she discovers a minuscule bathroom: toilet, sink, and a shower barely big enough to turn around in.

She pulls back the heavy dark brown curtains covering the windows at the far end of the room. The view is spectacular, if dizzying. More of those precarious air conditioners hang from buildings everywhere the eye can see. Wet clothes strung like flags run in a complicated web from window to window. The cars and people on the street below look like ants.

Stephanie turns back to the room. Four folding chairs hang neatly on the wall, a foldout desk secured next to them with a hook. There's a narrow single bed and a futon couch that looks like it opens for sleeping. Stephanie moves her bag to the bed.

Firsties! The refrain that had caused a million childhood battles with her brother leaps unbidden into her mind. *Catherine is right,* she thinks ruefully. *No matter how far you go, there you are.* The trick is not to forget your experiences, but to figure out how to harvest them and channel them, or as Stephanie gleefully rephrased it in her own words to Catherine one day in training, *"make them your bitch."*

Waiting for John, Stephanie fires off a quick text to let Catherine know she's in place. Then she turns again to stare out the window. Hong Kong. *Wow.*

POINTS FOR ATTITUDE

——

Jake Burrows, aka John Bernake, Hong Kong Island

REPORT

Arrived Hong Kong. Stevie Nichols and I are scheduled to meet Peter Lombard at his hotel in one hour, independent reports to follow as instructed. Additional information: Francesca Leigh is the legal attaché at the embassy who's been coordinating with local law enforcement. Senior Inspector of Police Alan Tsang is leading local efforts at his precinct in the Wan Chai District. Any information you can provide about either welcome.

Jake looks up from his laptop at Stevie, sitting cross-legged on the narrow apartment's single bed. She files a broken nail intently, seemingly oblivious to his scrutiny.

Her legs are encased in shredded skinny jeans. An oversized turquoise sweater slips off one bony shoulder, exposing a purple bra strap. Thick makeup rings her eyes. A shaggy mane of black hair tumbles around her shoulders. His sensitive nose can scent hairspray even feet away from her. *She looks like a suburban mall rat. What is Catherine thinking?*

He's only worked with Catherine before. Until Dakota Harris, his first solo run. But that had been a simple extraction. This is *an investigation.* And he's been paired with this janky-looking character? Catherine must know what she's doing. *At least I hope so.* Catherine claims to have logic behind every decision and methodology, but still Jake worries about their pairing.

"We should get ready to go over," he offers.

"Right." Stevie springs from the bed and slips on a pair of silver booties. "Ready."

Jake can't help but smile at her. *Points for good attitude.* It's odd; he suspects Stevie might be chronologically older than he is, but there's something young and eager about her, even with her tough-looking exterior.

"Give me a minute." He hits SEND on his message to Catherine. As he does, the sky cracks open and gobs of rain pour down, blurring the vista. "Might want a coat."

As Stevie digs in her suitcase, Jake shrugs on his own jacket and grabs one of the two oversized umbrellas sitting in a stand by the front door. Common Hong Kong courtesy or Catherine's usual meticulous attention to preparation? *Who knows?*

He's fighting jet lag. He's never had so little time for preparation and research. He's on the other side of the fucking world in a country and a culture he knows little about, despite the cram course he gave himself on the flight over. And a woman's life could hang in the balance. *I need to get my shit together.*

He runs a mental checklist of the basic tenets of interviewing:

1. Be a good listener.
2. Don't presume the answer to any question.
3. Pump up the Target; make him or her feel confident about speaking to you.
4. Never "one-up" the Target or make the Target feel foolish.
5. Don't disagree often and when you do, use disagreement tactically to move the interview in another direction.
6. STAY ALERT and FLEXIBLE.

There are nuances of course, and every interview subject brings his or her own circumstances and psychology into play, but these six core principles have led him to the unexpected successful extraction of information on multiple occasions. Jake has a deserved burgeoning confidence in his techniques as an investigative interviewer.

He's going to do the asking, as per orders, but both he and Stevie will write down their impressions of Lombard and his responses. He's grateful he's the one tasked with the interrogation; Stevie Nichols looks like she's more likely to smack an answer out of someone than elicit one through verbal probing.

The winds whip the torrential rain sideways, instantly turning their umbrella inside out and upside down, and they arrive at the Four Seasons Hotel soaked to the skin. Black mascara streaks down Stevie's face, giving her the look of a weeping clown. They stumble inside the hotel lobby, nodding at the uniformed doorman who opens the door for them. Hotel guests burst inside after them, laughing as they escape the downpour; others huddle by the revolving doors, debating if they're willing to brave it.

Jake's prior study of the layout of the hotel pays off as he confidently glides directly over to the bank of elevators leading to the guest floors. He silently hands Stevie a cotton handkerchief and gestures that she should clean up her streaming face.

"A hanky? You are fancy."

Jake ignores the barb and fishes a generic gray key card from his jacket pocket.

ACCESS BY HOTEL KEY CARD ONLY is etched on a brass plaque in English in front of the elevator bank. Jake presumes the Chinese characters below the words say the same thing. He finds himself holding his breath as he waves his card before the sensor, but the elevator lights flash to life and indicate car number 5 is descending to the lobby level. Catherine's shit always works. He doesn't know why he was nervous.

They ride upstairs in silence. When the elevator doors open on

the thirty-second floor, they face a console table adorned with tall
white orchids and a gilded mirror hanging above. Jake contemplates their shared reflection.

"Hang on a second. Let's clean up."

They do the best they can, finger-combing their hair and
straightening their wet clothes. Stevie dabs the rest of her mascara
away and suddenly looks younger, vulnerable and pink-faced.

"You ready?" Jake asks. Stevie gives him a quick nod and they
walk down the quiet corridor, make a left, and find themselves at
the door to the corner suite Peter Lombard had rented for his anniversary trip.

Jake raps on the door. Lombard opens it immediately, as if he's
been waiting for them. Perhaps he has.

**First Impressions of Interview Target: Peter Lombard is red-eyed
and haggard-looking, unshaven stubble rims his jaw. His hair is
greasy. He smells ripe.**

"You're the people Forrest sent?" Lombard slurs, his incredulity
apparent. "You're a couple of kids!"

"My name is John Bernake and this is Stevie Nichols. And yes,
Peter, we're here at the request of your employer." Jake shoots him
a disarming smile. "Looks can be deceiving, you know that. Can
we come in? Get started? What do you say, Pete? Is it all right if I
call you Pete?"

Repetition of the Target's first name is calculated to build rapport.

Lombard opens the door a little wider and ushers them in.
Through the far window of the sitting room the storm lashes on,
ribboning the plate glass with glossy streaks. Jake quickly assesses
the room's contents: a small round table with two dining chairs at
one end, a long beige sofa with a TV hung opposite, two red club
chairs, and a blocky wooden coffee table, on which sit the remains
of a savaged club sandwich and a bottle of beer. The sitting room

of this suite is larger than the entire apartment he and Stevie are sharing in Kennedy Town.

"We'll get right to it, Peter," Jake says, angling his wiry frame into one of the two club chairs. "Have a seat."

Stevie takes the other red chair and Lombard settles back down on the sofa, takes a swig of his beer. "Well, kids or no, and I meant no offense by the way, I'm damn glad to see you."

"Why is that, Pete?" Jake and Stevie both extract small notebooks and pens from the depths of their pockets. Surreptitiously, Jake switches the power button on the voice-activated recorder that stays there.

"You know why! My wife has vanished. It's been four days. No one seems to know shit."

Jake notes the collection of beer bottles in the waste can in the corner. "Okay. Let me start by asking you to tell us about the last time you saw your wife."

Lombard groans. "I've done this over and over again! How can a woman just disappear?"

"That's what we're trying to find out, Pete. So just take us through it. I know you're frustrated, but it's essential that we hear directly from you about every detail. We never know what might be important."

Lombard takes them through the timeline of his and Eva's arrival in Hong Kong, his missing bag, their arrival at the hotel, and her subsequent bath while he drugged himself to sleep. He walks them through awakening in the middle of the night and finding her missing.

"And after you realized she was missing? What did you do next?"

Lombard's face flushes a deep red. "I waited for her for a while. Tried to call her. When she didn't answer, I went shopping."

Jake knows this fact already. And the credit card charges support Lombard's claim. So, unfortunately for Lombard, does the Burberry shop assistant's story that he was flirting with her when he purchased a scarf.

Who flirts when his wife is missing? A suspect. Or at least an asshole. Jake knows that's likely what the local police are thinking. He and Stevie both make notations on their pads.

"What are you writing? Everybody is fucking taking this wrong."

"Taking what wrong, sir?"

"Oh, now I'm *sir*? What happened to your buddy *Pete*?"

Jake braces his shoulders. Lombard may be drinking, but he's sharp. He moves on to his next question.

"We've heard that there was some tension, arguing even, going on with you and your wife before she disappeared. Can you tell us about that?"

"Just a stupid argument. Nothing serious." Lombard laughs bitterly. "Although the way they've been looking at me around here, it's clear nobody believes that." He runs both his hands through his thick black hair.

"What was the argument about?"

"She was pissed that I surprised her with a trip to Hong Kong. I know, right? Ridiculous. Truth is, we've just been . . . I don't know, not connecting lately. It's why I planned this trip. To get us back on track."

"But Eva didn't look at it that way?"

"Eva . . . She's been having a hard time since we moved to London."

"How long ago was that?"

"Eight, nine months."

"You don't know for sure?"

A rueful look crosses the other man's face. "Nine. It's been just nine. But truth is, I've been working so hard it's all a blur."

"In what way were things hard for Eva?"

"She was lonely. She wasn't working because we were trying for a baby, and, well, that left her feeling isolated."

"That must have been hard for you," Jake offers sympathetically. "Balancing the pressures of your own work with an unhappy wife."

"Too right that. And I'm working this hard for us, for our future, which she well knows." Irritated frustration limns his words. "I know I come across as angry," he admits. "I'm just worried out of my mind."

"Tell us about the stranger. The one your wife said she was uneasy about."

"I still believe she was mistaken. I mean, what are the odds? I only even mentioned it, well, because . . . you know, like you said, anything that might help . . ." Lombard trails off. Takes a swig of beer.

"Tell us."

Lombard complies, sketching out the details Jake already knows.

"Do you have any idea who the man is that she was referring to?"

"No. Not a clue. But I'm sick I didn't take her more seriously. After the attempted break-in and then my suitcase . . ."

"You say it was searched?"

"Not just searched!" Lombard springs to his feet and grabs his now empty suitcase. "Look at this!"

The silky lining of the suitcase is slashed to ribbons.

"Does your wife know anyone in Hong Kong?"

"A few people from when she lived here. I gave their information to the police. I've reached out to them too, through Facebook, but no one has seen her."

"We'd like their names as well."

Lombard nods. "Sure."

"Are there any spots in the city that your wife liked to frequent?"

"Man Mo Temple. And she's a big fan of the aviary in Hong Kong Park. Most of the stuff she told me about was the usual touristy spots for the most part. Peak Tram. The Star Ferry. All that shit. And a few lesser-known places that locals had turned her on to, restaurants and such. Hiking trails." Lombard snaps his fingers. "One of them was Dragon Tail, something like that? Does that help?"

"Everything helps. We'd like a list, if you could write it up for us. Thank you."

"No problem."

"How are you feeling about the law enforcement response?"

"Just great," Lombard answers sarcastically. "They're practically printing placards reading 'guilty' to hang around my neck. Forrest had someone from our Hong Kong law firm come by, but he's an M&A guy, for Christ's sake. And that bitch." He shoots a look at Stevie. "Sorry. That *woman* from the embassy? Useless."

"Why do you think they've focused suspicion on you, Pete?"

Lombard's thick black eyebrows draw together. "Isn't it always the husband?" He exhales another bitter snort of laughter. "And people heard us fighting, I guess. But what couple doesn't? And that I went shopping." His cheeks mottle red once again. "It wasn't that I wasn't worried. I just thought she was trying to make a point. So I thought I'd make one too."

Jake lets silence hang in the room for a good long time. Catherine's taught him just how badly most people feel compelled to fill that empty space.

Stevie shifts position, a move Jake catches out of the corner of his eye as he steadily keeps assessing Peter Lombard. He silently wills Stevie to be still. He needs Lombard to fill the void.

Lombard examines his fingers. Clasps his hands and cracks his knuckles. Meets Jake's eyes and shrugs.

Jake finally leans across the wooden coffee table, his eyes beseeching. "Peter. What do you think has happened to your wife?"

"I have no fucking idea! You tell me. Isn't that why you're here?"

RING OF TRUTH

___

Stephanie Regaldo, aka Stevie Nichols, Hong Kong Island

REPORT

Yo, boss. All good here in this crazy-ass city, although this place you've got us staying in is one tiny squat. Good thing I've deduced my roomie bats for the other team, since we're right on top of each other; keeps us both out of trouble. Ha!

I know you want me to keep to business in these reports so here goes:

Peter Lombard appears to be a relatively healthy man in his mid-thirties. When interviewed, he showed evidence of anxiety in his speech patterns and also through his overall lack of attention to grooming and red eyes. No determination yet as to whether or not those symptoms are real or contrived. Lombard drank beer during the interview and appeared to have been drinking for some time, based on the bottles in his trash. I wouldn't assess him as drunk, but certainly "loose."

He answered the questions presented to him in a clear and consistent manner, and his replies generally conformed to the information he's given previously to the authorities.

Lombard's body language and involuntary physiological responses (use of defensive posture, reddening of complexion, etc.)

indicate he's uncomfortable discussing his wife and their relationship, but he also freely admits to them fighting the day they arrived in Hong Kong and claims it was trivial in the overall nature of their marriage. There are definitely some weirdo details in his story, but they're just odd enough that they might have the ring of truth. After all, we both know that truth can be stranger than fiction, don't we, boss? ·

As for the kid you've partnered me with here, and I mean kid, why is he lead? You ask me, he seems soft. And that's one thing you know I'm not, right? I hope you find this report more professional, like you asked.

Awaiting instructions.

"Stevie"

HOLLOW SUITS

———

Jake Burrows, aka John Bernake,
Hong Kong Island

Straightening his tie, Jake enters the square concrete block housing the United States Consulate General Hong Kong & Macau. His sharp suit fits like it was made to order for him because it was. His shoes cost almost a grand. His wardrobe is a suit of armor, an announcement of privilege and entitlement. He's right on time for his appointment with Francesca Leigh, the legal attaché, or legate, liaison for the Eva Lombard disappearance.

After clearing security with his false identification and passing through the metal detector, Jake gives the expected name to the petite, raven-haired receptionist. She offers him a seat. He declines. Looks at his watch. A silver-haired woman strides toward him with a flinty smile. She wears a neatly fitting dove-colored pantsuit, a white silk blouse, and a classic strand of pearls. Pearl studs adorn her earlobes.

"Hello. Mr. Bernake? I'm Francesca Leigh. Follow me and we'll go into my office." Her voice has the faint telltale lilt of a Southern upbringing. She pivots in her black suede pumps and moves briskly away. Jake falls into step beside her.

Once they're seated in Leigh's functional office, the niceties of coffee offers and observations about the humid weather behind them, Leigh fixes Jake with an evaluating stare as she slides her business card over to him. He doesn't pick it up or offer to reciprocate. Leigh's eyes narrow.

"Thank you for seeing me," he launches in smoothly, determined to control the flow of conversation. "As you know, our firm represents many of Holcomb Investments' interests here in Hong Kong. And of course, Peter Lombard works for Holcomb in London. I'm here to see if there is support of any kind we can offer. And also to inquire as to the status of the investigation, to the extent you have information you can share with me."

Francesca Leigh's icy blue eyes meet Jake's. A current passes between them. It carries the shared knowledge of the billions of dollars of Holcomb money that pass through Hong Kong. Leigh is a career diplomat; the twisted braid of money, politics, and diplomacy is one she must know well. It's why Jake led off the way he did, why his cover is that of an attorney working for Holcomb's Hong Kong firm.

"I can assure you that the Hong Kong police are taking Mrs. Lombard's disappearance seriously."

"Do they consider Mr. Lombard a suspect?"

A wry smile twists Leigh's face. "Isn't the husband always a suspect? But if I had a guess, I'd say she's with the ex-boyfriend."

"Ex-boyfriend?"

"Eva Lombard lived here in Hong Kong for a couple of months some years back. Had a pretty serious relationship by all accounts. Her sister says he was her last serious relationship before she married Peter. It stands to reason that if she was fighting with her husband she ran off to see her ex."

"You seem very sure that nothing bad has happened to her."

That wry flash of smile again. "Wishful thinking maybe. Don't ever want to think the worst has happened to an American citizen here in Hong Kong. And the statistics support that. Have you been in Hong Kong long, Mr. Bernake?"

"Just coming on two months. After a stint in the London office." Jake wonders if he always lied so effortlessly, or if it's a talent he's acquired since working with Catherine. He shifts his focus back to the legate's icy stare as she continues.

"Then you should know by now. The Triads control much of what happens in this city. Crimes against American tourists are good for nobody's business, so they control that too."

"Is there anything our firm can do?"

Leigh glances at her own business card, still sitting on the desk before Jake. "Excuse me, but are you even old enough to be a lawyer?" she asks suspiciously.

"I get that all the time." Jake smiles easily. "I'm older than I look." He leans forward, hands spread in supplication. "I'm sure they sent me because I'm a Yank. Not too many of us here in the Hong Kong office."

"Look. Random violent crime is rare here. I lay odds on a wife trying to teach her husband a lesson."

"I hope you're right. Nothing would make me happier than to be wasting your time, Ms. Leigh." Jake unleashes his most disarming smile.

"*Mrs.* Leigh. It's always a pleasure to meet another American in Hong Kong." She smiles, but Jake observes it does nothing to warm her chilly gaze. "What club do you belong to?"

"Aberdeen Marina. Came with my comp package." Another easy lie. But membership there would have come with an employment package as an associate at Kingsford, Downes & Faulkes, and he knows Catherine has added "John Bernake" to the rolls of the club if anyone bothers to check. To the law firm's website too, for that matter; she's always thorough.

"Perhaps I'll see you there. We have friends who belong."

"That would be my pleasure. Let me guess—Atlanta?" he hazards.

"Born and raised in Augusta," Leigh replies with the first warmth he's glimpsed. "You have a good ear."

Jake extracts a gold case and lays down a card with the embossed KD&F logo, enjoying the look of mild surprise on Leigh's face. Once again he appreciates Catherine's faultless attention to detail. "Feel free to call me if we can help in any way. That's my direct number." The number on the card will divert to one of Jake's cellphones.

"I'll do that. Thank you for coming in."

Ex-boyfriend. Funny how Peter Lombard didn't mention that.

STICKY FINGERS

___

Stephanie Regaldo, aka Stevie Nichols, Hong Kong Island

Flyers affixed with cellophane tape litter the plate glass windows of the Good Luck Dim Sum Shop, all but obscuring the patrons inside. If Stephanie hadn't been planted across the street for over thirty minutes already, she wouldn't even be sure that S.I. Alan Tsang had stopped in for his usual lunch. But, armed with knowledge of Tsang's habits as supplied by Catherine, she'd been in place to observe the policeman's entry. Luckily the cop's a creature of habit, stopping in to this place for a solo midday meal nearly every day.

Stephanie snakes her way across the crowded street, acutely aware of how very *foreign* she is here. How strange it is to be one of the few white faces among the many Asian ones. It makes her feel exposed, the anonymity she could take for granted back in the States a squandered, unappreciated asset, one she won't be quick to dismiss again.

She pulls open the door to the restaurant. It's a narrow joint, no more than one long counter crowded with stools. Clouds of steam rise in gusty puffs; there's the sizzle of oil and a lingering scent of burnt grease in the air. Tsang's seated at the far end of the counter, a bamboo basket before him. He shovels in great mouthfuls, barely taking time to swallow one greedy gulp before he pushes the next one in.

Luck is at hand again; the seat next to Tsang is empty. Stephanie perches on the stool and fixes a pointed look of longing at Tsang's lunch.

"I'm sorry, I speak no Chinese; do you speak English, by any chance?" Stephanie fixes Tsang with what she hopes is an expression of optimistic innocence.

Her quarry shrugs irritably. "Yes. How can I assist?"

"Oh, fantastic," Stephanie babbles. "If you could just help me order? Last time I tried pointing and I ended up with, god, I don't know, it might have been tripe, even though I'm not even sure I know what tripe is exactly, but I suspect something *totally disgusting*, by the looks of the stuff."

Tsang's expression shifts to one of mild amusement. "Anything besides tripe you'd prefer to avoid?"

Stephanie graces Tsang with a radiant smile. "You tell me." She leans over and inspects the contents of his bamboo basket. "What have you got there? That all looks yummy."

Gesturing with his chopsticks, Tsang points out the items in turn. "Pork bun, shrimp shu mai, soup dumpling."

"Perfect. I'll have that. Would you order for me? Thanks so much."

Tsang barks a few words at the counterman, a balding old man with hunched shoulders and a basketball-sized belly. They're speaking Cantonese, Stephanie suspects based on her research about the island, although she wouldn't be able to tell one Chinese dialect from another if they punched her.

Tsang returns to his determined demolition of the dumplings in front of him, eyes fixed firmly on the task at hand.

A cup of hot tea is placed in front of Stephanie, swiftly followed by her very own bamboo steamer. The counterman lifts the lid. Delicious scents tantalize from within, both savory and sweet.

A stab of hunger both primal and urgent hits her as she realizes it's been close to eighteen hours since she's eaten. She often forgets, only to be crippled with hunger when the pangs finally hit, something Catherine has lectured her about repeatedly. She bites into a pillowy dumpling that squirts hot broth into her mouth.

"Hmmm. Delicious."

She takes her best shot at engaging Tsang in further conversation, offering prepared tidbits about being an art student on a gap year. Stephanie prides herself on the attention to detail she's invested in her cover story and is eager for an opportunity to show it off. However, she receives only grunts and monosyllabic responses in return. Tsang finishes his food, pays with cash, and departs the shop without a backward glance. Stephanie follows suit a few moments later.

She blends seamlessly into the pedestrian surge, turns a corner, hails the first cab she sees, and settles inside it. She may not have succeeded in chatting up Tsang, but she does have his spiral notepad, neatly lifted from his jacket pocket and transferred to hers.

Stephanie cracks open the notepad, hoping for English, unsurprised to see mostly Chinese characters with the occasional English word scattered throughout: Thursday, American, Holcomb.

Holcomb. A shiver of excitement courses through Stephanie's body. She doesn't know exactly what she's looking at in Inspector Tsang's notes, but at least she's looking at something.

OUT

———

Peter Lombard,
Hong Kong Island

He's been drinking all day. Just beers, but sucked down in a steady succession since he woke up this morning. *Come to think of it, was that morning?* Peter realizes he's not quite sure what day it is. Or time it is. His sleep has been fitful, naps at odd hours, chunks of Ambien-induced oblivion tortured by fragments of disturbing dreams. A permanent buzz seems to encircle him, a prickly energy force field built of anxiety and uncertainty, interfering with rest and clear thought.

I'm going out.

He pulls on sneakers and, after a glance out the window, a rain jacket. Now that he's decided to go, he can't move fast enough. He shoves the hotel card key into his wallet and jams it into one pocket, his cellphone into another.

The hotel hallway's decorations in their muted, sandy tones with their vaguely Chinese, wholly corporate accents seem unbearably creepy to him all of a sudden. He races to the elevator and punches the DOWN button. The car *crawls* up to the thirty-second floor. Peter can't contain himself; he bounces back and forth from foot to foot, desperate to move, unsure what it will accomplish.

The elevator door slides open. *Finally.* Peter steps into the cab. Hits the LOBBY button. The elevator stops on the eighteenth floor, admitting two businessmen in sharp suits with flamboyant silk pocket squares. One addresses the other in what Peter guesses is Italian, resulting in guffaws of hearty laughter from his companion. Peter's suddenly conscious of his stubbled jaw and wrinkled, food-stained button-down, embarrassed by his agitation, furious at Eva.

When the elevator lands at the lobby, he bursts past the Italians, eliciting another round of laughter from the two of them and an ugly stream of consciousness inside his own head: *Fuckers. Are they laughing at me? Let's see how they hold up if their wives go missing! Eva. How dare you? Where are you? Fuck. How can I be this worried and this angry at the same damn time?*

A thick bank of dark gray clouds hovers overhead, and although the rain holds off for now, the blocked sun gives the streets an eerie, shadowless cast. It feels as if the entire world is holding its breath and waiting.

Agitated, directionless, Peter tugs at his unruly hair and mutters to himself as he strides wildly forward, oblivious to the larger world around him. He brushes and knocks into passersby and is cursed out more than once, and in more than one language.

Peter walks himself breathless and tired. His steps lag.

"What the . . . !" he cries as each of his arms is suddenly seized in a viselike grip. He's pulled into a narrow, garbage-strewn alley.

"Stop!" he shouts. "Help!" before a solid punch to his mouth leaves him spitting blood and, *oh fuck,* a tooth. *Were those brass knuckles?*

Peter tries to wrestle free of his attackers, but takes a knee to the groin that sends him crumbling to the filthy ground.

His head spins with agony; he thinks he might vomit. A hail of kicks rains down on him, curling him into the fetal position. *Please stop.* He thinks it, but his mouth can't form the plea.

Why? Why? Why are they doing this to me?

A pointy toe connects with his ear and leaves his skull ringing. Protectively, Peter curls an arm over his ear. He screws his eyes shut as a hand wrenches his arm away. Tenses as he waits for the next blow.

He gasps at the feel of the intimate brush of lips against his earlobe, more unsettling than the onslaught of kicks and hits. Recoils at the whisper that follows: "Get your bitch under control."

Peter lies there for an eternity after he suspects they're gone, long after the last stinging blow. His ears ring with a shrill whine. His entire body pulses with pain.

He chances opening his eyes, but his left one seems to be swollen shut. He pulls himself up into a sitting position with a groan. He wipes a handful of blood and spittle away from his mouth.

A tiger-striped cat sashays past him with a haughty twitch of her tail. Observing the cat's pathway, Peter's one good eye meets the impassive, black-eyed stare of an impossibly ancient woman seated in a white plastic chair at the far end of the alley. She methodically shells peas, uninterested in Peter's predicament. Next to her, an open door leads to a bustling kitchen, in which he can see four sweating men intently focused on their bubbling pots.

"Thanks," Peter mutters sarcastically. "So nice of you to call for help."

He hauls himself to his feet, wincing as each new injury announces its painful truth. He stumbles from the alley and back out into the street, nearly crashing into a pair of laughing young lovers who lose their gaiety upon seeing his battered face.

"Are you all right, mate?" The young man frowns.

Australian, Peter thinks, *not English. Why would it matter?*

"Clearly not," his girl adds. "Just look at him!"

"I think I was mugged," Peter rasps, although he knows a mugging is not the likely explanation.

"Get your bitch under control."

"What's the emergency number here?" the girl demands, fishing a cellphone from her backpack. "Zero, zero, zero, like at home?"

"I jus' wanna go back to my hotel. . . ."

"Got to get you to a hospital, mate."

"No!"

Peter can interpret the layers of complexity contained in the looks exchanged between the young couple.

We have to help. What if he's dangerous? Shouldn't we call the police? Is this any of our business? Are we safe? What should we do?

With a bruising rush Peter's thoughts turn to an incident early in his relationship with Eva. They'd just come out of a movie and were wending their way to dinner. After a long gray February, the first teasing hints of spring were in the air. Peter tucked one of Eva's hands inside his for the very first time as they strolled; he was conscious of a current between them and hoped she felt it too.

They were heading west on 57th Street toward Lexington when they saw another couple crossing the avenue in their direction. They were of similar ages to Peter and Eva, he'd guess, and alike in other ways too—the man wore a down vest the same make as his own, the woman's chestnut brown hair was close to Eva's own color. These assessments he made instantly and unconsciously. It was only later that he figured out that these surface similarities were partly why what happened next was so startling.

Cocooned by the warmth of his burgeoning intimacy with Eva, Peter was inclined to look at every stranger with a smile. But this pair practically threw sparks as they raged at each other, shouting expletive-laced insults at the top of their voices. He drew Eva to the side, protective, as the pair neared, but still they were up close and personal when the guy sucker punched his companion in the nose.

The woman howled. Blood spurted.

Eva gasped. Halted in her tracks. Her eyes met Peter's. In an infinitesimally brief exchange they had exactly the same kind of silent dialogue this Aussie couple is having now.

What do we do? Should we get involved? How dangerous is he? Is this? How can we leave that girl?

Peter had acted before he thought.

"Hey," he shouted, placing himself in between the puncher and both women. "Cut that shit out."

He saw a flash of pride in Eva's eyes; it pumped him up. He turned to the bloody victim. "Do you want to come with us? You should get some ice on that."

The woman's eyes blazed. "What the fuck do you think you're doing getting in our business?" One bloodied hand clawed out and raked Peter's cheek. He jerked back but not fast enough. He still has a little scar where she marked him.

Although it'll probably be buried under new scars now.

He had grabbed Eva's hand and they ran together, horrified, laughing, bonded. After their blood cooled, they'd talked for hours, starting with a shared abhorrence of the scene they'd witnessed, which led to a larger discussion about male-female dynamics and gender norms. Eva engaged and challenged him; he found it damn sexy. She'd cleaned his small wound, kissed it better, and the deep kiss they shared at the end of the night left them both breathless. The "Incident on Lex" became a chapter in the library of Peter and Eva's personal history, one of the threads in the fabric of their interwoven lives.

The couple they were then, the optimism and happiness he'd felt, all now seem as ancient and blank as the old woman he'd left back in the alley with her peas.

"I'm fine," he mutters at the Australian couple as he lurches away. "Don't worry about me."

"You sure?" The Aussie girl's nasal query floats after him. "You look like you took the worst of it."

He's not at all fine and he knows it. But what are these two kids with their strangled vowels going to do for him?

He feels invisible to the Asian pedestrians he passes; their eyes don't even flicker. White passersby, the expat and tourist crowd, avert their eyes from his bruised face and bloody shirtfront. He runs the tips of his fingers along his ribs and finds the lump that's swelling there. He staggers along in what he hopes is the direction of the hotel.

Frustrated, lost, hurt, and miserable, Peter catches his breath in front of a shop selling an astonishing variety of gaudy gold jewelry, bangles as wide as his arm and thick, flowing bibs of interlocking golden flowers or dragons roaring flame. A golden rooster, accented with a red enameled comb and wattle, sits among silk flowers in a glass box rimmed with fairy lights.

Eva would have laughed. Would have found just the joke to make him laugh too.

"Get your bitch under control."

What the hell did that mean? Peter's not sure, but doesn't the phrase imply that whoever did this to him didn't *have* "control" of Eva? Hope flutters in his chest.

Peter fishes in his pocket for his cellphone. Is not at all surprised to see the screen spiderwebbed with cracks. Not built to withstand a literal beating, after all. *At least it works,* he thinks as he presses a stored number.

"Forrest? It's Peter Lombard."

Pain, frustration, and pure relief at having someone *listen* color the barely coherent torrent that follows. Peter forgets about the time difference, the promise he made to himself to never appear weak in business, how very badly he craves Forrest Holcomb's approval.

Peter vents his fears about Eva, his many questions, his suspicion that it was the meddling of those two *kids* Forrest dispatched that resulted in his savage beating. Finally his stumbled words run out of steam as a petrifying weariness settles over his battered body.

I think I need to lie down.

He sags against the shop window. His knees buckle and he slides down against the plate glass until his ass hits the concrete, his legs splayed out in front of him.

"Peter? Can you hear me? Peter?"

Peter's hands drop to rest on his thighs and he looks at the cell-phone glowing in his right palm.

He can hear, even though Forrest's voice has gone faint. Peter contemplates lifting the phone to his ear, but he's not sure he can manage it. His hand resting on his thigh looks so very far away.

"Where are you, Peter? You need to get to a hospital. Call the police."

Peter nods. Right. Forrest's right. Of course he is. That makes total sense. Hospital. Police. He should definitely do that.

Nothing else makes sense. *"Get your bitch under control."*

WHILE PETER WAS STILL SLEEPING . . .

———

Eva Lombard,
Hong Kong Island, the Day of Arrival

Eva stops the cabdriver before they reach the address she's given him. The butterflies in her stomach demand she get out and walk. A practical realization also reminds her she has limited cash and may not want to use credit.

The walking does her good. She follows the curve of Bowen Road. The steps are as familiar as the ones she takes every day in London with Baxter. It's as if she was here yesterday, not ten years ago. Some things have changed of course, but she passes a tea shop that she and Alex used to frequent and is absurdly pleased to see the stooped and cranky old woman who runs it still calling the shots.

It occurs to her that Alex might not be home. Hell, he might not even live here anymore. But Eva knows the three-bedroom apartment on Bowen was a score when Alex got it—an inheritance from an aunt he barely knew the year before Eva and Alex met—and given the pricey nature of Hong Kong real estate, he would be unlikely to have given it up. Nor had he mentioned anything about moving when they last emailed, a few friendly lines back and forth the week of his fortieth birthday.

Eva catches sight of her reflection in a shop window. Her hair's a mess; her hand clutches her bloody scarf. She finger combs her hair. Checks her palm. Her cut still sears, but the bleeding's stopped. She's tied the severed strap of her shoulder bag into an awkward knot. The bag's unusually cumbersome because of the addition of the Leica and bumps uncomfortably against her right hip. She's got a fevered look in her eye; she can see that even in her blurred reflection.

Why am I here exactly? She doesn't know. She just knows Alex always made her feel safe. This thought propels her up the last stretch of hill.

His building looms proudly before her. It's a beautiful colonial-era apartment building with old-world charm featuring gracious balconies, but crowded on either side by a pair of modern, steel and glass monoliths.

Showing up at Alex's doorstep without notice after all this time suddenly reeks of folly. She thinks of Peter, her husband of seven years, snoring away back in their hotel room. How is it that the events of the last twenty-four hours threaten to erase years of trust in their marriage? *I can tell his Ambien snore from his regular snore, for fuck's sake! I know him.*

But think of how well Pete can lie. She never would have expected it of him, even if he tries to soften his deceptions about this trip behind the guise of "planning a surprise." Lying well is lying well and Pete's proven he can do it. So is he deceiving her about anything else besides their itinerary? She was *attacked*. That fact is inescapable.

Like any good reporter, she needs to know which questions to ask in order to figure out what the hell is going on: the who, what, why, where, and how that will shift the events of the last few days into clear alignment. But right now, she's coming up empty. *A safe harbor is what I need. Just for a little while.*

Eva applies a swipe of lip balm and grips her scarf a little tighter, unhappy to see a fresh well of blood bubbling up across her palm. She tucks the rusty and crusty cuff of her shirt up under the sleeve of her leather jacket. She scowls at her reflection. Not exactly how she envisioned seeing Alex again (if she ever did daydream about that and, okay, she will admit she has, but only if angry at Peter and a couple of glasses in), but it'll have to do.

Her eye is caught. A menacing shadow rises up behind her, stretching a clawlike hand toward her shoulder.

Eva freezes, her startled cry frozen in her throat as the shadow draws closer. A large hand descends on her shoulder and grips it tightly. Her body once again becomes inexplicably, maddeningly liquid.

She can do nothing but stay rooted to the spot and await her fate.

We have a dilemma . . .

An acknowledgment that virtually everyone's devotion has its sharp edge; a hard angle of selfishness in the face of drained compassion or personal risk. We're human, after all—kindness, empathy, all of these more evolved traits ultimately smack up against the ugly primal truth that the broken-legged lamb is usually best left for the lions.

THE OTHER HALF

Magali Guzman,
New York City and Hoboken

Maggie's day has been an education in how the other half lives. First she and Special Agent Ryan Johnson tracked down Betsy Elliott's friend Amanda Levine just as the mom of two was getting her kids organized for school and out the door of her Park Avenue penthouse. To achieve this stupendous feat, Amanda needed both a nanny and a personal assistant. The arrival of Maggie and Ryan, with their flashy badges and probing questions, seemed an irritation, concerns about Betsy and Bear's whereabouts overshadowed by the inconvenience to Amanda's *stressful* day.

Next they interviewed Jessica Brown, another friend of Betsy's. Upon hearing Maggie's last name, Brown broke into terrible *Español,* and insisted on reassuring Maggie "your people are welcome here." Never mind that Maggie, as well as her parents and *their* parents, were all born and raised in New Jersey. The snidely amused looks Johnson sent her as Brown mangled her way through a few more awkward Spanish sentences made Maggie itch to punch him in the gut.

Both women professed worry about their missing friend and horror about the "times we're living in." Amanda wistfully offered that maybe Betsy just needed a little "treat," as being a mother was "just so much to cope with. Maybe she flew to Paris to shop?" she asked hopefully.

Jessica was blunt and more cynical. She watched a lot of crime shows and she knew the odds of Betsy and Bear being alive diminished with each passing day. She dourly opined that their bodies would no doubt turn up soon. "New York provides a degree of anonymity, but everything comes out in the end, right?"

Both women declared themselves unaware of even a hint of strife in the Elliotts' marriage. "Rock solid." "He treated her like a queen."

Maggie reflects on the way these women live. Protected. Supported. Pampered. Oblivious? Perhaps willfully so? That certainly seems true of Amanda Levine. Jessica Brown, on the other hand, is correct that the ugly parts of humanity eventually show up everywhere. Except that Maggie's grimly aware that watching them on TV is distinctly different from the real deal.

Next up, they have an appointment with Rachel Ferris, the last of the three women Roger Elliott had identified as his wife's closest friends. Rachel's apartment building on East 77th Street is yet another doorman-guarded womb of wealth and safety.

The Ferrises' doorman announces them and Maggie rides up in the elevator mentally reviewing what they know so far. Betsy and Bear Elliott have been missing for fourteen days. There's been no word from her and no sign of her or Bear; it's as if they vanished into thin air. Nor has there been any follow-up to the ransom demand, despite its command to Elliott to gather the cash and wait for further instructions. The postmark revealed the demand had been mailed from the Philadelphia suburb of Berwyn, Pennsylvania. There is no known connection between the Elliotts and that town. The paper stock and envelope used for the demand were the house brand of a national office supply chain. No fingerprints were found on either envelope or letter. Further tests are pending.

The Ferris apartment is another magnificent tribute to wealth and taste, or at least the taste of a decorator. It's elegant to be sure, but also sterile, every perfectly angled *objet* studied and precise. A Nordic-looking woman in her twenties with a lilting accent introduces herself as "Kiva, Mrs. Ferris's personal assistant" and escorts Maggie and Johnson into the kitchen.

Upon Maggie's entrance, Rachel Ferris pauses with a spoon filled with a rich brown sauce halfway to her mouth.

"There you are," she gushes, as if they are long lost friends. Tossing her spoon carelessly down on the counter, Rachel brushes past the ponytailed man in chef's whites standing in front of the simmering pots on the six-burner stove. "Welcome. I hope you don't mind if we meet here in the kitchen. Armando's cooking for a dinner party we're hosting tonight and I need to taste as we go. Every detail needs to be perfect."

Maggie accepts Rachel's offers of a seat at the kitchen table and a cup of coffee, while Johnson declines. He takes up position near the kitchen door, notebook at the ready.

Maggie has her prepared questions, but quickly realizes that she should just let Rachel Ferris *talk*, which she seems to do without self-editing or interruption as her staff circles around her silently— the assistant pouring their coffee, the chef offering up a plate of scones still warm from the oven, along with jam and clotted cream.

"I never eat these." Rachel giggles. "I don't even let Armando make them usually. The temptation is just too much! But the *stress of tonight*! Just incredible!"

Maggie thinks about her mom, who raised five kids with no help and routinely hosts Sunday dinners for up to forty family members all without breaking a sweat. She bites into a scone and allows the buttery crumble to shut her mouth before she says something she regrets.

"We were expecting twenty, which is *just* about what our formal dining room can handle, any larger group is strictly cocktails only, that's our rule. Even twenty I don't like; we have to do two tables of ten and it just feels *cramped*. Sixteen at one table is really perfect. Eighteen is just awkward. And now Roger's canceled, of course, and Betsy's I don't know where, and I don't know what to do. And not only about the seating, although of course I do need to figure that out. That's enough of a stressor, but what about the party altogether. Should I cancel it?"

Rachel Ferris seems to finally have run out of gas. She turns limpid eyes to Maggie, eyes that beg for reassurance.

"Do you think you should cancel it?"

"It occurred to me. But Vaughn, that's my husband, thinks we have to hold the fort, so to speak. Our husbands just partnered on this joint venture in Long Island City. All of the guests are investors in the new complex or involved in the deal in some way. The party's the celebratory kickoff. But it doesn't seem right to me without Betsy and Roger here."

"So the party was important to Betsy?"

"Oh yes! We've been organizing it together. Every detail! The last two weeks have just been hell without her. And today, all day, I keep expecting her to call and confirm she'll be here early, at four, just like we planned. We were going to dress together. We have a glam squad booked." Rachel's voice is heavy with sadness and uncertainty. Her busy fingers crumble her scone to bits and pick out the currants, arranging them in a tidy little heap on the side of her china plate. "Vaughn and I have been going back and forth about it. He thinks it's important we go forward with tonight, despite the circumstances. To protect all of us, he says."

"Protect you from what?"

"Oh, I didn't mean! Protect the deal. The investment. That's all. It took years to put together and the ink's barely dry. And of course Roger's distracted."

"Can you think of anyone who might have wanted to hurt the Elliotts? Anyone with a grudge?"

"I wouldn't know. Roger and Vaughn play hardball sometimes

in business, I'm sure. But hurt Betsy? Never." Rachel Ferris shakes her head ruefully. "Do you think maybe she went off with Bear by herself?"

"Can you think of a reason why Betsy would go off on her own with Bear?"

"No. Just asking," Rachel replies, pushing her heap of currants around with an index finger.

Not a very good liar, are you, Rachel? "You know, Amanda Levine suggested Betsy went to Paris. So you're not alone in thinking maybe she left voluntarily."

To Maggie's surprise, tears spring up in Rachel Ferris's eyes. She struggles to control them, her Botox-ed facial muscles contorting obscenely in the struggle.

Another reason not to inject poison in your forehead, Maggie thinks. *Seriously ugly cry face.*

"I'm so worried about them."

Ah. A genuine human is lurking under the plastic surgery, after all. Maggie's tone softens. "Of course you are, Mrs. Ferris. That's only natural."

"Oh, call me Rachel. Mrs. Ferris is Vaughn's mother." She attempts a wobbly smile. "It's a feeling more than anything."

"What's a feeling?"

"It's not like Betsy said anything to me." Rachel folds into herself, crossing her arms and legs.

Maggie trusts feelings. Instincts. She wants to encourage Rachel to trust hers. "Anything might be helpful, Rachel. Betsy is a good friend of yours. You know her better than anyone, probably, other than Roger. And you're a smart woman. Smart enough to be able to sense things without necessarily putting an exact finger on what's up."

Rachel unfolds her arms. She leans forward toward Maggie, placing her elbows on the table. "That's exactly it. It's just a feeling. . . ." she says eagerly.

"So tell me. You never know. It might be important."

Rachel further crumbles her scone. Maggie observes that despite her proclaimed love for the treat, Rachel's only played with it and not consumed a single bite.

Her loss. Maggie crams in another delicious mouthful. *Totally worth a few extra laps in the pool.*

Rachel's beseeching eyes meet hers and Maggie knows she's got her. There's something Rachel Ferris desperately wants to share.

"Tell me, Rachel."

With a flick of their employer's wrist, the chef and the assistant disappear, melting soundlessly away.

Wow. A rich people superpower.

Rachel casts a glance at Johnson and his poised pen and then speaks softly, intimately to Maggie. "Like I said, Betsy never *said* anything to me about anything. But about six months ago, I think *something* happened."

"What kind of something?"

"I don't exactly know how to describe it. We were close, like you said. But Betsy stopped talking to me. I mean, she *spoke* to me; we talked all the time. But she stopped *confiding* in me. At first, I didn't even notice. She heard me out if I needed a good vent about Vaughn or the kids, and she can do an impression of my mother-in-law that cracks me up every time. But she stopped sharing anything really personal with me. The whole friendship became kind of one-sided. I even asked if she was mad at me at one point."

"Was she?"

"She said no. In fact, she acted like I was a little crazy for asking. Like everything was normal and I was being oversensitive. It kind of hurt my feelings, to be honest. But Vaughn and Roger are tied at the hip so I just kept my mouth shut after that. And like I said, we still talked. Every day, while we were planning this party."

"Can you think of anything that happened around the time you noticed the change in Betsy? Something that might have prompted it?"

"It was after they came back from a family sailing trip along the Amalfi Coast. Betsy's dream vacation; she'd been planning it for years. But if something specific happened there, she never said."

"Do the Elliotts have a good marriage?"

"Oh. Sure. They're great together. Our crowd jokes about it actually, because they outdo each other with gifts and romantic gestures. Puts the rest of us to shame."

"Do you like Roger Elliott?" Maggie sees the question throws Rachel off guard just a little.

"Everyone likes Roger." She giggles. "Isn't that the case? I mean, you've met him, right? The man's a charmer. It's the secret of his success."

From tears to giggles in under a minute. You are a piece of work. "Roger and your husband do a lot of business together?"

"Yes."

"So you've spent a lot of time with them as a couple?"

Rachel keeps her eyes steadily focused on the lumps of scone her nervous fingers are crumbling ever smaller.

Maggie waits. Then softly presses her, "Rachel. Is there anything else you'd like to tell me? Betsy's your friend. Don't you want to help me find her?"

"I do!" Rachel's defiant eyes meet Maggie's. "I just don't know anything for certain. And it's complicated. . . ."

"What's complicated?"

Rachel plunges a teaspoon into the clotted cream and swallows down the rich mouthful. "Let me just say this. Nothing and nobody's perfect, okay? Anything that looks perfect is a lie. Now I'm going to have to ask you to leave. I have a million things to do to get ready for tonight."

Rachel Ferris stands. Her Nordic personal assistant mysteriously reappears to help Maggie pull back her chair. The chef returns to the stove.

Wow. Another demonstration of the rich people superpower.

Maggie rises too, but hesitates. "Mrs. Ferris. A woman and a

little boy are missing. Your friend. Your son Sammy's playmate."
Maggie catches the emotional flicker in Rachel Ferris's eyes at the
mention of the boys. She presses on. "If there's anything else you
can share with me that might help bring them home safely, anything at all, you should tell me."

Rachel's eyes skid away from Maggie's and she busies herself
with the plate of pastry, handing it to her assistant. "You clearly
enjoyed Armando's scones. Here, let us pack you a few." She lets
loose that giggle again. "Better on your hips than mine."

The Nordic assistant bundles three scones into a white paper
bag with the letter *F* monogrammed on it in gold script and hands
it to Maggie. Their audience is over.

"What did you make of all that?" Ryan asks Maggie as they
descend in the elevator.

"Not sure. Something maybe happened that maybe changed
Betsy? Not much to go on there."

"These women are all fucking nuts."

"Finally something we can agree on, Johnson. Want a scone?
Better on your hips than mine." She apes Rachel Ferris's delivery of
the last line.

Johnson laughs, an honest guffaw. She holds out the bag for
him. He extracts a scone and takes a big bite, spilling crumbs across
his chest. "Oh, fuck me," he sputters, swiping at the mess.

Maggie reaches into the monogrammed bag and retrieves a
paper napkin that is likewise emblazoned with a letter *F* in gold
script. "Look," she says as she offers it to him. "A useful party
favor."

"*F* for fucking nuts," Johnson growls. Their eyes meet in a moment of shared amusement.

For a brief second Maggie thinks maybe she'll miss Ryan when
she starts her UC work. *Maybe.* She watches as he crams another
huge bite of scone into his furiously working jaw, while swatting
crumbs from his shirtfront.

No. Maybe not.

Later that night, Maggie's jaw rests heavily on the palm of one hand, the pointed V of her elbow anchored on the desk to prop up her nodding head. She's grateful to be home in her own apartment in Hoboken, snuggled into boxer shorts and an oversized sweat-shirt. She's been examining the copies of the security footage of the Elliotts' Park Avenue apartment building she'd had the FBI tech lab burn for her. She's been running through it for endless hours, but at least she's comfortable.

There are multiple angles to study, with cameras positioned out-side the entrance of the building, at several points inside and out-side the lobby, inside all four passenger elevators, on every other landing in the staircase, in the communal laundry room in the basement, inside the freight elevator, and outside the back service entrance.

To amuse herself, Maggie's spent the last hour or so creating a false narration for the characters that silently cross her screen. She dubs the orange-haired, perpetually fur-clad, and imperious ma-tron the Countess, describes the distant body language and sharp looks between a tense-looking husband and his uptight wife like a sports announcer calling a fight, invents a blood feud between two taciturn porters.

It may pass the time, but it's not getting her any closer to Betsy and Bear Elliott. *Overactive imagination.* That's what Maggie's mother always says.

She replays the footage of Betsy and her son entering the lobby the day of their disappearance, this time slowing down the speed. Something's different about this day from the earlier days in the week.

Maggie's pulse quickens. She begins scrolling backward through the footage, looking to confirm or deny her burgeoning suspicions.

Wow. I'm right. In the course of Betsy's comings and goings with Bear she always had a nanny in tow. But not the last time she was seen in the lobby. Deep in Maggie's belly a warning bell chimes: This means *something*.

Maggie runs her fingers through her hair, sifting through the myriad questions that emerge as she processes the implications of her discovery.

The ugly drone of a buzzer interrupts her thoughts. Maggie rises and answers the intercom. "Yeah?"

"Me."

She presses the buzzer.

When the double knock comes, she's ready at her apartment door with two freshly cracked beers and a smile. "*Hola*, brother mine," she says as she offers Diego a bottle. They are the youngest two in their family, but their bond goes beyond that. Diego's a street cop in Newark. The siblings share a genuine calling for their careers in law enforcement.

"Yo." He holds up a bag from which wafts the tantalizing scent of Chinese takeout.

"About time. I'm starving. Get in here. I want to run something by you."

After they've had their fill of food and a second beer each, Maggie launches in with a short preamble to set the stage. Then she gets to the point. "So I'm looking at the footage from the building and I notice that Betsy always has a nanny with her if she goes out with the kid. *Always*. That's weird enough, you ask me, given she really does seem into the whole motherhood thing, like genuinely. What's weirder, though, is that the doorman told me the Elliotts always have three nannies on rotation, but in the last week, there are only two women I can identify as nannies on the security footage."

"So maybe the doorman was wrong. Or maybe they were short-staffed that week. I hear that happens to rich people."

Maggie tosses a pillow at him. "I'll short-staff you in a second."

"That does not sound like something a sister should say to her older brother."

"You're absolutely right. It was disgusting and I don't apologize."

Diego tosses the pillow back at Maggie. "Don't we have an episode of *Walking Dead* cued up?"

"We do."

"Magali. You can stop running so hard. You made it into undercover school in the FB-fucking-I. This'll be someone else's case in five minutes. Stop and smell the roses, kid."

How can she push after that? She grabs the remote. After the episode and a shared pint of mint chocolate chip, Diego bids Maggie good night.

"Get some sleep, Mags. You look like shit."

Maggie throws some shade right back. "That sweet tongue must be the reason the only woman that'll hang with you is me. And I'm reconsidering."

"Speaking of which, my friend Carlos asked about you again, but I told him . . ."

"Maggie doesn't date cops," they finish in unison.

"It's a sensible policy," says Maggie.

"Yeah, sensible for the men in blue that are spared you." Diego sticks his tongue out at her.

"Adiós." The door closes behind him. Maggie eyes the temptation of the firm mattress and soft pillows beckoning to her through her open bedroom door, then sinks back down in front of her laptop. She combs through the security footage one more time, now familiar enough with the routine of the building to sort tenants from staff from visitors. She zooms in on blurry faces and stops on individuals that appear even mildly out of place or awkward, jotting notes and questions on a yellow legal pad.

The third time she notices the slender figure in the hoodie, she begins to suspect the girl is deliberately hiding her face. Clad in high-top sneakers, jeans, and a navy blue sweatshirt with the hood pulled tight around her head, the girl has her face averted regardless of the positioning of the camera. She appears in the lobby twice in one day, stopping in the morning to talk to the doorman on duty, waving goodbye when she leaves a few hours later. On footage from the following day, Maggie finds her slipping into the service entrance using a key. It's impossible to guess the figure's age; she's so scrawny and small she might still be a preteen waiting for a growth spurt.

But maybe not. Maggie catches sight of the slender figure greeting Betsy and Bear in footage taken outside the front of the building. They seem familiar, the slender girl putting a hand on Betsy's shoulder and bending down to talk to Bear.

Maggie freezes the image and hits a couple of buttons. An enlarged, glossy copy of the trio spits from the printer. Maggie stares at it. The camera has caught something quite extraordinary that Maggie hadn't even noticed while the image was on her screen: The slender figure bending to talk to Bear is at precisely the right angle to have her face reflected in the side-view mirror of an idling Lincoln Town Car.

Spinning back to her keyboard, Maggie zooms in even closer, enlarging the reflection, playing with the balance between the size of the image and clarity of detail.

Gotcha. Instinct sings in her heart and guides her mind, next steps falling into place before her like dominos. She's increasingly able to trust this feeling and knows she'll need to in order to be successful in the field. *In order to stay alive.*

Maggie prints an enlargement of the face in the mirror. Examines the blurred features revealed.

Not a preteen, a woman. Maybe in her twenties? Thirties? Hard to say as her face looks weathered, like she's spent a lot of time outdoors. Shaggy black hair. Remarkable blue eyes. Intelligent. Urgent. Guarded. Fierce.

Or am I reading all of that into her?

Maggie laughs at herself as she climbs into bed. She's probably just someone who lives or works in the building. What kind of danger could that skinny little woman threaten?

Overactive imagination. Just like Mama says.

SMACK!

——

Catherine,
Mexico City, Mexico

I'm deep asleep when I feel her gentle hand on my shoulder, hear her soft whisper in my ear.

"Let's go, Cathy. Let's go."

I know I should wake up, but I can't. A pull as strong as an undertow keeps my limbs snug in my warm, heavy blankets, my eyes closed. I want to drift away on the tide.

Will we get out in time?

Not if I can't wake up. But I don't care, I snuggle my face deeper into my pillow. *Maybe if I don't wake up everything will work out differently this time.*

I stretch my limbs and they expand, child-sized arms and legs lengthening and widening, growing a soft down. And then I'm no longer in the flannel of my nursery. I'm wrapped in sheets of impossible silken softness, my body moving liquid and hot under Holly's. He slides inside of me and I cry out, desperate for him, urging him deeper.

I want release so very badly. I'm on the verge, about to cry out.

A sound snaps me awake.

I'm trembling, from my dream, from my lizard-brain alert system screaming danger. I focus my eyes, pushing the shadows back into their corners. *Where am I?*

Gabi's house. Mexico City. I'm positioned on one of the two sofas in the open plan main floor, the first line of defense for the Harris family sleeping (along with Gabi) on the floor above.

SMACK!

I hear it again, the noise that busted my uneasy sleep wide open.

Taking my stun gun from its hiding place underneath a cushion, I slide down off the sofa in front of the fireplace and onto my hands and knees on the bamboo floor. Quick glances left and right reveal nothing out of place. I creep slowly around the edge of the sofa and peer out across the shadowy expanse of the house.

All seems quiet. The stairs to the second floor are empty. I can't see behind the kitchen island, but there's a stillness in the air that belies another's presence.

SMACK!

My head whips around and finds the culprit. The door to the terrace is open, swinging in the wind. I'm certain I secured it before I went to sleep. *Did I?*

I hesitate a moment. Cover the upstairs first? Or secure the residence? Taking advantage of the darkness, I crawl along the floor toward the stairs, the safety of the Harris family my top priority.

When I reach the stairs, I sprint up them as quietly as I can. Cock my head around the landing.

Clear.

I check Dakota's room, opening the door with a soft click that doesn't even register on the sleeping teenager. I close the door just as softly.

Next, Steve, Lisa, and Finn.

The door to their room squeals as I open it. Steve and Finn slumber on, but Lisa startles awake and stares at me with terrified eyes, drawing the coverlet protectively up around her shoulders.

I put a finger to my lips, signaling she should stay quiet. "Stay here," I mouth more than say. She gives me a jerky nod.

The bathroom in the hallway is similarly quiet with no sign of any intruder or disturbance. I push open Gabi's door. Her rumpled bed is empty.

"Gabi?" I call softly into the dark room. No response.

Light falls in a rectangular yellow block from the open bathroom door on the left side of Gabi's bedroom. I sidle toward it, nerves prickling, stun gun raised, and take a look.

Empty. A bite plate, the kind used to prevent the wearer from grinding teeth, sits on the bathroom counter. I run a finger along it and discover it's still damp.

Where's Gabi?

I head back down the stairs. When I reach the main floor, I flick a switch and flood the space with light. Clear. I check the door leading down to the garage. Locked. I flick the lights off again.

I'm heading for the terrace and if anyone is out there, I don't want them to see me coming.

Crossing to the open terrace door, I roll my shoulders to relax them; my clients are safe, the house almost secured. The door must have jostled loose in the wind. Or maybe Gabi's out there, unable to sleep.

Shielding my body with the wall, I peek my head around to scan the terrace. My eyes struggle to make sense of what I see, shadowy lumps and things that go bump under a dark and smoggy sky.

All seems clear. I take a few steps out just to be certain. My eyes adjust.

Clear.

I don't know if I'll get back to sleep tonight but at least all seems to be well.

The bullet crushes into the frame of the door mere millimeters from my ear. I spin and duck into a crouch. A second bullet whizzes through the doorway and explodes a terra-cotta pot full of prickly cacti.

"Catherine, are you all right?" Gabi's voice is tight with tension.

"Are you?"

"Yes."

"Who's shooting?"

"Me!"

"Then stop. It's just me out here."

Gabi must have hit the switch because the terrace is abruptly flooded with light. She appears in the doorway, a pistol in her shaking hands.

"What the hell?"

"I heard a noise." Gabi gestures with the gun. "So . . ."

"Yeah, well, next time, ask before you shoot."

I brush past Gabi to find the Harris family huddled at the top of the stairs. With arms and legs spread wide in front of his wife and children, his body poised to pounce, Steve's face is a caricature of fear. Little Finn clings to his mother, his face buried in her neck. Lisa strokes his back and murmurs in his ear. Dakota looks like a little girl rather than the defiant teen that has been flouncing around with an arrogant attitude for the last couple of days.

"Sorry," I reassure. "False alarm. Go back to bed. Just a door in the wind."

If it was only that simple. Poor little Finn retreats deeper into himself, flapping his hands, repeating a cry of "Kota, Kota, Kota." An oppressive weariness settles over Dakota's face as the boy springs away from his mother and claws onto his sister. She sinks to the floor, weariness replaced by resignation as she holds her little brother and rocks him, stilling his hands in hers.

"Okay, Finny. You're okay. It was just a bang." She repeats a variation of this for what seems like a very long time as Lisa and Steve stare helplessly at each other over the heads of their children.

Dakota finally takes the boy back to sleep with her. I take Gabi's pistol and empty the remaining bullets. Insist she put the weapon back in the gun safe located in the garage. I watch her do it and then pocket the key.

"Just as long as I'm here." She knows how I feel about guns. This incident has proved my point. If there's a gun around, someone is a hell of a lot more likely to get shot.

"I'm sorry," Gabi offers. "I got it when Mia went away to school."

"Why don't you make Steve and Lisa some tea. I'll be right up."

Gabi lingers; I can tell there's more she wants to say, but I don't want to hear it right now. "Go."

I sweep through the house methodically, starting down here in the garage. The *fruta* van is in place; keys in the ignition, ready for an easy escape should that become necessary. Gabi's car, a Range Rover, is squeezed in beside it; the automatic garage door is secure. I come back upstairs. I check every window and recheck the newly secured terrace door. As far as I know, no one has picked up on our trail, but it's better to be careful in all things.

Steve, Lisa, and Gabi sip the dregs of a pot of chamomile tea. I join them, perching on a stool at the kitchen island.

The Harrises are both very pale; Steve has one steadying hand placed on top of his wife's smaller one.

"It was all supposed to be different," Lisa says, so softly I can barely make out the words. "This year. All I thought I was looking at was adjusting to Dakota being away at school, what that would do to Finny. She's amazing with him, you know, the only one who can always get through when he's really . . . struggling."

Her voice grows even softer. I find myself leaning closer to hear.

"And my poor baby girl. Thought she'd finally be able to be a normal teenager." Lisa shifts so she can look directly in Steve's eyes. "I know you're doing the right thing. But is it going to cost us everything?"

Her husband stares helplessly back at her, his face lined with regret, sorrow, the desperation of not knowing if it will, in fact, cost them everything.

"Not if I can help it," I interject. "Look, that gave us all a scare but it was a false alarm. We're safe here. You'll testify. And then it'll all be over."

Anxiety clouds both of their faces despite my reassurances. I can't blame them. Our nerves are shot.

"You two should try to get some sleep."

"The door. It might have been Finny," Lisa responds. "He likes locks. He plays with them. I should have told you. It's impossible to watch him every second." The tired anguish in her voice is painful to hear.

"Don't worry about it. That door's on me either way and it won't happen again."

The Harrises head upstairs. Gabi opens her mouth to speak but I shut her down with a look. She drifts upstairs as well.

I'll never get back to sleep so I check all my devices: three laptops, a dozen phones. I take on the task of downloading reports from operatives in the field. With Holly stirring my dreams, I start with Hong Kong.

As software decrypts Jake's latest, I sort through the tangle of images that haunted my sleep tonight. My mother. Holly. I know what links them. For me they were both the epitome of *safe*. Safe is something I haven't had much of.

Self-pity. Screw this. *I hate it.*

But Holly did make me feel safe for a time, and at a point in my life when I needed it badly. He's never once asked me for anything after I turned down his offer of marriage, and he's unquestionably offered resources when I've needed them along the way. I'm anxious to see what Jake and Stephanie have to report. I can't let Holly down. I won't let him down.

SHANGHAI STREET

Jake Burrows, aka John Bernake, Kowloon

"It's so humid. And the pollution. How can this city be so clean and so gross at the same time? Where are you taking me, anyway? And why are you the one in charge? No one's given me a good answer to that question yet."

Stevie's grievances and whiny questions set Jake's teeth on edge. He's had just about enough of her buzzing around him like an irritating fly. He catches a glimpse of her shaggy hair and querulous eyes in the reflection of a store window as they pass. He snakes even faster through the chaos of Kowloon's Shanghai Street, half-hoping he'll lose her.

Goods spill from open shop fronts like seeds burst from pods: kitchenware including woks, steamers, skewers, rice cookers, knife blocks, cutting boards, and cauldrons; sinks, faucets, showerheads, and porcelain toilets; rolled bolts of fabric; brightly colored boxes of cleaning products; exotic fruits, Chinese herbs.

The air is heavy, ripe with moisture. A dark green garbage truck with a powder blue cab rumbles past, drowning out Stevie's incessant whine. *Thank god for small favors.*

Jake checks the address he has scribbled on a piece of scrap paper shoved into his front pants pocket. He directs Stevie to enter a particularly unappetizing-looking entryway. Paint peels from a battered wooden doorframe. A smell like boiling cabbage fouls the air.

"The fuck?" she mutters. "What the hell is this?"

Wordlessly, Jake presses the elevator button. The cab descends with a grotesque squeal. He pulls back the hand-operated gate and gestures that Stevie should enter. She does, but not without glaring at him.

"You could talk to a person, you know," she volleys. "That's how a partnership works."

"You could shut your mouth for one goddamn second too, you know. That's how *this* partnership will work."

"At least tell me why you dragged me all the way over here."

Jake clams up. He doesn't know what to expect when these elevator doors slide open. But he can't tell Stevie that. She's challenged his authority every step of the way. He's following Catherine's instructions and that has to be enough. They ride up to the fifth floor of the building in silence, an acrid scent of burnt grease assaulting his nostrils.

The elevator grinds to a stop. The doors open. Jake blinks. The grungy street and creaky elevator fade away as his eyes rake over a large, modern open space, with shiny white floors. The entire footprint of the building is subdivided into a series of red lacquer–framed mini-offices, each equipped with a desk, a chair, and a state-of-the-art computer terminal. Each module's hung with gold curtains. Some are drawn, but most of the units seem to be unoccupied. The pulsing blue of countless screens gives the room an underwater glow. Incense burns on a small altar to their right.

Cedar? Sandalwood.

A tiny Chinese woman comes forward to greet them, her small frame overwhelmed by an oversized flowered blouse layered over a pair of checked trousers. She moves like a young girl, fluid and confident, but as she gets closer, Jake sees she's ancient; her face webbed by thousands of fine lines, her eyes a bottomless, impenetrable black.

"I was told to ask for Gracey," Jake informs the old woman. "Rhonda Daly from Manitoba is a mutual friend."

The old woman snaps her fingers. Two teenage boys materialize to flank Jake and Stevie. They're both slender; one wears dorky glasses. They hardly seem threatening, but Stevie backs away. "Whoa, whoa, what's this?" she protests.

"Just come on," Jake hisses. The teens lead them down an aisle separating one of the rows of "offices" from another and into a module of their own.

Jake settles in front of the computer and goes to work, fingers racing over the keyboard. Stevie leans against the red partition and crosses her arms over her chest. "We came all the way over here to use a computer?"

"Uh-huh." Jake keeps his attention on the screen.

"And you couldn't tell me that, why?"

"Because you annoy me."

That finally shuts her up. Jake continues on silently as the teenage boys re-enter, bearing a tray with two cups of hot tea and a bowl of fresh orange slices. They place the tray on the desk and depart.

"That's a nice touch," Stephanie opines as she helps herself to an orange slice.

Jake ignores her. He's found what he's looking for: Eva Lombard's Facebook account. The profile picture features Eva and a huge furry dog with an eager expression. The animal is also prominently featured in her posts. "Baxter at Buckingham Palace," "Baxter at Kensington Gardens," "Baxter at Trafalgar Square." Jake briefly admires Eva's eye for composition before getting down to business.

The woman has no privacy settings, lucky for Jake, potentially foolish for Eva. No one's life should be an open book; Jake's always believed that. His very lack of a social media presence had been a determining factor in his joining the Society; Catherine had told him so. Facial recognition software is getting increasingly sophisticated and more easily obtainable; it's harder and harder to be a ghost. It's one reason Jake now rocks a beard.

In a matter of minutes, he's narrowed down the list of Eva's friends to find those currently living in Hong Kong. There are seven in total, but only four have relatively frequent interface with Eva: Alexander Blake, forty years old; Heather Haas, thirty-one; Daniel Haas, Heather's husband, thirty-three; Yuan Dai, twenty-nine.

The Haas couple's posts reveal a six-year marriage and an even longer relationship. Yuan's revealed as a woman by her profile photograph, in which she sports impish hot pink pigtails. Jake tries to recall if Francesca Leigh referred to an ex-boyfriend or just an ex?

Boyfriend. Alexander Blake seems like their best option.

"I have a name for the ex-boyfriend. Alexander Blake."

"Wonderful. But it's not like we couldn't have used any computer to find that out." Stevie stuffs an orange slice in her mouth and gives Jake a goofy orange peel smile.

What the hell is Catherine thinking putting the two of us together?

Jake averts his eyes from Stevie as the old woman who'd greeted them at the elevator enters. She's trailed by the two teenage boys, who tote a large cushion with a fanciful pattern of birds and flowers embroidered across the fabric. The boys set the pillow down on the floor and back out of the space, drawing the curtains.

In one smooth motion, the old lady drops into lotus position atop the pillow, coming to rest with her upturned hands loosely held on her knees. She raises her right palm upward and gestures to Stevie.

"Give it to me," the old woman commands in a chilly voice.

Jake shoots a glance at Stevie. *Does she know what the hell this woman's talking about?*

She must, as a sheepish expression crosses her face. She fishes in her jacket pocket and extracts a notebook. Hands it over as she's been instructed.

"What the hell is that?" Jake barks.

Stevie shrugs. "Notebook I lifted off Inspector Tsang."

"And you didn't think to mention it to me?"

"Catherine told me to make the play. Not you. Pot calling kettle anyway, asshole."

Jake burns. If Eva Lombard is in real danger, this partnership may implode before they can ever get to her.

Stevie gives him a punch on his shoulder. "Lighten up." She gestures to the old woman, who is poring intently through the detective's notebook. "At least now we know why we're really here."

TROUBLES

Peter Lombard,
Hong Kong Island

He's starting to feel a bit better, hovering *above* the pain instead of tightly held in its steely grip. He attributes this, correctly, to the pills the nurse handed him about forty minutes ago. He holds an ice pack in place over his right eye. Lifts it to gingerly test the swelling underneath. Winces.

The pink curtain surrounding his hospital bed draws to the side, revealing Inspector Tsang. He raises an eyebrow as his eyes assess Peter's battered state.

"How are you feeling?"

"Been better."

Tsang asks a series of questions and Peter answers them to the best of his ability.

"I was going stir-crazy. I needed to get out of the hotel. I went for a walk with no destination in mind. I was just walking along when I was jumped."

"No, I never got a good look at my attackers. I was distracted, and then it all happened so fast. Then I was trying to protect my head. Although I did a shit job, obviously." Peter punctuates the last comment with a wry laugh and a wave of the ice pack.

"Yes, only one man spoke, although I'm sure there were at least two, maybe three?"

"Yes, the man spoke English."

Tsang asks if Peter can remember what the man said and Peter hesitates. Repeating the threat seems a betrayal of Eva somehow, as well as an admission of a chasm between him and his wife that he's uneasy exposing to Tsang's inquiring stare.

" 'Get your bitch under control,' " Peter finally allows. The harsh commandment hangs starkly in the disinfectant-flavored air. Tsang's eyebrow flickers upward yet again. He leans in close to Peter.

"Do you know what he was referring to?"

"No idea. But don't you see? He must be talking about Eva. This proves something's happened to her."

"What trouble have you brought with you to Hong Kong, Mr. Lombard?" Tsang asks in a tone so low and mild Peter has to strain forward to hear him.

Peter jerks back as Tsang's softly spoken words land like a punch. "What? I've just been attacked. My wife is missing! And you want to make me the bad guy here? I don't think so."

"Why are you so defensive? What aren't you telling me?"

"Nothing. I swear. Now please go. I have a headache and want to rest."

Tsang doesn't move. "It doesn't work that way, Mr. Lombard."

Peter fumbles for his phone. Finds the contact number for Francesca Leigh and presses CALL. Defiantly raises his one good eye to meet Tsang's impassive stare as he hears the ring on the other end.

Peter's defiance sputters as his call switches over to voicemail. After the beep that follows Francesca's recorded Southern lilt, Peter leaves a message: "Mrs. Leigh, this is Peter Lombard. I need you to call me as soon as possible.

"Okay," Peter says to Tsang. "We're done. I'm an American. A victim of a crime. I've cooperated with you every step of the way and now you come at me with accusations? Get the hell out of here. I've left word at the consulate. My next call will be a journalist."

Peter realizes he's shaking. Also, that he's not entirely sure what his rights *are* as an American in Hong Kong. But his bluff works. Tsang backs off. Asks a couple of questions confirming details of Peter's attack, *just to show he's still the authority figure,* Peter suspects. He plays along and answers. *No sense in antagonizing the cop any further.*

Tsang wraps it up and informs Peter that he'll be in touch, a tinge of warning in his tone. Peter exhales as the cop disappears behind the pink curtain. Realizes he hadn't even been aware he was holding his breath.

Peter knows he'll go completely insane if he stays in the hospital another second. He hates them as a general rule, heavily associated as they are with the loss of his mother to breast cancer when he was twenty-four. *Why are the curtains in this ER the exact pink linked to American breast cancer research?* They feel like another kick in the teeth, summoning loss and grief and anger that Peter would rather keep buried.

Minutes after Tsang departs, Peter signs out of the hospital over the attending physician's objections. *They* might want to monitor him overnight "just in case" because of his head injuries, but Peter needs action. He has a plan. Of sorts.

First things first, he's going to fill the prescription for pain pills the doctor provided. Then back to the hotel for a shower and a change of clothes. If the Hong Kong police and Forrest's fancy *undercover operatives* can't track Eva down, maybe he can. Enough of waiting on other people. The more he thinks about it, the more excited he gets. He's going to do something. Finally.

Because at first he believed Eva had left him. That she'd decided his grand romantic gesture was too little too late. He's been ashamed, as he knew on a gut level that the blame for the fissures in their marriage lay more on his shoulders than hers. It wasn't his schedule and commitment to his job; those he knew Eva respected and accepted. It was his patronizing attitude toward her loneliness, her hobbies, and her coping mechanisms, including and especially drinking, that had widened the gulf between them.

A small flare of hope rises. *Maybe she did leave me.* Peter shudders. *God, that I should even consider that the better possibility.*

Hard to buy now, though, not after my own attack.

He's able to fill the prescription in the pharmacy adjacent to the hospital lobby and he swallows two more pills down dry right away. He's "lucky," they told him back at the ER. Bruised ribs, multiple contusions, two broken fingers, one lost tooth, and a possible concussion, but it could have been "way worse." *Slim comfort.*

By the time a taxi drops him at his hotel, Peter's floating on a cloud concocted from drugs, pain, exhaustion, and disbelief. He shoves a wad of bills at his driver and enters the lobby conscious of the muted but appalled reactions to his appearance that greet him. A toddler with two blond braids catches sight of him from the safety of her stroller and bursts into tears. Her distracted mother turns to see what's causing the alarm and snatches her little girl away from Peter's path.

Great. Now I scare kids.

He's grateful that he rides up to his floor in an elevator that's otherwise empty. He feels certain that all he needs is a shave and a hair wash, a crisp shirt, and a fresh eye. He's going to figure out what the hell is going on. Find Eva. Make things right.

He strides down the hallway. Waves his key card in front of the door and watches the sensor click from red to green. He pushes open the door.

At first he can't make sense of what he sees. Stuffing spills from the savaged guts of the sofa and two armchairs in the suite's sitting room. The coffee table has been upended, one leg snapped off. The contents of the shopping bags from his ill-advised spree are dumped on the floor, the expensive items sliced to ribbons.

Peter freezes in the doorway. He knows he should get the hell out of there. But he puts one foot forward. And then another. *Who is doing this to us? What the fuck is going on?*

He stands in the middle of the room. The curtains are open, the ever-changing and always-spectacular view of Victoria Harbour on display. *I should leave,* he thinks, as he stays motionless.

What's that reflected in the glass? Is someone here? He turns, Eva's name on his lips, praying he'll see her behind him, back safe, with an easy explanation for *everything.* For any of it.

His head shatters in pain.

I didn't think I could hurt again so much so soon is Peter's last, but not very useful, thought as everything goes black.

WHILE PETER WAS STILL SLEEPING . . .

——

Eva Lombard,
Hong Kong Island, the Day of Arrival

They're laughing about it now, of course, she and Alex. How after he grabbed her shoulder she froze like a deer in headlights. How she'd struggled to make sense of the towering "giant" behind her before it was revealed to be the father with his son perched on his shoulders, their weird shadow even further distorted by the angle of the light. How they gaped at each other soundlessly for a few moments as Eva's eyes traveled up above Alex's head to the little boy's face (an adorable kid with the exact same smile as his father), and then back to meet Alex's astonished eyes. How he'd finally sputtered, "Why didn't you tell me you were coming?" before swinging his child down off his shoulders and enfolding her in a crushing hug.

Upstairs in his apartment, over tea and a plate of ginger cookies, while little Ian plays nearby, Eva shares her account of Peter's surprise trip. She knows Alex's sharp; he's clearly noticed her injured palm and disheveled appearance, but hasn't said anything about it. Yet.

"So how long are you here for?"

"Ten days."

"Do you want me to take a look at that hand?"

To her utter shame, hot tears scald Eva's eyes. Her throat closes;

her nose is suddenly clogged. She looks away from Alex and at his happy little boy busily constructing a Lego spaceship on the coffee table in the living room.

I can't get Alex involved in this. Whatever this is.

"I should really be going," she chokes out.

"Don't be daft. You need attention," Alex replies easily. He escorts her into the kitchen. She drifts along with him limply, unable to resist.

I do need attention. Attention's exactly what I need.

He winds the blood-soaked scarf away from her palm and drops it down in the sink. "Oooh. That looks nasty," he says, inspecting her injury. "Want to tell me about it?"

She's not sure what to say or how to begin. Her suspicions seem ridiculously far-fetched on the one hand, but then again . . .

She shakes her head. "No, not just yet."

She lets him run warm water over her wound and clean it with soap. He wraps her palm in a clean dishcloth and has her sit down on a stool at the kitchen counter while he opens a first aid kit. "Upside of that little lad," he says, gesturing to the bandages, ointments, and swabs nestled inside the box. "I'm ready for anything."

The antibacterial ointment stings in that way that tells you it's doing its job. Alex layers Eva's palm with clean gauze and winds her hand in more gauze strips so it's well padded. He secures the bandage with adhesive tape.

The stinging subsides, but her hand throbs painfully in rhythm with her heartbeat. "Here, live large," Alex suggests, as he hands her four aspirins and a glass of water.

After she swallows the pills and drinks most of the water, Alex takes the glass away from her and sets it on the counter. He lifts her bandaged hand to his mouth and kisses the crescent of flesh where her thumb curves into her palm, a tender corner the gauze doesn't cover. "There. A kiss to make it better."

A shiver of shameful desire courses through Eva's body. If only his son wasn't in the other room . . . *My god. What is wrong with me?*

"So, Eva Bean. What's going on?"

The use of her old nickname chokes Eva up yet again. She wants to confide in Alex, but she suspects she will sound delusional, her suspicions that Peter wants to have her killed utterly absurd. She questions everything, including her own motives in seeking out her former lover. *Did I manufacture a crisis in my head to send me back to Alex? But what if I'm right? Clearly something ugly is intruding into my life.*

"I don't know how to begin," she finally stammers.

Alex gives her an appraising glance. "Okay. We've got to get out of here in about fifteen in any event, as I have to drop Ian at his mum's. Then you and I can have a proper talk. Maybe involving alcohol." Alex turns his head to call to his son. "Ian, mate, we've got to go. Start putting the Legos away."

The boy's sunny disposition disappears. Ian thrusts out his lower lip in a pout. His bottom lip begins to tremble. He beats his small curled fists against his thighs as an ear-shattering howl escapes his throat.

Alex is up and on his feet immediately, sweeping the boy into his arms. "Come along," he soothes his son, as he turns his head back to Eva. "Sorry about this. We're in a stage. I need to take him into his room and work through it with him. You'll be all right for a few?"

"Of course."

Alex carries the boy down the hall. Eva's jumpy. Can't sit still. She buzzes around the apartment idly noting both the changes and the things that have remained the same in the decade since she's been here. *I remember that antique chest. That lamp is new.* All the while her mind fevers with a combination of fear, anxiety, excitement, lust, shame, and confusion.

A framed photograph catches her eye. She and Alex, during their long ago summer fling, sitting side by side on a red silk loveseat. Eva remembers that loveseat with a pang. They'd fucked for the first time on it, and many times thereafter. A more practical brown suede sofa is now in its place. In the photo they are demure, fully dressed, no hint of the carnality they'd shared there so many times. They clasp hands. Both of them face the camera. Their thighs press up against each other's, a hint of their fire. They look happy. And so young.

Sadness wells up and will not be denied. Eva gives in to a deep, longing regret for roads not taken; relationships squandered or neglected, the futile game of asking *what if*? If she had stayed in Hong Kong, given her and Alex a real chance, who knows what might have happened? Maybe that could have been her little boy in the bedroom; her patient husband dealing with a tantrum.

The doorbell buzzes, snapping her out of her unhappy reverie. She cocks her head to listen; is Alex going to answer the door? It seems unlikely; neither the boy's cries nor his father's calming murmurs have abated.

The buzzer sounds again. Eva knows the building. If someone was coming from outside they would need to be admitted through the intercom system. She pads over to the front door and looks through the peephole. Two men stand outside, both clad in dark blue boiler suits with matching insignias in white on their breast pockets.

"Yes?" she asks through the closed door.

"We're here to take a look at the HVAC," one of them volunteers.

"One minute." Eva takes a second peek through the spyhole. Their features are distorted by the fish-eye lens, but she can make them out well enough. Both men are Chinese. One carries a toolbox. Eva walks down the hall and knocks softly on Ian's door. "Alex, some men are here about the HVAC?"

He comes to the bedroom door and cracks it open. Alex holds Ian balanced on one hip, the little boy's face nestled into the curve of his father's neck. Ian's face is red, he gulps big mouthfuls of air, but he's calmer.

"What about it?" Alex asks.

Eva *feels* the blood drain from her face. Alex notices. "What's wrong?"

"I don't even understand what's going on myself. But a man attacked me with a knife earlier today. That's how my hand got cut."

"What's that got to do with my HVAC?"

"It wasn't just some random mugging! Someone's been following me. Since London! I came to you because I trust you, always have, but I can't let you get involved."

"Involved in what?"

"I don't know. But if you didn't send for repairmen . . ." She gestures to Ian. "On the off chance these men tracked me here, we should get out of the building and away from here as quickly as possible."

Alex shifts his boy to his left hip. "Let's use the kitchen exit."

With a rush of pure gratitude, Eva remembers why she loved Alex: this easy acceptance, this calm and kind understanding. With a bolt of anger, Eva remembers Peter calling her paranoid. *Or was that a mind fuck? Is Pete the reason I need to be paranoid?*

"Do you need anything? Or can we just go?" she whispers.

"I've got wallet, keys, phone, and kid. I'm good. You?"

"I've got my bag."

"All right then. Let's go."

Eva and Alex make a beeline for the back door. A key hangs next to it on a hook on the wall and Eva remembers, plucking it from its perch and using it to unlock the door. Alex ushers Eva through and follows, his son held tightly in his arms. Eva closes the door behind them and turns the key in the lock from this side.

They are halfway down the first flight of stairs when they hear pounding behind them. Fists. Feet. Eva can't tell exactly.

But whatever the source of the racket, it certainly doesn't sound like a couple of routine maintenance workers thwarted in their attempt to fix an HVAC unit.

Eva trips down the stairs even faster, glancing behind her to see Ian clinging to his dad, his recent misery transformed into delight by this sudden ride. The little boy releases a chortle of laughter. "Go, Papa!"

As they come to the turn of the next landing, Eva draws up short and Alex bumps into her from behind. "Cover Ian's eyes!" she whispers. There are two bound and unconscious men stripped to their underwear and bundled in an unceremonious heap. Eva notes the slow rise and fall of their pale chests and gratefully realizes they're not dead.

Alex cups one hand over Ian's eyes, and they skirt past the men and down the next flight of stairs.

When they reach the musty vestibule with the door leading into the alley, an entirely new round of fear claws its way into Eva's belly. *Who's to say there aren't other men lying in wait? What if it's too late? What if I've already brought danger to Alex and his son?*

She pulls the door open a few inches and peers outside. Sheeting rain renders the alley a gray-wash watercolor painting, objects indistinct, their edges uncertain. They don't know what's ahead of them, but Eva knows danger is behind them.

There is no other choice. The only way is out.

BOUND

Peter Lombard,
Hong Kong Island

When Peter emerges from the fug of unconsciousness, his first thought is much like his last thought before he blacked out. *Hurt.*

He jerks and discovers he's bound, legs tied at the ankles, wrists behind his back. His eyes pop open as he struggles against the ties binding him. He appears to be in his destroyed hotel suite, he can determine that much. He unsuccessfully tries to spit out the gag clogging his mouth.

"Oh good, you're awake," says the man looming over him. It hits Peter like a bucket of ice water: This is the man who accosted him at the airport, the man Eva accused of following her. *She was right.*

"I'm going to take that gag out and we're going to have a conversation."

Peter nods. *Take it one step at a time.*

The man reaches over and pulls the cloth from Peter's dry mouth.

Peter spits out shreds of cotton and croaks, "Where the hell is my wife?"

"She's a tough one." The man smiles without any warmth whatsoever. "Look what she did to me." He gestures to his swollen nose and scraped-up cheek.

"Good for her," Peter retorts.

"Maybe. Maybe not."

"What the fuck does that mean?"

The man's face contorts into a grimace of sick pleasure that makes Peter's skin crawl. "What does she know, Lombard?"

"About what?"

"Okay. Let's try something else. Where is it?"

"Honest to god, I don't know what you're talking about." Peter stares at him, thoughts racing. *I need time to think.* "Can I get some water?"

The man strolls into the bedroom of the suite. Peter's cellphone lies on the floor mere inches away from his bound feet. *Can I reach it?* He strains to try. He hears the suction pull of the minibar refrigerator. Then the door slamming shut.

"Here," his captor says, lifting a plastic bottle of water to Peter's chapped lips. Peter sips at the cold liquid, greedy eyes still on the cellphone. *So close.*

"Just give me the camera, Lombard."

"What camera?"

"And I heard you were a smart guy. Don't make me hurt you more."

This is all insane. Peter thinks it. Then he says it out loud. "This is all insane. I have no idea what you're talking about."

His assailant fixes him with cold eyes. Cracks his knuckles, the *snap, crackle, pop* sound of it unnaturally loud. He laughs; it sounds like sandpaper. "You don't know what she has, do you? Am I right? Does she even know?"

He takes Peter's face between his hands and squeezes just hard enough to make every inch of Peter's battered head screech in pain. "For a smart guy, you're kind of a dumbass. Where is she?"

"I don't know. I wish I did. At least she got away from you."

A ready fist connects with Peter's nose and his head explodes. *I'm literally seeing stars.* Blood runs down into his mouth, hot and metallic. He spits. Spits again.

"Stop making this harder than it has to be. Where's her camera?"

"With her, I presume. She has it with her all the time."

"Well then. We have ourselves a problem, don't we?"

WHILE PETER WAS STILL SLEEPING . . .

———

Eva Lombard,
Hong Kong Island

Her heart pounding, Eva leads Alex out of the dank vestibule at the base of his apartment building's back stairway and into the sheeting rain. Alex shields Ian from the downpour as they hustle through the back alley and load the boy into Alex's old BMW, which is parked nearby.

As Alex pulls into traffic and drives, Ian chatters happily, oblivious to the strained atmosphere between the adults in the car. Eva tries to catch Alex's eye, but his gaze vacillates between the rain-slick roads ahead of him and wary glances in the rearview mirror.

As they pass an elegant, doorman-attended apartment building, Ian squawks, "You drove right by Mummy's!"

Alex laughs it off. "So I did, silly me." But the anxious look he slides at Eva tells her his drive-by was deliberate. "I don't think we're being followed," he murmurs to her. "Still, I don't want to take any chances. I'm going to circle around."

A lump forms in Eva's throat. When she thought of seeking out Alex, she never suspected she would endanger him, or his son. *Stupid twat.*

"I'm so sorry, Alex. Why don't you just let me out? If anyone's following us, they'll stay on me and you and Ian will be out of it."

Alex's eyebrow cocks archly in a way that is so familiar to Eva it hurts. That very raised eyebrow had punctuated the probing questions he'd asked her in his sexy London accent when she'd first been drawn to him.

"I don't think so, Eva Bean. What kind of arsehole do you think I am?"

He grins at her then, and despite the fear and confusion that plague her, Eva feels a ray of hope. *I have someone on my side.*

Alex makes a call. He arranges to drop Ian at his ex-mother-in-law's antiques shop instead of at his ex-wife's, claiming an unexpected work obligation will keep him near that part of town. There's a well-worn and weary pattern to the rhythm of their argument that Eva can detect even listening just to one side of it. But Alex prevails. He disconnects the call. "We're going to see Po Po," he tells Ian. "Your mum will get you later."

Alex pilots the BMW through the Sheung Wan District and onto Hollywood Road. A turn onto a side street and Alex bundles Ian out of the car and into the waiting arms of a smiling, elderly Chinese woman.

Once Alex is back in the car, Eva's grateful that he doesn't immediately pepper her with questions. They sit quietly for a spell, listening to the sound of the driving rain. Alex turns the ignition and pulls away from the curb.

"Where are we going?" Eva asks him.

"That depends on what you want to tell me, Eva Bean."

COLONIAL GEM

—

Stephanie Regaldo, aka Stevie Nichols, Hong Kong Island

Heavy rain sheets down, prettily but perilously blurring both light and sound through the windshield of their speeding taxi. The streets are slick and shiny with rapidly forming puddles. From the dry comfort of the backseat, Stephanie peers out the streaky window to check an address as the cab finally slows.

The building's a relic from another time, crammed between two towering columns of modern, glistening glass and steel, and much shorter than its neighbors at only six stories. The real estate sites refer to the edifice as a "colonial gem." Stephanie found images of the structure online before they came over in person, so she knew not only the marketing term but what to expect: pale stucco with gracious archways, terraced balconies iced with wrought iron, mullioned windows, sturdy wooden doors. All dwarfed by two of Hong Kong's most aggressive and modern towers, which encroach from either side. Alexander Blake's apartment is on the top floor of the "colonial gem."

Stephanie turns to her partner. "Well, that's the place. What now?"

"Let's see if anyone's home." John hands a wad of Hong Kong dollars to the taxi driver.

Stephanie adjusts her hood and tightens the collar of her jacket. *Here goes nothing.*

She plunges out of the taxi and into the downpour. Hustles to the arched portico surrounding the front entrance. Even though she was only exposed to the storm for a matter of moments, fat drops of rain roll off her as she shakes off her mad dash. *Like a dog after a bath.*

She turns expectant eyes to the cab.

John swings his legs out of the taxi and plants his shiny leather shoes firmly on the drenched asphalt. From this seated position he pops open an oversized umbrella, jackknifing his body up and out of the car only when the umbrella reaches full span.

"Afraid of a little water?" Stephanie calls, baiting him. She can't help it. *He's a pussy.* "What? You gonna melt?" She snickers as one of his expensive shoes scuffs through a puddle deeper than it appears. He ignores her.

A series of names in block type align against a brass-framed panel of buzzers. John presses the button reading: A. BLAKE. They wait. Nothing. He tries again. Shrugs.

Stephanie extracts a chamois bag from inside her jacket. "Keep the umbrella angled toward the camera," she instructs, nodding in the direction of the lens positioned on the front of the portico and aimed directly where they're standing.

Shielded by the circle of dripping black, she examines the options in her kit and selects a long skinny pick. With a practiced thrust she jams it into the lock securing the door. Two quick turns and the lock pops open with a satisfying *click*.

Stephanie relishes the look on John's face, a mix of admiration, shock, and repulsion, all fueling unasked questions. "Come on in," she says. "It's fucking wet out here." She swings the door open and strides in with confidence.

Acting like you belong somewhere is half the battle.

The lobby features a massive circular marble table. An equally massive crystal chandelier is centered above it; the faceted pendants send prisms of rainbow dancing around the room. A vase brimming with exotic tropical flowers sits on the table's heart. Stephanie's sure they're fake; the colors are too improbably vibrant to be real. She plucks away a waxy green leaf. Is surprised to find it oozes sap on her fingers.

There's a single elevator directly ahead of them and a gracious marble stairway to their right. The lobby's deserted, the only sound the steady drum of the relentless rain outside. Stephanie beelines for the elevator.

Alexander Blake's apartment door proves to be just as easy for Stephanie to pick as his front door. This time, she's cocky enough to give John a happy little wink just before the bolt turns. As the door opens, a security system beeps ominously. Stephanie heads for the keypad located to the right of the entrance. Punches in a series of numbers. The beeping ceases. Stephanie ushers John inside and closes the apartment's front door softly after him.

They listen intently, poised for fight or flight. But if anyone's home they remain undisturbed by the intrusive alarm. Or quietly hiding. Stephanie takes a step deeper into the apartment.

"Do I even want to ask where you learned to pick locks like that?" Jake inquires, trailing behind her.

"I don't know, do you? Does it matter? I got us in, so let's look around."

"And the keypad?"

She shrugs. "As soon as we got a name back at Gracey's, I did a little digging. It's remarkable what you can find online if you're even a little bit clever. I hacked into Blake's computer. Stupid sap has a folder marked 'PASSWORDS' on his laptop."

She turns her attention to examining the vestibule of the apartment. The boss has taught her how important careful observation can be. Observation without judgment even more so, although way harder to achieve, all of our preconceptions insistent on obscuring what is often right in front of us.

A boldly patterned area rug covers most of the hardwood floor. A console table to their left holds a bowl of keys, a stack of mail, and a browning, half-eaten apple atop a square of paper towel. Next to the table is an umbrella stand containing a large, well-made, classic black number and a bright green child's umbrella with bulging froggy eyes. Underneath the table sit a pair of men's sneakers and a pair of child's rubber rain boots, the same emerald green as the frog umbrella.

The entryway opens up into an enormous sitting room, one that screams money. Stephanie's beginning to get an eye. Not so much for fashion, there she likes what she likes. But for architecture and design. She can recognize quality now. Hungers for it. She casts greedy eyes over the possessions of Alexander Blake.

A finely knotted silk rug on the floor. Deep chocolate brown suede couches. Armchairs upholstered in coordinating fabrics and accented with plump contrasting pillows. Enameled vases filled with fresh flowers. Antique Asian chests and tables with intricate detail. A serious-looking oil painting of a landscape hangs prominently. There's also more evidence of a child: a heap of dress-up clothes in a basket, topped off with a fireman's hat, picture books housed in a small set of shelves, a half-constructed Lego spaceship on the coffee table.

A pair of French windows lead out to a terrace and she follows their call despite the rain.

The view is both beautiful and weird: The rake of the mountainside provides a sharp angle down to the misty gray city below. The shiny neighboring towers loom overhead, giants dwarfing the smaller building. Rain beats down in a steady stream. Stephanie shuts the door firmly.

Further investigation reveals three bedrooms. One's kitted out in a masculine style. A substantial bed, heavy furniture in dark wood. A second tidy, Star Wars–themed room is obviously designed for a little boy. A third bedroom appears to be used as an office, although a stack of bright plastic bins full of toys has invaded the space.

A quick glance reveals the kitchen is huge by Hong Kong standards, efficiently designed with late model appliances. There are two full bathrooms and one guest powder room, all recently remodeled. The place is empty.

"I'd say he was here not too long ago. And left in a hurry."

"Why's that?"

John ticks each contributing clue off his fingers. "One, the apple in the front hall. Browning, but not rotten. Two, the Lego project in the living room. Did you notice? Every other toy or book is picked up and in its proper place. It's all a little OCD for me, but whatever. Three, the umbrellas and rain boots. Why would you go out on a day like today without them unless you were getting out in a hurry?"

Stephanie glances at him with surprise. Maybe he's smarter than he looks; these are reasonable assumptions. Nonetheless she retorts, "I'm not sure the umbrellas and boots prove anything. Maybe they own more than one set each. And what if the kid's allowed to have one project out at a time? You don't know anything about this guy. Maybe he's strict. If I learned anything from the boss, it's not to jump to conclusions."

His face tightens. He turns away. It's not that she thinks she's wrong; she knows she's not. It's just that she also knows that the harsh way in which she delivered her reply scalded more than she intended. *Fuck. Why do I always feel so rough?*

"I'm going to take a look in the office," she says, eager to be away from her partner for even a few moments.

Stephanie brushes past John and settles in front of Alexander Blake's computer. Her fingers fly across the keyboard and she settles comfortably into his cushy desk chair. *You can tell it costs just by sitting in it.*

She quickly pieces together a portrait of Blake, accessing his bank and credit card statements, email accounts, phone records, and other files. He works at the Hong Kong Convention and Exhibition Centre as a lighting tech. She suspects there's family money too, though, given this apartment and the man's fat bank balances. His son, Ian, likely the apartment's other occupant, is four years old. Blake shares custody with the boy's mother, a woman named Kristen Chen.

She's about to do a deep dive into Blake and Kristen's relationship when she senses a presence behind her. Stephanie swivels in the luxe desk chair and turns a smile on for John, hoping to soften things between them. Her smile fades when she sees his pale face. "What is it? What did you find?"

"It's Eva Lombard's. It matches the description her husband gave us. It was in the kitchen sink."

He holds out a rose pink scarf, streaked with rusty red. "And I'm pretty sure this is blood."

Stephanie's pretty sure he's right.

TRACKS

——

Jake Burrows, aka John Bernake, Hong Kong Island

The bloody scarf belonging to Eva rendered Stevie uncharacteristically quiet. She'd agreed with Jake that their next logical step was approaching the other people the missing woman knew in Hong Kong. They'd gone to the Haases' apartment first simply because it was closest.

Now that they're there, she remains mute. Jake's tempted to give a little shit back to her, *"What's the matter, afraid of a little blood?"* He restrains himself, both mildly concerned by her shift in demeanor and grateful for relief from her never-ending carping. Also, he's got his own reactions to blood; finding that scarf hit him sideways too. If he pokes the bear there's no guarantee she won't poke back.

The rain's abated at least. Jake assesses the mirror-glass clad tower rising above them, reflecting heavy banks of clouds and a first sweet sliver of sunshine. He's never seen a city like this. Even after years of living in Manhattan, he's dazzled and overwhelmed. Every structure ridiculously tall, gleaming and modern, cut into an island that's itself all sharp rises and angles, banked by green only where the sheer pitch of the mountainous terrain renders construction impossible.

He tells Stevie to wait outside. For once she doesn't protest or challenge. He hopes to hell she gets her shit together fast, whatever it is that's going on.

What if Eva's here? What if she's hurt? What if she's not? Then what? He needs a partner he can rely on no matter the circumstances. He checks his phone again. Still nothing from Catherine since he sent an SOS about the discovery of the blood-streaked scarf in Alexander Blake's deserted apartment.

Jake springs into action when he sees a woman with a baby carriage struggling to open the front door of the Haases' building. He greets her with a smile and a friendly word, holding the door and helping lift the pram over the lip of the doorway.

Once again, Jake marvels at just how *right* Catherine sometimes is. Sometimes, if not always. But it is true that with the right clothes and attitude, Jake can enter places of wealth and privilege without a second glance. And not just enter, *blend into,* access and information just handed over to him. Within moments he's learned the baby's name is Devin, the mother's, Pam. Of course she knows the Haases. She and her husband, Charlie, are great friends with the couple. But Daniel's in Germany. And Heather won't be home now. She'll be at the club. For little Kelby's ice-skating lesson.

It doesn't take much longer for Jake to learn that the Haas club of choice is the Aberdeen Marina Club. At least that's a stroke of luck; Catherine's cover took care to put him on the rolls there.

He tells Stevie they are headed for the club. They may not find Eva there, he's painfully aware of that, but he needs a trail of any kind.

Once they are settled in yet another taxi, Jake decides he has to say something. "You all right?"

"Fine."

"Okay. It's just that you finally stopped giving me shit, so I figured you must be in a bad way."

A hint of a smile flickers across Stevie's face. She punches him in the arm. Hard.

"Ow! What the hell?"

"Thanks for caring." She gives him a dazzling grin, good humor seemingly restored. "Sorry about that. I'm back."

Jake rubs a hand over the sore spot where she punched him. "Yeah, I fucking hope so. And don't hit me again."

"You need to toughen up."

"And don't start telling me what to do again! Listen to me. You have your way of getting into things and I have mine. Take my lead at this next place."

The Aberdeen Marina Club lives up to its name, circling as it does a harbor dotted with sleek and sexy watercraft: sailboats, powerboats, a small armada of kayaks, a stand of Jet Skis. The uncertain weather has left the dock full, ropes lashed and tarps secure.

The multistory building housing the club is designed around the view, with banks of glass windows facing out to the water. The glare prevents any view inside no matter how fiercely Jake squints.

He cautions Stevie one last time. "Just keep your mouth shut. Follow along and don't interfere."

She does as she's told as they enter reception and are directed to a concierge for "new member" counseling. She's a polished stone of a girl in a vaguely nautical uniform. After Jake provides his (fake) ID and introduces Stevie as his visiting sister, the concierge takes them through a map of the facility, and a briefing of its amenities (gym; spa; several restaurants; tennis courts; two swimming pools; a baseball team; several spaces dedicated to kids, from a nursery for babies to a "chill" space for teens; a bowling alley; and, yes, an ice-skating rink).

The alabaster girl smoothly glides from describing the club's delights to a review of the club's strict membership policy and code of conduct. Jake hears Stevie's snort and gives her a light kick on the ankle. She scowls at him and he flashes her a broad grin in return.

The concierge offers to arrange a tour, but Jake demurs, claiming a pressured schedule. He tells the woman they'll just take a quick peek around and return on a day when he is better able to give a tour the proper attention.

The dry chill of the ice-skating rink makes him shiver in his damp clothes. Jake takes in the unruly row of five small children on the ice, stumbling and shrieking in front of a cheerful instructor imploring the kids to bend their knees. He scans the bleachers and identifies Heather Haas, an exhausted-looking woman with two toddlers in matching pink squirming on her lap.

"Just hang back," he whispers to Stevie, as they thread their way through the stands. The rink is brightly lit, sharp, clean white and royal blue. The ice looks freshly groomed.

"Heather?" he jovially addresses their Target. "How good to see you again! John Bernake. We met at a party at Pam and Charlie's."

It's fascinating to watch Heather Haas's exhausted face struggle to place him. The war between confusion and societal politesse plays out until she can compose her features in a tentative smile. Jake knows it's partly the setting that buys him this allowance. Merely being in this club "places" Jake for Heather.

He takes a seat without asking and admires Heather's twin girls. He makes faces at them until both toddlers are giggling. Stevie settles in several rows behind them.

Jake asks Heather to point out Kelby on the ice. She softens even further with Jake's familiar use of her son's name and gestures to a boy with a determined set to his jaw pushing his way across the rink. Jake capitalizes on her obvious pride, commenting about the boy's skill with admiration. He turns the conversation to the expat experience, the particular nature of friendships formed among strangers in a strange land. Pam and Charlie for example, such good people.

Heather follows him down this path. "Yes, these friendships are really like no other. If it wasn't for people like Pam, I would have lost my mind with three kids under the age of six. It does bond people, doesn't it? Having to adapt to living in a place you may have never even visited before?"

Jake leans in and speaks softly. "And you've heard, of course, that an American woman's gone missing? Awful."

All color drains from Heather's face. "I knew her," she whispers. Corrects herself, "*Know* her. I just mean I knew her when she lived here."

Jake's about to press further when he's startled to see the concierge striding toward them with a look that could only be described as furious. He glances behind him. Stevie is gone.

"I'm so sorry if I upset you." Jake extends a hand for Heather to shake as he rises. "I'm sure I'll see you around again, but I've got to be going now."

Heather looks startled but nods accommodatingly. "Of course. So nice to see you."

Jake offers each little girl a high five and ambles away from Heather and toward the concierge. She heads him off at the top of the aisle. "Mr. Bernake," she says in a tone as cold as the ice on the rink. "Security found your sister on an office computer trying to break into our membership files. I'm afraid we're going to have to escort you both from the club immediately."

PINCH

———

Stephanie Regaldo, aka Stevie Nichols, Hong Kong Island

The pinch of the guards' hands on her biceps is all too familiar. Stephanie concentrates on relaxing her body even though every muscle screams to twist and punch her way out of this. It's only the realization that John's steady stream of bullshit actually seems to be cooling the fury of the concierge that keeps her still.

She has to admit to some admiration. He's a walking lesson in what Catherine touts as the importance of acting "as if." He blends a combination of embarrassed outrage at his "wild sister," and a hushed whisper about "her problems," with a promise that she'll never darken the door of the club again, and somehow gets them cordially escorted to the front door with his own membership privileges intact.

Stephanie rubs her arms where the guards had gripped her. She chances a look at John's face. His mouth is set in a grim line. He strikes out down the street without a backward glance.

Shit. Stevie runs after him. "Look, I'm sorry—"

"Don't talk to me."

"Where are you going?"

"*I'm* going to the restaurant Eva Lombard's friend Yuan Dai owns. You can go to hell as far as I'm concerned."

"Hear me out. . . ."

John whirls around to confront her. "Are you kidding me? Why should I? Didn't I tell you to hang back? I was just getting somewhere with Heather Haas!"

"Hey, I said I was sorry. And I have to give you credit; you handled that stone-cold bitch concierge with some real chops."

He tugs his hair in a gesture of frustration that's becoming familiar to Stephanie, then keeps on walking.

"That story about your 'troubled sister' came pretty easy." Stephanie trails after him. "Close to home?"

Bull's-eye. John stops again and turns. "I've had it with you. We can't work together." But despite the force of his words she can see she's touched a nerve. There's raw pain in his eyes.

"The blood on the scarf," Stephanie persists in a low voice. "My father and brother were murdered while I was away for the summer. I was sixteen and visiting my mother. I came home and found the bodies. But the first thing I came across was my brother's bloody T-shirt in the front hallway. The bodies were next. They had been there, in our house, for three days before I arrived."

She raises her eyes to meet his, her own raw pain exposed. "Seeing that scarf, I don't know, it got under my skin. I'm sorry."

"My parents were both murdered," John replies tersely, without adding any details. Stephanie takes this as a peace offering.

They stand there silently for a moment; then, gently, she touches his arm. "To the restaurant then?"

He nods.

When they're settled in yet another taxi, Stephanie casts a questioning look at John, but he keeps his head resolutely turned away from her and stares fixedly out the window at the teeming streets. It's only when they climb out of the taxi that John addresses her again.

"As long as we're stuck here in Hong Kong, we have to work together."

"Yes."

"Then stop being such a pain in the ass."

She smiles up at him. "I'll do my best."

The taxi deposits them outside a shiny multilevel mall monstrosity, an assault of trademarked signage announcing the presence of every major European designer.

"The restaurant's here?" Stephanie asks doubtfully.

"Upstairs."

They enter the mall and ascend on an escalator. Everywhere Stephanie looks there are people weighted down with shopping bags bulging with luxury goods. *Where does all this money come from?* Stephanie's life before the murders was very much a blue-collar existence, her father working construction and her mother relocated to Hawaii to "find her bliss." And after the murders—well, that's a dark hole that she'd prefer not to think about. But bottom line, Stephanie's never had money. Never particularly lusted for it either. It's only now she's beginning to understand the freedom and privilege it can provide.

Yuan Dai's restaurant is enormous. A factory really, with a glass-enclosed kitchen thrumming with white-clad chefs. A perky young hostess with an unflappable smile mans a check-in stand at the front entrance, busy handing out buzzers to the many waiting patrons. Jake waits his turn and then asks for Yuan instead of a table. The hostess's smile doesn't waver. She nods politely. John shoots Stephanie a look and then repeats his question.

"Yuan Dai? Is she here? I'm a friend of her friend Eva Lombard."

Two very thin young men appear by the hostess's side. They nod politely to Stephanie and John and gesture that they should follow them. The men are in their late teens or early twenties, Stephanie guesses. She also guesses they're not waiters.

Stephanie shoots John a look that screams, *I hope you know what you're doing*, before obediently falling into step.

The men remain mulishly silent, despite John's attempts at conversation. *His bullshit doesn't work everywhere.* Stephanie can't help feeling a little bit smug. She assesses their two companions; she can probably take both of them, as long as they're unarmed.

They're led through the tumult of the eatery: waitpersons delivering trays of steaming noodles, chattering patrons, screaming babies, the bang and clatter of plates and cutlery. There's not a single empty table.

At the far end of the restaurant, next to the fishbowl of a kitchen, is a door forbiddingly marked in red Chinese characters. If Stephanie had to hazard, she'd guess those characters made up the equivalent of STAY OUT. Nonetheless they follow the boys through the door.

When it shuts behind them with a solid thump, the noise and chaos of the restaurant disappear like a puff of smoke. The corridor is dull and plain. Gray Pirelli rubber tile covers the floor and taupe concrete walls sport incongruously cheerful orange stripes zigzagging across their widths. Or at least Stephanie thinks they're intended to be cheerful. Whether they're succeeding or not is another story.

The men escort them to a closed door. One raps sharply on it. A woman's voice barks a command from within and one of the two opens the door. Stephanie peers in around John's shoulder. A woman sits behind a massive ornate desk. The whole room is outfitted in antiques, genuine, as far as Stephanie's marginally trained eye can discern. Intricate inlays of ebony and mother-of-pearl enhance the desk and a matching credenza. The chairs are all upholstered in embroidered silk. A collection of vases, each one more beautiful than the last, fills the shelves of a long, low bookcase.

The woman now rising to inspect them is very slight in stature; her shiny black hair is dyed platinum blond on the ends. She wears oversized Chanel glasses, a complicated black outfit involving a multitude of buckles and oversized snaps, and a pair of insanely tall platform sneakers.

John extends a hand for the woman to shake and Stephanie has to suppress a snicker when she ignores the gesture and circles around both of them like a prospective buyer skeptically assessing a purchase.

"Are you Yuan? My name is John Bernake. We're looking for Eva Lombard."

"And why might that be?" The woman's voice is surprisingly firm and strong coming from someone so diminutive.

"We've been hired by the firm that her husband works for. He's desperate to find her."

"Well, maybe. But he's not the only one looking." Yuan Dai snaps her fingers. Their two escorts pull out Glocks that they point at Stephanie and John respectively. "So why don't you tell me a little more about why you're looking for my friend Eva?"

Trust is a fragile thing. . . .

Hard to earn. Easy to fracture. Nearly impossible to truly repair after breaking.

Have you ever heard of Kintsugi? It's a Japanese technique used to repair broken pottery with seams created of resin and gold. Some believe the repaired vessels are more beautiful than the originals. But just like in Kintsugi, the fissures mending broken trust that may appear to be an enhancement are often revealed to be gleaming but still fragile scars, reminders of the hot pulsing blood pumping to our battered hearts.

Do we lie to ourselves when we affirm: "I can get past this. We can get past this"? Isn't the impossibility of doing so almost inherent in the repeated assertion?

Why do we hurt each other so? I wish I knew.

TRUTH OR DARE

——

Magali Guzman,
New York City

Maggie waits in the cold marble lobby of Roger Elliott's flagship Manhattan office building as the uniformed security guard behind the desk checks her credentials. She's dug deep into Elliott, even deeper after the hint from family friend Rachel Ferris that perhaps paradise wasn't perfect, after all.

Mostly she's been impressed. The guy inherited a boatload, which should make him a shithead almost automatically in Maggie's opinion, and yet she likes him. He'd been born into a Manhattan empire but had also been a smart, key player in early development of the outer boroughs and had expanded his company's interests into a diversified portfolio of investments, primarily tech companies. Remarkably, he's pretty clean as far as she can tell, practically squeaky, particularly for someone whose gnarled roots sprang from New York real estate, as that is an especially fetid swamp.

Elliott's office on the top floor of the building is nothing like the empty and chilly lobby. The place hums with workers; there's energy and excitement in the air. An exquisitely dressed, young Indian American man greets her and nods at her politely but doesn't offer his own name as he escorts her to Elliott's domain.

He's on the phone when she enters, and Elliott gestures that she should sit as he finishes up his call. She does, sharp eyes roving over his environment, open ears parsing what she can of his conversation.

His office is mostly what she expected: expensive furniture, state-of-the-art electronics, family photos, a doorframe basketball hoop. A large collection of astronaut memorabilia housed in Lucite boxes and a gigantic brass telescope aimed out the plate glass window. Her research had revealed space exploration is an obsession of his.

Elliott wraps up his phone call and addresses Maggie. "I'm losing my mind. I only come in because work is at least a distraction."

"I understand that." Maggie gives him a disarming and complicit smile. *No judgment here. The story of my life too.* "Have you gotten any further instructions?"

Elliott bristles with anxiety; a muscle twitches in his cheek. "Nothing. What have you learned?"

"Special Agent Johnson is meeting me here, sir. We can brief you together."

"He called to say he was running late. Please just tell me what you know."

Johnson called Roger Elliott but couldn't be bothered to even text me? That prick. Any good feeling Maggie harbored toward Ryan as a result of their shared moment over Rachel Ferris's scones dissipates immediately and irrevocably.

She briefs Elliott on the forensic information the Bureau has collected. She glances at her watch. Johnson is twenty minutes late. *Screw it.*

"How was your wife's relationship with Rachel Ferris?"

Elliott looks confused. "With Rachel? Fine. What's Rachel got to do with this?"

"Would you say Betsy and Rachel were close?"

"Thick as thieves." He winces. "Why?"

"Would Betsy have confided in Rachel?"

"Oh yes, I see where you're going. Yes, she might very well have. Have you spoken to Rachel?"

"I have. And I'm figuring out how to say this delicately, but of all your friends and neighbors, she's the one person who sensed that maybe something had changed with Betsy the last few months. Or changed for you and Betsy."

He stares at her, then offers up his palms. "I'm an open book. Ask me anything. Literally anything."

There's something *off* about his insistence. No man in Roger Elliott's position can afford to be completely transparent. *Why is his lawyer not here? Did Elliott and Johnson conspire to leave her alone with Elliott? To what end?*

Maggie gets *that tingle,* the one that tells her she's just on the edge of an unknown *something,* creeping closer to a turn or a revelation in a case, a feeling she's come to respect.

"So *did* something change in your relationship with your wife?"

"Absolutely not. Give me a polygraph if you want to."

"Sir, no one is asking you to do that."

"I know. But actually, I'm insisting you give me one."

Maggie feels it again. *That tingle.* "Well, sir. If you insist."

Later that day, as Maggie greets Terry Addis, she's reminded of how much she likes working with him. They've run a number of polygraph exams together and she always finds Addis excellent. It's not about how he attaches wires or reads printouts. It's his careful collaboration with agents in preparing the questions to be administered and his deft handling of the subjects that make him a good colleague.

She's briefed him on all she knows to date. Together they've crafted the series of ten questions they are about to put to Roger Elliott. When they enter the examination room, Roger Elliott waits for them, his suit jacket flung across the back of his chair, his shirt-sleeves rolled up.

He offers his arms to them as they enter, along with a charming, self-deprecating smile. "Ready for slaughter."

He's eager to confess something, isn't he? Maggie gives him her most welcoming smile in return. "Let me introduce Terry Addis. He'll be conducting the exam."

Elliott nods at the tall, thin African American man with the square-framed glasses. "Hello."

"Nice to meet you, sir," Terry replies.

"But before we hook you up to the box," Maggie continues, "we want to go over a few things with you. Make sure that you're comfortable with the procedure and also with the questions we'll be asking you."

Elliott can't hide his surprise. "You're going to tell me the questions in advance?"

"Yes, sir."

Maggie takes him through all of the technical details first. Sensors will be attached to his fingers and his chest. His blood pressure will be monitored. There are also sensors in his seat cushion.

Then she explains that once he's all hooked up they'll give him a baseline question. "Terry will ask you how many fingers he's holding up. He'll hold up two, but you say three. That'll give us a reading of how a lie appears on your particular graph."

For the first time since making his demand for a polygraph, Elliott looks uneasy. "Don't all lies show up the same?"

Maggie flashes him a reassuring smile. "Actually, no. That's why we do the baseline. But it's nothing to worry about, Mr. Elliott. We only compare you to you."

Elliott relaxes. Maggie wonders what he's thinking. She can't get a handle on this guy and it pisses her off. *Surety,* that's what Maggie likes, as a person in private life, and even more so in conjunction with her work.

"So let's review the questions. Ready?"

"Sure."

"Okay. Number one: Is your name Roger Deacon Elliott? Number two: Are you married to Elizabeth 'Betsy' Baer Elliott? Number three: Are you the father of Bear Elliott? Number four: Would you describe your marriage as a happy one? Number five: Do you know the whereabouts of your wife and son? Number six: Have you ever done something for which you could be extorted? Number seven—"

"What kind of question is that?" Elliott interrupts, hackles again on the rise.

Maggie beams at him. "Mr. Elliott, sir, you requested this exam. You don't have to do it. You're free to go at any time. But, let me ask, is there a reason that question bothers you? Because if there's something you want to tell us, even if it's unrelated to your family, we can iron that out right now. A business issue, maybe?"

"Of course not. Don't you think I would have told you if there was something going on that would have put Betsy and Bear at risk?"

"I'm sure you would have, sir."

Maggie waits, half convinced Elliott is going to bail and half hoping he'll be tempted to spill something that might give them a lead. But while he shoots his cuffs, cracks his knuckles, and purses his lips—all classic delaying tactics—he doesn't give anything up.

Finally Elliott assents to continuing with the exam, and they go over the full list of questions with him twice. Number seven: Do you believe your wife left involuntarily? Number eight: Do you have any idea who might have kidnapped your wife and child? Number nine: Do you and your wife argue? Number ten: Can you confirm the date and time you last saw your wife and son?

Then they excuse themselves and take a tactical break before they hook him up. *The stew. Let him wallow in it.*

When they re-enter, ready to get things going, Elliott seems equally eager. Terry attaches all of the monitors and checks his equipment.

"Are you ready?" Her question is directed to Terry but it is Elliott who answers.

"Yes. Let's do this."

"Okay. I'm going to step out now, and Terry will conduct the exam."

Maggie exits the room and enters the adjoining room equipped with a one-way mirror. Terry establishes Elliott's baseline. Maggie keeps her eyes razor sharp as Terry moves into the body of the questions. She knows well enough that the polygraph will have its own reveals, but she trusts her observations and instincts too. When Terry has taken Elliott through the questions once, Maggie re-enters the examination room.

"There. That wasn't so bad, right?" Maggie smiles at Elliott and he looks relieved.

"That it?"

"Actually, we're going to give it another go. Three times is usual. We'll be right back."

Another calculated break, this one just a shade longer. This time Terry mixes up the order of the questions. Maggie sees Elliott's cheek twitch as he realizes the progression has changed, but he doesn't comment. Then another break, this one even longer than the last.

After round three, Maggie again asks Elliott to wait. She and Terry sit down to review the results.

Terry frowns as he runs his finger along the readout.

"What? Spill," Maggie urges.

Terry adjusts his glasses. "I think he's telling the truth when he says he doesn't know where his wife and kid are or who might have kidnapped them. But look here and here," he continues, pointing at the readout. "He's lying about their marriage being a happy one. Same as he's lying about never having done something for which he could be extorted."

"So maybe he does know more than he's saying?"

"There's consciousness of guilt reflected in this exam. Roger Elliott is hiding something. Which fits with his insistence on us administering the exam."

"I see where you're headed. If Betsy and Bear's disappearance is tied to something Roger Elliott got himself mixed up in . . ."

"And if he had reasons for keeping that something on the down low, like it was illegal . . ."

"He could be compelled to find a way to confess to what he *doesn't* know in order to protect exposure of what he *does*. I agree with you about the psychology, Terry. The only problem is that we're not mind readers."

DIZZYING HEIGHTS

—

Eva Lombard,
Kowloon

Hong Kong Island as viewed across Victoria Harbour from the Kowloon shoreline was pretty impressive a decade ago; now it's like nothing Eva's ever seen. Ricocheting lasers, flashing neon, a tightly packed crowd of buildings that coordinate a light show every night shortly after sunset.

The first time Eva had seen the Hong Kong skyline from the Kowloon side had been a magical night ten years ago when Alex had taken her to an underground party on the rooftop of a not quite finished skyscraper here. Love had been her drug that summer; everything they did together was magic and she would have followed him anywhere.

The second time was when Alex brought her to this hideaway four nights ago.

Guilt threatens to eat Eva from the inside out. She's not contacted Peter since she's been stashed here. She's drifted into a dangerously unreal bubble where time is elastic and her moorings to "real life" frayed.

She's also come perilously close to sleeping with Alex. She flushes as she remembers how they had collided together after finally finding a safe haven in this apartment on the forty-ninth floor of an eerily nearly empty skyscraper. After the rush of their escape from his apartment, both of them had been urgent and hot. Their kisses had been both familiar and heart-stoppingly new.

Eva had been the one to call a halt, pulling away, apologizing. Alex has been a perfect gentleman since. But he's been back to the apartment to bring her food and other supplies, and she can't deny that her hand has lingered on his or that she thrilled when his arm accidentally brushed her breast.

The shore opposite her window ricochets with a fresh display of colored lights. The hotel where she left Pete sleeping taunts her by adding to the show with a rainbow-hued arc that streaks the night sky.

Guilt. Fear. Confusion. Suspicion. Just add some sour lemon and stir. The perfect anniversary cocktail. But funny—I haven't wanted a drink since I landed in Hong Kong.

Eva turns away from the view. She wanders the peculiar apartment that is both her prison and her safe house. Cartons containing flat screen TVs, Bluetooth speakers, and laptops are stacked against every wall. One bedroom is stuffed to the gills with designer handbags, real or counterfeit, Eva can't determine. The furniture is limited to a pair of cots, one long sofa, a couple of rudimentary chairs, and a folding card table. For all of the luxury of the building's construction and design, the apartment itself resembles a warehouse.

But chief among the hideaway's assets is a garage that connects to one of the giant malls thronging the area. Once you've parked inside, it's relatively easy to disappear into the maze of connected corridors and underground passageways, elevators and stairways, retail and apartment buildings.

Eva had agreed it was best and safest that she remain here while Yuan and Alex tried to find out a few things about her predicament. But her bizarre surroundings coupled with her bird's-eye view of the hotel where she left her husband are constant reminders of the wretched turn her life has taken.

The reunion with her old friend Yuan Dai was no exception to the ridiculous, fantastic, completely inescapable fact that Eva's life has spiraled into a spy novel. It was Alex's idea. Eva followed his suggestion blindly, somewhat surprised the two were still in touch. She'd been their common link that summer ten years ago. They'd always sort of bristled at each other back then. It turned out they still do.

But Yuan ran a restaurant empire now. And her boyfriend was an "uncle," a senior member of one of the local Triads, which meant she had access to protection and the vast underground network of knowledge the Triads collected about everything happening in Hong Kong. Relying on Yuan's connections would be safer even than the police, Alex had assured her.

This apartment is one of Yuan's; she apparently owns several in this largely empty tower. The building itself, Alex had told Eva, is so sparsely populated because it's a dumping ground for rich Mainland Chinese looking to hide assets offshore. It's eerie knowing not a single other apartment on this floor is occupied.

Safe, said Alex. *Creepy,* insisted Eva.

She pokes around in the meager offerings in the refrigerator and comes up with a papaya. As she pares away the skin to get at the soft pulp, Eva composes an email to her sister in her head, one that she knows she will never send. Her phone is dead, but that's almost beside the point. How could she send something this absurd?

TO: Jenny Fitzgerald Mooney
FROM: Eva Fitzgerald Lombard
RE: Adventures abroad!

Dear Jenny,

Remember how I was complaining that I was bored? Well, this week has turned into an object lesson in the admonishment to be careful what you wish for! I'm a fugitive in Asia, hiding out from an unknown threat in a likely criminal's apartment, estranged from Pete, and on the brink of adultery with the "one that got away." How's that for excitement!!!

The rap at the door makes her jump. She checks the time. Alex isn't due back for hours. Cautiously she makes her way over to the peep-hole embedded in the door's center and peers out. She sees the now familiar face of one of Yuan's soldiers, introduced to her as Henry. Eva unlocks the door and pulls it open. Henry pushes a man and a woman she's never seen before into the apartment. He follows them in. Yuan trails behind.

"Who are they?" Eva spits, rapidly assessing the couple: Caucasian, likely American, both a little younger than she. The bearded man is well dressed, the woman a little trashy. They certainly don't look like they belong together.

"My name is John Bernake," replies the bearded man. "And this is Stevie Nichols. Forrest Holcomb hired us to find you."

"Forrest hired you?" The revelation does nothing to calm Eva's nerves. Not with the mental gymnastics she's been engaged in while she's been stranded here in her fortress. *Who would want to attack me? How is Pete involved? Who can I trust?*

"Your husband is beside himself with worry," Bernake continues. "I'd like to contact him to let him know you're all right."

"No!" The word shoots from Eva's mouth and hangs suspended in the air by her vehemence. Yuan nods and a Glock appears in Henry's hand.

Bernake raises an eyebrow, but he continues, his voice even. "Eva, I can see that you're scared. I don't know why, but I can tell you this—I've met with your husband. He's wrecked with worry about you. Why are you afraid to let him know you're safe?"

Eva shoots a look at Yuan. She knows Yuan wouldn't have brought these people here if she hadn't done some vetting. "I need to speak to my friend," Eva tells Bernake. She pulls Yuan into the designer-bag-packed bedroom and closes the door before the interlopers have a chance to respond.

In the exchange that follows, Eva learns that Yuan has investigated the pair to the extent she could, their key validator being a woman named Gracey who runs an Internet café. Gracey was able to vouch, if not for the pair themselves, for their employer, a dark-net-based organization that Gracey has relied on from time to time for certain unusual deliveries.

"For her Internet café?" Eva asks with a little snark. She's still astonished that Yuan, her carefree "girls' night out" drinking buddy, has morphed into a Triad-connected entrepreneur.

Yuan shuts her down. "You ask too many questions. You always have."

"Hazard of my profession."

"Maybe. But I suggest you stop asking and tell them what you know. They might actually be able to help you. Gracey doesn't vouch for anyone lightly."

Eva strides out of the bedroom. Peers first into the man's eyes and then the woman's. Both meet her gaze evenly. *What do I have to lose at this point?*

She asks the pair to sit. They do, perching side by side on the edge of the sofa. Henry leans against the wall opposite them, his gun casual in his palm. Yuan swings herself up to perch on the edge of the card table.

Eva paces as she speaks. "I think it all comes down to a photograph I took back in London," she begins. "I was taking a picture of something else altogether. But after I took it, one of the two men in the background of the image started following me."

She continues, taking them through their flight to Hong Kong and her movements up until now. "The guy who attacked me in the park is one of the men in the photo. And at first I couldn't place the other one. But I think he might work for Forrest too. So tell me, who do I trust? Why should I trust you? I don't know if I can trust my own fucking husband."

Suddenly wobbly with the relief of laying it all out there, Eva drops down onto her haunches. "I don't know if I can trust my-self," she murmurs. She squeezes her eyes shut, making a wish for a different truth.

Stevie Nichols addresses her in a soft voice, inflected with a familiar New York tinge. "Eva," she says. "Keep your eyes closed for a minute."

Eva's eyes snap open.

"No, I mean it," Stevie presses. "Close your eyes." Her tone is both soothing and commanding. Eva complies. *It's a relief to be told what to do.*

"Think about Peter, Eva. Your husband. The man you promised to love and honor. You two made a commitment to each other. You *chose* each other."

Eva flashes on the silver-framed, frozen image from their wedding left behind on the dresser in their London townhouse. *God, London seems like a long time ago. Our lives in New York another lifetime. How is this real? How can Pete and I be so far apart? How can it be that I'm terrified of him?*

Eva's snapped back from her fearful musings by the woman's low tones. "You pledged yourselves to each other in front of your friends and family. Promised to love and honor each other through good and bad. What a lucky thing to want to make those promises to another person! A rare thing. A beautiful thing."

A wisp of the song they'd picked for their meticulously re-hearsed first dance spills into Eva's thoughts. She can practically feel the warmth of Peter's hand on her lace-clad waist. *That had been a beautiful day. Pure happiness.*

"Think about the first time you kissed Peter."

Oh, that first kiss. All melt and yearn and promise.

"Think about the last time."

Did I kiss him before I left the hotel? Eva can't remember. Then the memory floods into her. *Yes! I kissed him on his forehead before I left. I thought about coming back to make a baby.*

She sways. Sinks down from her haunches so she's sitting cross-legged on the floor.

Stevie continues in her soothing voice. "We've met your husband, but you *know* your husband, Eva. Could that man know-ingly put you in danger? I don't think so. Not the man we met. It's obvious he loves you, that he's worried sick about you. Let us take you back to him. And then the two of you can figure out whatever's going on together."

The thought of actually being face-to-face with her husband after the events of the last few days is paralyzing. Eva's poised perilously on a balance beam, as terrified of falling into the abyss of *knowing* the truth about Peter as she is of *not knowing*. Sickened by her doubts, she can only croak out a feeble "I don't know."

Stevie nods. "I understand you don't know who or what to trust. I get it. I have trust issues myself. You're kind of a fool if you don't. But look at it this way. Your friend Yuan went to considerable lengths to protect you, yet she brought us here. And we can all go to Peter together. Talk to him. You owe that to your marriage. If he's involved in any way in trying to harm you, we'll get to the bottom of it and be there to protect you. Maybe you two are on the same side, after all. I bet you are. Talk to him, Eva. Find out the truth."

Eva's so tired of running. Tired of being scared. Ready, she hopes, to figure out what's going on *with Pete*. Even if that truth is the worst thing imaginable. She tips off the balance beam and falls: She has to *know*.

She opens her eyes. "Let's go."

SKILLS

Stephanie Regaldo, aka Stevie Nichols, Kowloon

Stephanie settles Eva Lombard into the backseat of Yuan's Tesla. Henry's at the wheel. Yuan graciously offered them the use of her car and driver, before vanishing into the night. Stephanie suspects Henry is actually there to keep watch on them, not provide a service.

"You're secretly a romantic," John says quietly as she shuts the car door.

Stephanie snorts in reply. "Hardly. I didn't believe a fucking word of that crap. Our job is to get her back to her husband. I would have said whatever it took to get her to come with us. I just played a hunch. It's her fucking anniversary."

She circles the car in order to climb in next to Eva, enjoying the stunned look on John's face and leaving him to ride shotgun.

They drive in silence. Henry's aggressive, cutting off other cars and laying on the horn. Stephanie keeps close watch on Eva, who tightly grips the edges of her seat with every swerve. She's very pale; dark shadows bruise the tender skin under her eyes.

Eva wilts even further as they pull into the circular driveway of her hotel. Henry says something in Cantonese and the valet hops to, bowing and scraping obsequiously as they climb from the Tesla sedan.

But Eva's not the only one looking ragged as they enter the hotel; John is distinctly green. "He's a maniac!" he mutters, gesturing at Henry. "Nearly killed us half a dozen times on the way over here!"

"We're on the verge of 'mission accomplished,'" Stephanie hisses. "Pull yourself together."

The lobby of the hotel is thronged with well-dressed patrons. Live music floats out of two different bars, soft jazz from one corner, bluesy rock from another. That pleasant buzz born of cocktails, conversation, and laughter permeates the space, rising upward in gusts to the vaulted ceiling.

The four of them pierce this fizz of happy like a needle pricking skin. They ride the elevator to the thirty-second floor in weighty silence. Eva draws back into one corner, wary eyes following the illuminated numbers flashing above the door.

PING!

The elevator door slides open. Stephanie leads the way down the hotel corridor to Peter and Eva's corner room. The DO NOT DISTURB tag hangs on the doorknob.

Eva turns to Stephanie, her eyes anxious. "I don't know what to say to him."

"As soon as you see him, I'm positive you'll know exactly what to do and say," Stephanie reassures her. "Trust yourself. Trust him."

"Okay," Eva breathes as she waves her card key in front of the lock panel. "Here goes nothing."

Stephanie catches John's eye and gives him a little wink. To her astonishment, he rewards her with a lopsided smile.

Eva opens the door and pushes it open. Gasps.

Peering around her shoulder, Stephanie sees why: The room is in chaos, the place well and truly trashed. The tables are upended; the decorative furnishings broken, clothes scattered. A shattered glass ice bucket lies in glittering pieces amidst a puddle of water.

"Stay back," Henry urges, pushing past them, gun drawn. He disappears inside.

"Oh my god," keens Eva. "What's happened now?"

"Stay calm," Stephanie commands her. "We'll find out."

Henry returns moments later. "Empty," he reports.

John steps into the room and surveys the damage. Stephanie and Eva follow. Henry turns away, punching in a number on his phone and conversing in rapid Cantonese. Stephanie guesses that he's reporting up. She and John are going to have to do the same soon enough.

Whoever had been here had been thorough. Not only is the living area of the suite ravaged, all of Eva's and Peter's clothes are dumped in unceremonious piles. Empty drawers hang open. The bed is stripped, the mattress gutted. The minibar hangs open and empty, its former contents scattered in front of the glow of the gaping door like crushed offerings to a god.

Stephanie pushes open the door to the master bathroom. There's a bloody towel on the bathroom floor. Not blood soaked (Stephanie has seen blood soaked), but heavily *splattered*, certainly. Stephanie's gut twists at the scent: iron, copper, death. Glancing at John she realizes she's not alone in her reaction; he's gone pale under his gingery beard, a muttered expletive escapes his lips.

He turns Eva back before she can enter the bathroom. "Check the closet first," he snaps, steering her away.

"Is there something in the bathroom?" Eva demands, charging past them both.

"Eva, wait!"

But Stephanie's too late. A low moan torn from somewhere primal crawls from her mouth in an attenuated stutter, "Unhhh . . . unhhh . . . unhhh . . ."

At that instant Stephanie feels a moment of real kinship with Eva. She'd known instinctively how to *play* her—*let's just be girls talking about boys*—all that bullshit. But now, this woman with the fancy education and clothes, the opulent hotel suite and loving husband and family, this woman who had every damn thing Stephanie didn't, now they are linked forever in a sorority of a different sort, all of their other differences be damned.

They've seen the shed blood of a loved one and known uncertainty about its meaning. Stephanie's trail of blood led to the murdered bodies of the two people she'd loved best in the world. Eva's path is still unfolding.

Stephanie feels it like a current between the three of them—she, John, and Eva. Her own story didn't have a happy ending. From what little John's told her, his didn't either.

This is why I want to do this, Stephanie realizes with sudden resolve. *Because I want to give other people happier endings.*

"We're going to find him, Eva," Stephanie promises. "He's going to be all right."

Eva Lombard gulps in a breath. She tears her gaze from the spattered blood and offers Stephanie a wretched smile. "Well, you found me, didn't you? Okay. Let's go get him."

Well, shit. That's a surprise. I was sure she was going to fold.

Stephanie likes Eva more for the offer, but she's already saddled with one lame-ass partner and she's not taking on another. *No effing way.*

STRANGER

——

Jake Burrows, aka John Bernake, Kowloon

Back in Yuan's safe house on the forty-ninth floor of the apartment building on Kowloon, Jake paces the polished wood floors and thinks he might lose his mind. His inclination for action (equally matched by Stevie's, he has to reluctantly admit) had been quelled by Henry's insistence that if anyone was going to locate Peter Lombard in Hong Kong, it was going to be the Triad network, not these two American strangers.

Faced with the stark reality that this is indeed a task best left to Yuan's foot soldiers, Jake allowed himself to be brought from the Lombards' hotel room back to the apartment in Kowloon along with Stevie and Eva Lombard. But he can't stay still.

His jittery mind keeps bouncing from the blood in the Lombards' suite to a different bloodied hotel room back in Paris, still probably the worst day of his life (even though he's had plenty of others that could qualify: *The day Mom went missing. The day Dad was found murdered*). But that day in Paris is still the topper. It was the day all of the mysteries of his family began to unravel, and Jake learned the ugly way that love isn't enough to conquer evil and that fear can corrupt even the most solid affection.

Jake knows he has to send a report with the latest information to Catherine, but a kind of defiant obstinacy has kept his fingers from the keys. They are supposed to be *helping* people. That's what he signed on for. And he guesses that they are. But not for the first time, Jake questions Catherine's methods as well as his involvement in her operations. *Was it necessary to drug and kidnap Dakota Harris? Why is he paired with Stevie Nichols? Has Catherine told them all she knows about the Lombards? And if not, why is she shielding information from them? How did this become his reality? Waiting on Triad soldiers while marooned in an apartment that looks like it belongs to a fence!*

A fierce nostalgia grips Jake. A hunger for the time *before* his life was a map of love, loss, and heartache, his own as well as other people's.

Stevie interrupts his reverie by slapping a magazine shut and getting to her feet. "I'm going to go out to get us some food. You okay staying with the princess?"

"Of course."

"You all right, dude? You look like a wreck."

"Thanks."

Stevie puts a hand on his arm to get him to cease his relentless pacing. "It's not like I give an actual shit about how you're feeling, but we've got a job to do here and I can't afford to have you knocked off your game."

"Your solicitude is touching."

"You can 'big word' me all you like, but I'm serious."

"Do you ever question what we do, Stevie?"

"What?"

"Or Catherine's methods?"

"Look, if you're having some kind of crisis of conscience, stick a pin in it until this case is over and then do it on your own time. And to answer your question, no. I'd be dead if it wasn't for Catherine. I owe her my life and she has my complete loyalty."

"I feel like I joined up with her because I had no other choice—"

"That's just looking at it wrong. It was my only *and* my best choice. I bet that's true for you too."

"Aren't we all just a fucked-up bag of tricks?"

His question is rhetorical but Stevie answers. "Yeah, so? Tell me who isn't fucked up. And you think that scared woman in the next room cares about the respective sacks of shit you and I are toting around? She just wants to be safe. As long as we can do that for people? I'm good."

Jake nods. He has to admit Stevie is growing on him, with her direct manner and proud spirit. "Fair enough. What kind of food are you getting?"

She gives him an impish smile. "Chinese. What else? Might as well enjoy it while we can."

RUSTLE

Peter Lombard,
Tai Po District, Hong Kong Island

Although he was brought in blindfolded and he's been locked in a dingy, windowless bedroom since his arrival, Peter has been able to determine precisely the kind of establishment into which he's been deposited. His clues have all been aural: the constant chime of the front doorbell, the rustles and titters of girls assembling, the bumps and thrusts and moans leaking through the thin walls.

He'd heard about the hookers in Hong Kong from colleagues. When he announced this trip, tips had been shared: Prostitution is legal in Hong Kong—for single women acting as sole proprietors; but for real fun, go to a brothel. There you'll also find gambling and any kind of excess your heart desires.

Peter had brushed most of this talk off, reminding his boisterous friends that this was *an anniversary trip with his wife*. He'd endured some teasing about his Boy Scout ethics, but it was good-natured all in all, and he put up with enough of the banter to be one of the boys. Now he's desperately trying to recall any other tidbits he'd gleaned that might help him out of this mess: The girls are in rotation—Hong Kong to Beijing to Shanghai and back again; the brothels are Triad controlled; the attitude within them "anything goes," which has allowed for some pretty dark shit to go down.

Peter wonders why he's still alive.

One thing about being a captive: It gives you time to think. In his mind, Peter has turned over the steps that led them to take this trip to Hong Kong a thousand times. His original thought had been Paris; that much was true. Why *did* he shift direction to Hong Kong?

He remembers talking about the planned trip to the City of Lights at a dinner party Forrest and Miranda Holcomb hosted. He'd watched Eva from across the room, noting that she seemed out of sorts, and also that she was knocking back glasses of white wine with alarming frequency. A romantic week in Paris seemed just the thing to get them back on track.

But then Hong Kong had come up, and all at once it had seemed like the ideal choice. A little more exotic, as well as a more personal destination, given Eva's history with the island. Once the seeds of the trip had been planted, the roots flourished, the tender shoot rose upward, and the leaves unfurled. Peter requested an extra few days off given the distance they were traveling. He dug into research in order to pick the perfect luxury hotel and the finest restaurants. He'd planned and booked and schemed with a sense of anticipatory thrill, bursting with a sense of pride over having created an experience for them he was sure Eva would treasure.

And look how that all worked out. For the hundredth time in an hour, Peter struggles to understand how he got here. A week ago, he was in London, a normal guy with a normal set of problems. He plucks nervously at the sour-smelling, floral-patterned sheets smoothed over the bed that fills most of the cramped room. He thinks about the possible sources of that sour smell and stands.

A commotion erupts. He hears banging. Shouting in Cantonese. Doors slamming. A girl's shriek. *What the hell is happening now?*

Heavy footsteps stomp down the hallway in his direction. Peter tenses. Glances around the room for any possible weapon and comes up empty.

The door to his room flies open. That kid with the hipster beard who works for Forrest stands there, legs firmly planted, hands on his hips. He has a baseball cap with the Cardinals insignia jammed on his head, mirrored shades obscuring his eyes.

"Come with me," the kid orders.

Peter meekly follows him out of the dingy bedroom and into a poorly lit corridor. He takes furtive glances at the rooms he'd passed blindfolded on the way in. Girls circulate, mostly Chinese, a few blond Slavic-looking women. Cigar smoke billows pungently from one open door. A glimpse inside reveals gambling tables. Half-naked girls bring drinks and proffer lighters. Yet another room reveals rows of mounded silk pillows on which patrons recline, smoking opium. Peter's eyes meet those of a gaunt man exhaling a roiling cloud of smoke: Black, fathomless pools set in yellowing whites stare at him blankly. Peter averts his gaze.

As they near the front door, a pair of bulky bouncers blocks their way. Peter gives the kid a panicked look. *Now what?*

To his shock, the kid shouts something in Cantonese, anger bristling from him like a porcupine's spines. The bouncers let them pass.

Peter follows the kid out into the street. A rush of gratitude hits him as he greedily breathes the moist night air. He turns furtively to see the building in which he'd been held. A squat five-story structure painted a brilliant robin's egg blue, with wrought iron bars on all the windows.

"Thank you," he says to Forrest's emissary.

"Hurry up," urges the kid, guiding him down the street and around the corner.

"What the hell did you say to them?" Peter wonders.

"Damned if I know," the kid replies as he stops in front of a pair of idling Tesla sedans. He rocks back and forth on the balls of his feet. "She wrote it out for me phonetically." The kid gestures to a petite Chinese woman standing in front of the cars. The ends of her black hair are dyed platinum. She's clad in thigh-high boots and a red and black minidress laden with silver buckles. She's flanked by two Chinese men armed with Glock pistols.

Peter instinctively backs away.

The woman growls something in Cantonese that sounds like a bark. The men beside her lower their weapons.

"Peter Lombard. Good to meet you finally." The woman's voice is mellifluous, lightly accented, her English perfect. She extends a delicate hand for him to shake. "I'm your wife's old friend Yuan Dai.

"We must keep moving," Yuan continues. "I sent your friend inside on the pretext he was on orders to move you from the Triad that controls that brothel. Supplied him with just the right things to say to get you out of there. But there's no guarantee we won't be followed."

She gestures Peter and the kid toward one of the waiting Teslas. "You go now. And try to stay out of trouble. In fact, I suggest you all get the hell out of Hong Kong as soon as possible."

Yuan Dai. Peter remembers that name. He'd messaged her through Eva's Facebook. Her advice to get the hell out of Hong Kong seems eminently sound. He'd like nothing more once he finds his wife.

At least I'm out of captivity. Peter climbs in the backseat of the waiting sedan, despite the question screaming silently in his mind: *Is this frying pan to fire?*

The kid climbs in after him and slams the car door shut. The driver pulls away and the Tesla silently accelerates from zero to over a hundred kilometers an hour in mere seconds.

"Holy crap!" The expletive bursts from Peter as he grips his seat.

"Yes, his driving takes some getting used to," the bearded kid replies, stripping off his sunglasses and baseball cap.

"What just happened back there?" Peter asks. "How did you get me out?"

"I apparently said I had orders to move you to another address on the authority of a high-ranking member of the Triad that controls that brothel."

"And they bought that?"

"Maybe not," the kid says after a worried glance out the back window. "Henry. Black BMW. I think we're being followed."

"I know we are," the driver replies grimly as he cuts a hard right, wheels squealing.

Henry slams around the corner. Blasts through a stop sign. Peter closes his eyes in terror. Opens them again when Henry lays on the horn. Immediately wishes he hadn't.

Henry screeches through a crowded intersection just as the yellow light turns solidly red. Horns blare in protest, but they narrowly make it through. Their pursuer is blocked by the instant crush of traffic.

"Nice!" The kid pounds his fists on his thighs with excitement.

Peter thinks he might throw up.

They twist and turn at a reckless speed, finally slamming to a halt inside the maintenance bay of an auto repair shop. "We change cars here," Henry commands.

Peter climbs out of the Tesla and discovers his legs are rubbery. He's grateful when the kid grips his arms and escorts him to a Porsche Cayenne.

"Have you found Eva?" Peter asks, afraid to hear the answer.

"Yes. We're taking you to her now."

A riptide of relief surges over him. "She's okay?"

"Scared, a little banged up, but fine."

Peter offers up a silent prayer of thanks. Allows himself to be bundled into the backseat of the Porsche. Begins to rehearse what he will say when he is reunited with his wife.

RESPECT

————

Jake Burrows, aka John Bernake, Hong Kong Island

Jake is pumped. *That was fucking awesome.* He feels drunk on the danger of their escape, by his ability to bluff, by the success of their mission. Plus, he has a whole new respect for Henry's skills. He's definitely taking a defensive-driving class when he gets back to the States. Settling more comfortably into the cushy leather seats of the Cayenne, he shoots a glance at Peter Lombard. He's pale and shaky.

"You all right?" he asks.

"I'll live."

Lombard leans his head back against his seat and closes his eyes. His lips move, but Jake can't make out his words.

As Henry pilots the Porsche, Jake takes a glance out the back window. They seem to be away free and clear.

Yuan had learned Peter was being held in a brothel controlled by a Triad at war with her own (rather than one of the three with which her gang has a mutually cooperative ecosystem). Since a favor could not be asked, a bluff was constructed, one intended to shield Yuan and her gang from exposure of their involvement by sending in Jake.

Catherine will respect that play. Jake does too. And looking at

Peter Lombard's bloodied features, Jake feels a swell of unexpected pride for his part in releasing this man from his captors.

He remembers how Catherine saved him just as he was going to step off a ledge to his own certain death and realizes just how far he's come. And that he wants to go farther. For one thing, he misjudged Stevie. She's brighter than he gave her credit for, more emotionally intelligent too. She handled Eva Lombard like a champ. Their skills are actually kind of complementary.

Maybe Catherine knows what she's doing, after all.

The corner of Jake's mouth curls in a hint of a smile. *Maybe she does.*

REUNION

Eva Lombard,
Kowloon

She'd picked at the food the scrawny dark-haired girl with the New York accent brought in. She knows she needs to eat, but her stomach is as jumpy as the rest of her.

When she hears the scrape of a key in the lock, Eva is on her feet instantly. Her "protector" (this ridiculously skinny girl Eva's sure is younger than she) steps in front of her.

The door opens and in walks Peter, accompanied by Henry and the man introduced to her as John.

"Oh my god, Pete!" Eva exclaims, elbowing past the girl. "What happened to you?" His face is battered and broken; he moves stiffly. "Where have you been?"

"Where have *you* been?" he chokes out. "I've been worried out of my skull."

"Mostly here," Eva responds, gesturing to the apartment.

He opens his arms to her, but she hesitates. She stares at him, her husband, a man she thought she knew better than anyone, who she now fears is a stranger. A liar. A danger? His arms falter. A wounded look deflates his face.

Eva takes his hand, leads him into a bathroom, and closes the door behind them. She needs to be alone with him, to look in his eyes.

She notices a tremor in his legs. Hastily, she pulls the toilet seat down and gestures that Pete should sit. He sinks down quickly. She turns the faucet, letting cold water flow onto a washcloth. She wrings it out and dabs gently at Peter's face, clearing away crusted blood.

Where to begin?

A million uncertainties are jumbled together in Eva's fevered mind. *Who did this to him? Was it the same man who attacked me? Why? What trouble are we in? Are we even "we" anymore?* She's choked into silence by the mass of it all, so concentrates on tending to the myriad bumps and bruises on Peter's face.

He winces and she pulls the cloth away. "Are you okay?"

"No," he snaps. "I'm not. How could I be? I put you in danger. I promise you, Ev, I had no idea."

"No idea about what? What's this all about?'

"I don't understand entirely. But I think I was used as a mule to get something into the country."

Eva releases an involuntary yelp of laughter. "Peter. Listen to yourself."

"I'm not joking. My bag came back to the hotel trashed, the lining cut open. Do you know how much stuff just slips past X-ray machines? And if my suitcase *had* been flagged it would have been my ass in a sling. What if they picked it up at the airport once the bag got through security and safely to Hong Kong? Got what they needed out of the bag once it was in the country?"

"They who?"

"That I don't know."

"Even if you're right, why come after us? If they got whatever was in the bag?"

"I don't know that either. But, Ev? I never should have doubted you about being followed. I'm sorry. I'm sorry about everything."

Eva stares at her husband. His story could be plausible. It's certainly preferable to the notion that he wanted her killed. Despite his swollen eye and broken mouth, he looks more like the man she married than the stranger she feels like she's been living with for the last nine months.

A hard knot of sickening dread settles inside Eva's belly. This connects back to Forrest Holcomb, one way or another. It must, if she's right and the man in the photographs she took at the Sly Fox works for him.

Peter worships Forrest. And even if she can convince Pete that his mentor and idol is involved, how the hell can they pit themselves against one of the richest and most powerful men in the world?

Particularly since they don't have a clue about what is really going on.

A REPORT

___

Stephanie Regaldo, aka Stevie Nichols, Hong Kong Island

REPORT

Well, boss, we done good. The happy couple is safe and united. But I don't think that's the end of the story. Peter Lombard reports that all this fuss is about something hidden in his suitcase. This is his deduction, mind you, based on the fact that his luggage got lost on the way to Hong Kong and the lining was slashed when he got it back. This much we do know: Eva Lombard took several photographs of a pair of men in London. One of the men began stalking her after that encounter. He attacked both her and her husband in Hong Kong.

The second man in the photograph has been identified by Peter Lombard as working for his boss, Forrest Holcomb. I've attached copies of Eva's photographs to this email. Please advise. And, boss, I know you may not appreciate this sentiment in the way in which it's intended, but I'm having a blast.

Stephanie hits SEND on the encrypted email. Nothing to do now but wait.

DARK HEART

——

Catherine,
Mexico City, Mexico

We're all prowling like caged cats.

The fissures in the Harris family are deepening under the stress of waiting. Lisa and Steve circle tensely around each other. Dakota is surly. Finn remains the volatile and often unreachable hub of this family's centrifugal force.

Steve Harris is ready. I've practiced with him time and again. I'm sure he'll make a credible witness. My plan to fly him back to the States to be deposed is firmly in place. I've also filmed his statement for a timed release to the media. Knox Pharmaceuticals can bring on all the high-powered lawyers and low-morals thugs they want; we are going to win.

The Harrises will be safer after Steve's testimony is on the record, but they will have made powerful enemies. Silence may no longer be a motive for their deaths but revenge may very well be.

I haven't broached this with them yet, as I'm taking one thing at a time, but it will be my recommendation that after the trial the Harrises disappear into completely new lives, courtesy of the Burial Society. I expect that to be a difficult conversation.

Another difficult conversation will have to be had with Gabi. The incident with the gun has left me sour and unsettled; our usual easy understanding feels irrevocably compromised. This is the last time I will come to this house in Mexico City, but Gabi deserves a proper goodbye.

From across the expanse of the room I watch her cooking, bare feet firmly planted, quick fingers kneading dough, chopping onions, tearing cilantro. Lisa Harris plays with Finn, using lumps of dough to make little snowmen. Steve Harris reads one of the U.S. newspapers Gabi brought in earlier today. Dakota's disappeared upstairs with her trove of English language celebrity magazines, "desperate," as she announced, "for some fucking life."

Turning my attention to my laptop and a variety of incoming reports, I open a missive from Stephanie that's just been decrypted on my end. It contains good news, in that the Lombards are safe and sound, but my gut twists as the attached photographs load into view. I recognize the man Peter and Eva Lombard identify as working for Holly: Derrick Cotter.

Cotter's a fixer for Holly, I know that much, although I have never asked too many questions about the specifics of his job description. Having my own secrets made me reluctant to press Holly on his. All I know is that Cotter came up from the same rough neighborhood that spawned the future financial titan Forrest Holcomb. Best friends since they were six, absolute loyalty is their creed.

These photographs certainly suggest that Derrick Cotter's involved with the Lombards' attacker. But why? What is Cotter protecting? Or after?

I consider Peter Lombard's deduction that he was used as a mule. I wonder, and not for the first time, exactly what services Derrick provides for Holly. Has Derrick gotten his hands dirty so Holly can keep his clean?

I am broken. Therefore Holly must be too. How else could he ever love me? The startling and vicious stab of insecurity skewers me, as old as my soul.

Maybe it's *not* only Derrick who's gotten his paws dirty. Maybe

Holly's hands are filthy. Have I been unable to see the blackness within him because of my own dark heart? *Have I idealized a man who represents the very things I despise?*

My fingers fly along the keypad of one of my phones before I even know what I'm doing. Holly picks up on the second ring. He grunts a gruff "Hallo," his voice deep and scratchy. A woman's voice in the background mumbles sleepily, a phrase I can't quite make out. I imagine his wife, Miranda, in a satin eyeshade and a filmy peignoir, irritated by this callous interruption of her beauty slumber. "Hallo?" Holly repeats, his tone impatient. "Who is it?"

I hang up the phone.

Have I been played? Used? I can't talk to him until I think this through. My brain is spinning.

Why *did* Holly enlist me to look for Eva Lombard? Surely it can't be the innocent concern he expressed for a valued employee and his spouse. Not if he's involved in some way with the assaults on them. *But why then?*

Was he afraid he'd gotten the Lombards unwittingly involved in something for which he felt responsible? Holly knows enough about who I am and what I do to know my code doesn't extend to protecting criminals. Quite the opposite. Was he trying to make things right for the Lombards in some way?

There I go again, looking to keep him up on that fucking pedestal. Why should I believe he respects my code? What do I really know about the man anyway? He's no more than a body I traded fluids with a long time ago.

What if he's setting me up? What if I've put Stephanie and Jake in danger of exposure? Or worse?

Why is my experience of love irrevocably coupled with an expectation of betrayal?

Hell. I know the answer to that question, as much as I want to avoid it.

"Let's go, Cathy. Let's go."

My brain is buzzing again, my heart pounding. Despite the audible static I'm positive I'm radiating, the Harrises and Gabi seem oblivious to my state.

I saunter into the kitchen. Admire Gabi's ingredients and Finn's snowman. I casually crack open a bottle of añejo tequila, welcoming the acrid scent in my nostrils. I pour a shot and slug it back, relishing the scorch of the liquid down my throat. I need to think.

"Let's go, Cathy. Let's go."

I leave the shot glass on the counter and take the bottle of tequila out onto the terrace.

Holly. The last time I saw him, he asked me to meet him in Paris. I didn't ask why. It was shortly after his marriage to Miranda, a London wedding designed to rival a royal's. I'd followed the breathless tabloid reporting of the affair, celebrity invites, rare sky-blue sun-orchids imported from Tasmania, Swarovski crystal centerpieces, every choice designed to flaunt excess. Holly's not averse to a show, but I suspected this particular event was all Miranda.

We'd met at our usual hotel, the Mandarin Oriental. Fell into a fevered tangle of limbs, our hunger for each other untarnished by time, distance, or his new marriage. Then we talked for hours, sharing our thoughts on everything from global politics to cryptocurrency to the Paris spring collections, before proximity stoked our physical fires again.

As dawn broke outside our windows, Holly finally drifted into slumber. I stared at the softened lines of his sleeping face. Our love was perfect within the private hothouse we crafted when we could, although I suspected it would bloom bright and then rapidly wither out of it. Just like the rare orchids Miranda demanded grace her wedding.

I tamed one of his wild brows with an index finger. Planted a soft kiss on his bearded cheek. I got dressed and crept out while Holly was still sleeping. That was over two years ago.

Now I must face the truth. I may have deluded myself about everything: the man, the belief that in at least this one relationship

I had a kind of home. *Or maybe that's exactly what I had, except more of the sick and twisted kind of home that is all I've ever known.*

I tip back the bottle of tequila. Take a few long swallows as I stare at the bruised lavender sky.

TAKEN

—

Eva Lombard,
Kowloon

A vicious pounding on the front door of Yuan's hideaway sends Eva running from the bathroom, Peter at her heels. Stevie's poised on her tiptoes at the peephole, peering out.

"I think it's your friend Alex," she reports.

Stevie steps aside and Eva takes a look. It is Alex. He's red-faced and haggard, short of breath. Eva flings open the door.

"What is it?" she entreats. "What's happened?"

"They've taken Ian," Alex rasps. "I got a text."

"What did it say? Who's taken him?" The knot of dread already nestled in Eva's belly expands tentacles throughout her entire body.

"They snatched him right off the street. He was with his mother! Just outside her flat! They want your camera with the card you used when you took those pictures at the Sly Fox. They'll kill him if we go to the police!"

"When do they want to meet?" The question comes from John.

"Dawn. The text says we're to go alone to the Star Ferry car park and wait."

"Which side?" John wants to know.

"This side. Kowloon." Alex's eyes skitter across the people in the room as if seeing them all for the first time. "Ev, are you all right?"

"I'm fine," Eva reassures him, although she's anything but. *Stupid twat*. She's gutted with guilt. She brought this on Alex and Ian. She puts a hand on Alex's shoulder. *I'm so sorry*. She becomes aware of Peter's burning gaze and lifts her hand away.

"You must be Peter," Alex says to Peter. "But who in bloody hell are you two?"

"Long story," says Stevie. "But we're here to help. I'm Stevie and this is John."

Alex turns to Eva. "Can they help?"

"They've done decently so far," says Peter, inserting himself into the conversation. "But you have me at a disadvantage. Who's Ian and who in *bloody hell* are you?"

A fresh wash of shame churns into the guilt that already threatens to overwhelm Eva. "Pete, this is Alex Blake. Old friend from when I lived here. He helped hide me. But that's hardly the point. Ian's his son. He's four."

A terrible silence descends over them.

John is the first to break it. "There's something off about their demand," he says thoughtfully. "How do they know you haven't copied the photos? Given them to the police already, for that matter?"

"I haven't," insists Eva.

"Right, but they don't know that," John replies. "That might be our first order of business. Make some copies and build a fail-safe. But still, why didn't they even *ask* whether you'd duplicated them?"

"You know," Peter says slowly, "when I was attacked in our hotel room, the guy said something about 'not even knowing what we had' with Eva's photographs. We still don't. Two men at a table together means nothing unless one of them has beaten the crap out of you. Without us, there's no evidence of any crimes we know about or can prove."

"In which case, if I were them," interjects Stevie cheerfully, "I'd make sure you were all dead."

Eva catches the admonitory look John gives Stevie. "What?"

Stevie questions him in response. "These assholes have made it clear they're desperate to hide whatever it is they're up to. I'm just being realistic."

Another sticky silence descends.

"I think Stevie and I are off the radar for these folks, am I right?" John finally asks thoughtfully. "We've been behind them and around them but never in full view."

"Except for the brothel," Stevie chimes in.

"True enough," John agrees. He strokes his Vandyke. "But all they'll remember is a beard, sunglasses, and a baseball cap."

"What are you thinking?" Eva demands.

"I'm weighing our advantages," John answers. "Figuring out what they know and what we know."

Eva watches as John and Stevie look at each other, engaged in a wordless communication. It's absurd to put their faith in these two barely grown kids, but are they the only chance they have?

Alex breaks the silence. "Screw your help! This is my *son* we're talking about. I'm doing exactly as they say. You, me, and the camera are going, Eva. No one else."

Peter bristles. "Absolutely not. There is no fucking way *my wife* is going there alone with you. I'll go instead."

Stevie steps between the two men. "Now, now, boys, don't make me give you a time-out," she says, raising admonitory hands. In other circumstances it would be funny; they are each a head taller than she.

Alex defiantly meets Peter's stare. "He's *my* son. I'm calling the shots."

Eva's eyes flicker between the two men's hardening features. Her heart sinks.

This is all my fault. A child—Alex's child—is in danger, and it's all my fault.

Stupid twat.

She has no choice. She will do whatever Alex wants.

GUILT

Magali Guzman,
New York City

Maggie has never seen Special Agent in Charge Bates this furious. She, Ryan Johnson, and the four other agents who have been actively pursuing leads in the Betsy and Bear Elliott kidnapping case stand awkwardly before him as Bates gives directives in a voice sharp as cut glass, steam practically rising from his silver-haired head.

It's been learned that the younger sister of one of Roger Elliott's aides lives in Berwyn, Pennsylvania. This young woman had followed her brother's instructions to wear gloves, extract the letter addressed to Roger Elliott from the larger envelope in which it had been mailed to her, and then mail it back to Elliott so it was postmarked locally from Berwyn.

Stupidity won out, as it so often does with criminals. The aide didn't tell his sister the details of the scheme because he was afraid she would gossip. But she'd been following the details avidly, lording her tenuous connection to the headline-making case over her friends and classmates. When an intrepid reporter at the New York *Daily News* leaked the first word of the ransom note, little sister saw it online and began to wonder.

When the wider press began to pick up on the story, Elliott got ahead of the game. He made a television appearance in which he admitted to manufacturing the ransom demand, but also argued his motives were noble: Neither the police nor the pricey private investigators he'd hired had any clues about the whereabouts of his wife and child. He just wanted to literally make a federal case out of it in his desperation to find them.

Furious at Elliott for the deception and with no known grounds for federal jurisdiction, Bates shuts the entire investigation down. His last order is for a detailed accounting of all monies spent on "this bullshit." The agents are dismissed.

"What a fucker," opines Johnson about Elliott as the agents thread through the hallways of the Federal Building and back to their cubicles.

"I feel for the guy a little," Maggie confesses. "Desperation makes people do stupid shit."

"Sure it's not a crush, Guzman? I see the way you look at Elliott. Sure you're not going to set your hooks for the rich widower?"

"Fuck off, Johnson."

"Oh, that's original."

"Like your shit is? You're stuck in some last century version of toxic masculinity. You don't deserve original. And anyway, maybe Betsy and Bear are still alive."

"Elliott really got you drinking his Kool-Aid, didn't he? You taste anything else?"

"Johnson, you waste so much time being a dick, I don't know how you get anything else done." Maggie ducks into the ladies' room.

She doesn't need to pee, but splashes some tepid water on her face and twists her hair up on the top of her head, shaking off Johnson's stench. She glares at her reflection in the mirror.

Johnson's right about one thing: She does feel sorry for Roger Elliott; the urgency of his concern feels genuine to her. More than that, though, she's irritated by the puzzle.

Where are Betsy and Bear Elliott? People slip through the cracks; Maggie knows that all too well. No woman or child should be able to vanish off the face of this earth without a trace, but it happens all the time, horrible but true. It doesn't usually happen to the well-off and well-connected, though. That these two, with all of their assets and social infrastructure, should have done so is even more perplexing.

Unless it was voluntary. Unless Betsy used those very assets and connections precisely in order to disappear so seamlessly. Maggie turns that possibility over in her head. Up until now, the Bureau's focus has been radiating outward from the ransom note. But with the note discredited, could the answer lie somewhere back in the myriad interviews and statements taken from the Elliotts' friends and neighbors? *Someone* must have a clue about where Betsy and Bear are. Even if they *are* dead. She'd snapped back at Ryan, but she too knows the statistical odds.

Maggie sighs. Speculation is useless. This investigation is over. *Finito*. Bates couldn't have been clearer about that.

She can't help it that in the back of her mind a series of questions, suppositions, assumptions, and re-examination of those assumptions ticks steadily on like clockwork.

A woman and a little boy are missing. How can she just let that go?

MIST

Eva Lombard,
Star Ferry Car Park, Kowloon

Low-lying fog snakes across the darkness of Victoria Harbour and wends its way through the largely deserted parking lot in front of the ferry terminal. Eva, Alex, and Peter enter the lot three abreast, Eva in the middle. No more than a handful of cars along the perimeter are visible because of the dark skies and thick mist. Three dormant, tethered ferries gently rock on the current.

Eva glances at Peter but can't read the expression on his face. She takes a peek at Alex. His features are creased with worry; his hands balled into fists. Her own cut palm pulses hotly underneath its white bandage.

They reach the center of the car park. The very first hints of dawn lend a pink tinge to the gray shroud covering the pier. Alex spins in a circle, eyes scanning hopelessly for a glimpse of Ian. Tension explodes out of him. "Okay. We're here. It's dawn. We have the camera. No police. We did everything they asked." He shoots an angry glance at Peter. "Except for bringing along this fuckwit."

"Shut up, asshole," Peter snarls in reply.

"Shhh," Eva soothes. "That's not helping. We need to stay calm. All of us."

Time passes interminably slowly as the three of them wait. Eva's eyes dart everywhere and nowhere. The fog plays tricks on her. She imagines sinister figures only to see them evaporate into harmless wisps as the light shifts.

There are so many questions, so many things left still unsaid with both of these men, all of which must remain unspoken until Ian is reunited with his father.

If he's reunited with his father.

If we all survive past morning.

Eva hears their footsteps first. Three men emerge from the fog. The man in the middle she recognizes as the man who attacked her in Hong Kong Park. He carries a terrified-looking Ian in his arms. The other two men are Chinese, unknown to her. Both carry guns. Beside her, Peter and Alex stiffen.

"Hey, mate," Alex says as he reaches for his son. "It's okay. I'm here now. Everything's gonna be okay."

But the white man holds tight to the child. "Good of you to show up, Lombard," he says congenially. "After all, you were supposed to be the collateral before you staged your 'daring escape' from the Golden Pheasant. We never would have had to go for young Blake here if you had just stayed put. Truth is, you *all* made this *much* more difficult than it had to be."

"Let's make it easy now then," Peter says. "Here's my wife's camera. The card is still inside."

"Give me my son," Alex demands, stepping forward.

"What about copies?" the man demands, holding the little boy at arm's length from his father.

"There are none." Eva tries to keeps her gaze steady as the stranger's eyes bore into hers. She desperately wants to look away. She's never seen eyes so *empty*.

"Start walking. All of you," the stranger commands. He gestures to a white panel van that had previously been obscured by the fog. Its back doors hang agape, revealing a shadowy interior promising only menace. "We're going for a ride."

Alex explodes. "No bloody way! Yes, there are copies! Copies that will be delivered to the authorities with instructions to investigate you in connection with our deaths!"

A soft laugh burbles from the man's throat. It chills Eva to the core.

"I thought as much. Good to know who's a liar and who speaks the truth. But no mind. I'll be out of Hong Kong by the time your bodies are discovered. So let's get a move on. I have a plane to catch."

DIVIDE TO CONQUER

———

Peter Lombard,
Star Ferry Car Park, Kowloon

I am not dying here. This one burning thought consumes him.

I won't let you die here either. Peter reaches for Eva's hand, wanting to give her a squeeze of reassurance, but her attention is fixed on the sobbing child held in the stranger's arms. Peter realizes he's never seen her look so sad.

"It's all right, mate," Alex reassures his son. "I'm right here."

"They've got nothing to do with us," Eva implores the child's captor. "He's just a baby, for pity's sake. Take the camera. Do what you want with us. But let this man and his son go."

"It's all about Alex, isn't it, Eva?" Peter spits at her. "Has it always been about him? That why you were so hot to get back to Hong Kong?"

She wheels on him, her face white with fury. "That's what you want to talk about now, you selfish prick? Your *feelings* are hurt? This whole stupid trip to Hong Kong was your idea in the first place!"

Ian starts to weep, a terrible hiccupping sound.

"I've had enough of this shit!" Peter yells at the top of his lungs. He throws his hands up in the air and strides rapidly away in the exact *opposite* direction of the panel van.

And in that instant, he remembers who it was who'd actually

suggested Hong Kong when he'd been planning Paris. *Derrick Cotter. Of course it was.* Peter can see the moment it happened that night at the Holcombs' dinner party, playing in his mind like a silent movie on a loop.

Will these be the last thoughts I have?

"Come back here!" orders the man holding Ian. "And shut up!" he yells at the boy. In response, Ian only sobs louder.

"Screw you!" Peter shouts as he stalks farther away. "My life may be over, but that doesn't mean I have to make it easy for you!"

He keeps his pace steady and his back turned on the gunmen, knowing any second he'll hear an unmistakable bang, followed by the feeling of the burning sear of a bullet in his back.

Instead, he hears rapid footsteps. His arms are seized in a manner identical to when he was beaten in the alley.

He struggles against the viselike grips, but he's dragged to the van kicking and yelling. It's only when one of the men trains his weapon on Eva that he finally gives in to their commands to shut up. But his calm is momentary. As soon as he's shoved in the back of the van, he dives for Alex. "You motherfucker!" Peter shouts as he aims blows at his rival's head.

Eva gathers up little Ian and shields him with her body. "Peter! Stop it!" she yells.

The two Chinese men pull Peter from the back of the van and roughly escort him to the front passenger seat. The white guy is at the wheel. He turns to Peter with a sickly smile. "Really, man, that's how you want to go out? Whining over some bitch? Man up."

One of the Chinese men pushes Peter into the front seat and squeezes in next to him. The other disappears from view. Peter hears the back doors of the van slam shut.

The driver turns the ignition. Starts to drive. Peter sneaks a glance at the gun held casually in his guard's lap. The driver notices. "Don't get any stupid ideas," he admonishes. "You know, Lombard, sometimes it's just better to accept—"

Thud! A slight dark-haired figure collides with the front end of the van and flies across the windshield. Tumbles to the ground where she lies ominously still.

"Holy shit!" Peter cries.

The driver brakes. Swears. Drums his fingers on the steering wheel for a moment and then reapplies pressure to the gas pedal.

"You can't just leave her there!" Peter grabs for the wheel. The van swerves. He feels the pressure of the gun muzzle in his right side. He lifts his hands away from the wheel and raises them in surrender.

"You're right actually," the driver says softly, braking to a stop. "She might be a witness. If she's alive. If she's dead, there'll just be questions. Put her in the back with the others," he orders his companion.

This man has zero regard for life. None. Peter's stomach churns. He thinks of Eva's face, how she recoiled from him when he went after Alex Blake. *This can't be how it ends.*

Peter exhales as the barrel of the gun pulls away from his ribs. His guard climbs out and disappears from Peter's view.

He hears a muffled shout.

"What's happening?" the driver barks out the window. There's no reply. "Get out of the van," he orders Peter, who hesitates. "Now!" The driver pulls a gun and Peter obeys.

The dark-haired girl lies splayed facedown on the asphalt. But curiously, the Chinese man lies curled and inert right next to her. The driver gives him a nudge with the toe of his shoe, but he remains motionless. "What the hell?" he exclaims as he kneels to check his fallen man's pulse.

The driver is rising up, an annoyed sneer on his face, when Peter sees John Bernake come up behind him and plunge a hypodermic needle into his neck.

As he does, the woman on the ground leaps to her feet: Stevie.

Apparently she's perfectly fine.

THE PLAY

Jake Burrows, aka John Bernake,
Star Ferry Car Park, Kowloon

Jake drives the needle into the Target's neck and depresses the plunger. The gunman flails and his weapon fires, the crack of the shot echoing hollowly.

"Fuck me!" Stevie yelps, clutching her right calf. It's streaming blood.

The Target struggles to get off a second shot. Then the fentanyl hits, and he goes limp. Jake makes sure he's out before taking possession of his gun.

Jake signals that Peter should stay put but isn't sure he needed to bother. Lombard's white as a ghost, his eyes fixed on the blood pouring down Stevie's leg. He puts a hand on the van to steady himself.

Stevie, *god love her*, is hobbling over to the back of the van just like they planned, her would-be attacker's gun firmly in hand. She took a car hit and a bullet and is still going. *My own little Energizer Bunny.*

Jake's in position flanking her when Stevie flings open the back door of the van. But the gunshot that winged Stevie also killed any element of surprise.

Their remaining Target may be outnumbered and outgunned,

but he has the mouth of his weapon pressed firmly against Ian's pulsing temple. Alex and Eva flank this grim tableau, matching looks of horror on their faces. The little boy is frozen in terror.

Oh shit.

"There's no upside to that move," Jake assures the gunman softly. "Hurt the boy and we have no reason to let you take another step. But if you get out of the van and give us the boy, we'll let you go." The man drags the boy toward the doors, gun still in place against the tender skin of his temple. As the gunman reaches the lip of the cargo space, he peers out cautiously, eyes darting.

"If you're looking for your *colleagues,* I'm afraid they're out cold. Take your chance, friend. Give us the boy and go while you still can." Jake lowers his weapon and gestures that Stevie should do the same. The gunman thrusts Ian into Alex's arms and leaps from the van.

Both Jake and Stevie raise their weapons. He backs away from them, his gun trained on Jake, his eyes searching, trying to make sense of the whereabouts of his accomplices. He never sees Peter Lombard coming. Lombard jams a needle in the Target's neck with a conviction and precision that Jake can only admire. *Damn. And first time out.*

The Target crumples. Lombard looks like he might not be far behind.

It's a miracle, but Stevie's play worked. *Fuck, that was close. Nobody dead. That's the real miracle.*

Peter Lombard releases an amazed "Holy shit," as if he's parroting Jake's thoughts.

"Nice work, partner," Stevie praises, offering her fist to Jake for a bump.

"You too. Keep pressure on that," he adds, looking at her bleeding leg.

"What now?" Eva asks in a shaky voice.

"We pile them into the back of the van. Lock it and take the keys. Then a call to your friend Yuan is in order, I think. So let's get them locked and loaded and us out of here," Jake says. "Before anyone else shows up."

VICTORY

———

Stephanie Regaldo, aka Stevie Nichols, Hong Kong

Stephanie can't wait to file a report with the boss. *That was effing amazing!* Things got dicey for a minute there, sure, but Catherine is the first one to tell you that the unexpected is always to be expected. Stephanie feels tremendous pride in having been the major architect of the Victory at Star Ferry, as she's named the adventure in her own mind. (She's not yet sure about sharing that title in a report.)

Her assumptions behind the play were reasoned: at least three men, men who were likely expecting to be in full control of the situation, banking on fear about the boy to keep their victims' toes to the line. Probably armed.

Therefore, Stephanie proposed, they needed to rely on their wits, including her assortment of essential and proven con artist techniques, the element of surprise, and whatever tools they could conceivably muster up in the few short hours before dawn. They had planned for multiple scenarios.

In the end they employed the revered "act crazy ploy" (building on the obvious antipathy between Peter Lombard and Alex Blake), as a means of utilizing the classic "divide and conquer maneuver." A fortuitous use of the time-honored "car flop" sealed the deal.

It was Alex who knew of the twenty-four-hour drugstore where anything can be purchased for the right price, Jake who'd hastily refined Stephanie's plan to make sure all of them were armed with loaded hypodermics as a precaution. Both Lombards played their roles well when it all ultimately came down, with Peter Lombard in particular rising to the occasion. Even Alex Blake handled himself admirably considering the stress the man was under. Good teamwork all around.

What happened with the kid (or what *nearly* happened, *thank you Jesus, Mary, and Joseph*), that is something to learn from. She'd hoped they wouldn't bring him to the meet, after all. Made some of her calculations based on that hope.

And there's the problem with relying on hope right there.

Something else to talk over with the boss. What could have been done differently? Were there things they missed along the way? Stephanie laughs a little at herself; she used to hate school and now she is such an eager pupil.

She takes a last look around the tiny apartment she's shared with John Bernake these last few days. She's going home with at least one souvenir, a throbbing bullet wound in her calf. She kind of likes it. It's badass and makes her feel worldly.

Oh yes, darling, I get all my bullet wounds in Hong Kong.

WINGS

———

Eva Lombard,
Hong Kong Island

She'd lied to Peter, of course. But telling him the truth just seemed like too much damn trouble and trouble's one thing Eva's had quite enough of lately, thank you very much.

She and Peter are headed to the airport in just about an hour. She said she was taking a quick walk. He'd offered to come with her, but she'd shaken her head and watched the resentment flare in his eyes. The very air between them is thick with doubt and mistrust. Peter wants to talk, *finally*, but she's just not ready.

So here she is, sneaking off to meet Alex at the aviary in Hong Kong Park.

Birdsong fills the air as a glorious variety of winged creatures flit from perch to perch, rendered captive by the netting that surrounds the entire complex. Bird feeders hang strategically, offering up a variety of treats: sunflower seeds amassed in one; fresh fruits skewered onto the carved wooden spikes of another.

Eva shudders, thinking about the last time she was in this park. She looks down at her bandaged hand. When she looks up, Alex's shining gray eyes meet hers.

"So you're off then?" he asks.

"Yes. Today. Alex, again, I'm so sorry. . . ."

"Stop it, Eva Bean. All's well. I'm going to take my kid to Surrey for a bit to see his grandparents just to be on the safe side, but Yuan tells me I don't need to worry. Kind of afraid to ask exactly what she meant by that, so I didn't."

"She's something, isn't she?"

"She's definitely grown on me." Alex smiles at her, that same sweet smile that always made her weak in the knees. "But hey, I trust if I ever find myself on the run in London, I can count on you to return the favor?"

"You can count on me to return the favor wherever you are," Eva says and means it. "I literally owe you my life."

A pair of bright green parrots with navy and red feathered heads squawk and squabble as they quarrel over a suspended chunk of pineapple.

"Could have been different for us, you know. If you'd stayed." His tone is wistful.

"Oh, Alex, don't think I haven't played that game." Eva sighs.

She looks away from him, pretending interest in the flight of a snowy white bird with a scarlet head and perky yellow beak. Alex cups her chin in his hand and tilts her face back to look at his.

"Hey, Eva Bean. We are where we are. You had a scholarship waiting and a career planned in New York. I understood then and I understand now."

"And yet I followed a man to London." She says it bitterly.

Alex lifts her wounded hand to his lips and kisses that sweet little crescent of skin between her thumb and forefinger just above the bandage. A jolt runs through Eva. "Maybe just follow yourself for a bit," he advises softly. "And if that brings you back to Hong Kong? Even better."

"You're kind of too good to be true." Her eyes sting with tears.

"Oh, I doubt that," he replies. "Let's be realistic. We had a summer fling ten years ago. And then shared a life-or-death adventure. If it was just me with my usual late work nights, custody battles, and dirty socks, you'd see right away just how not good it is."

He kisses her, lightly, sweetly, this time on the lips. "Stay in touch, Eva Bean. Don't take a decade to come back next time."

FLIGHT

Peter Lombard,
Hong Kong Island

He burns to ask, even though he's sure he won't like any answer she provides. He's pretty sure he knows the answer already. Peter swallows the question and steals a glance at Eva's profile. Her eyes are closed, her face upturned to receive the warm sunshine streaming in through the taxi's streaky window.

They're headed to the airport. They've spoken little since she returned from her walk. They agreed to trash their shredded clothes. Packed what was salvageable. Peter arranged recompense to the hotel for the damage to the room and reserved the taxi to the airport. That just seemed simplest, given that Eva was crystal clear she wanted to get out of Hong Kong as soon as possible.

Not that he's longing to stay here himself. And what's he going to do when he gets back to London? Go to the authorities? Confront Derrick Cotter? Confront Forrest? *And say what exactly?*

He longs to talk things over with Eva, but the gap between them seems monstrous and insurmountable.

"Did you sleep with him?" It wouldn't have been Peter's first question had he been at all strategic, and it shouldn't have been under any circumstances, but it's the one that finally snakebites its poisonous way out of his mouth.

"Alex?" Eva responds, opening her eyes and meeting his. "No. But I wanted to. I kissed him."

Peter feels both relieved and angry. *Better to know the truth than be played for a fool.* Something about the calm clearness in her eyes encourages him to press on. "Why didn't you come to me, Eva? After you were attacked in the park?"

She keeps her gaze steady. "I thought you might be trying to have me killed."

"Wow." It's all Peter can muster.

"I know," Eva replies.

Peter stares out the window of the taxi without seeing anything at all.

"I'm not deciding anything right now," Eva finally offers cryptically. "I don't think you should either."

"I love you." He turns to her and attempts a smile. "Even though you pegged me for a killer."

"I know," she replies ruefully. "But you see the problem, right? You think I'll cheat on you the first chance I have. I've guessed everything from you having an affair and dumping me to plotting to have me killed. No matter how you look at it, we have . . . issues. If we have a road back, it's a long one."

"Don't say *if*," he entreats.

"I'm sorry, Pete. But we still don't know what kind of shit Forrest Holcomb got us involved in. I don't even know if I'm safe. Or if Alex and his kid will be! I was going to tell you at the airport, but you might as well know now. I changed my ticket. I'm not going back to London with you."

ADRIFT

——

Eva Lombard,
Somewhere over the Pacific Ocean

TO: Jenny Fitzgerald Mooney
FROM: Eva Fitzgerald Lombard
RE: Paris!/Oops not so much

Heya Jen, and guess what? I'm coming home! Long story short, we went to Hong Kong instead of Paris and things got decidedly weird from there.

Short story long, I've been lying to you for months. I hate London. Pete and I are in a place, well, complicated is an understatement. I'm trying to sort out what to do about Bax, keep him in the kennel in London or have him shipped home, but I don't think I'll know the answer until I'm back in New York and decide how long I want to stay. I'm planning on taking a cab right from JFK to your house, so tell the kids Auntie Eva is on her way! Then we'll plop them down in front of the TV and banish Bill to his man cave. We have a lot to cover.

xo E

Eva hits SEND and settles into her first-class seat. She waves away the flight attendant offering up a tray crowded with glasses of champagne. For the first time in a long time she feels clear, and she wants to stay that way.

Piecing together truth is a challenge . . .

And there are no absolutes. Perspective creates a kaleidoscope of viewpoints. Isn't this what confounds us all?

The justifications for lying are myriad, the consequences of falsehood often less harsh than the truth.

And then of course, there are the lies we tell to ourselves. . . .

FLIRT

Magali Guzman,
New Jersey

Her plate piled high with a dazzling array of food including lasagna, salad, and garlic bread, along with *tostones* and *carne guisada,* Maggie scans the backyard of her parents' house looking for a place to settle. The two long picnic tables are crowded with relatives, eating, joking, and talking animatedly over one another. Clusters of folding chairs are dotted about, people cradling plates of food in their laps. Children shriek as they run wild in an enthusiastic game of tag. Maggie smiles. She loves this chaos.

She spots her brother Diego and dodges a couple of nephews as she makes her way over to him. He's in a folding chair, shoveling food from a plate on his lap.

"You're late," he greets her through a mouthful of lasagna. "You remember Carlos, right?" He gestures to the man seated next to him, a stocky guy with buzzed hair whom Maggie's met a few times, a cop who also works at Diego's precinct.

"Of course," Maggie says. "Good to see you, Carlos. Welcome to the madhouse."

Carlos rises. "Take my seat. I'll get another." He sets his plate on the ground and goes off in search.

"He likes you," Diego opines, forking in another mouthful of food.

"Don't be stupid," Maggie retorts. "He just has manners. Unlike you."

"Where've you been?"

"Chasing something."

"I don't like the sound of that."

"Look, I was going to bring this up anyway, so I might as well do it now. Can you quietly run a photo through DMV facial recognition?"

Diego stops chewing. Swallows. "What are you doing?"

"It's no big deal." Maggie aims for nonchalance.

"Don't bullshit me, Mags. If this was official you'd use official channels."

"Okay. Look, there's a woman. She appears in the security footage from the Elliotts' apartment building—"

"*Anda pa'l carajo!*" Diego protests. "Do you want to blow up your whole career?"

"Of course not. I'm just running down this one last lead. This woman interacted with both Betsy and Bear; I saw it. The doorman at their building swore she sounded local; he remembered because their other nannies were British. It's a hunch and a long shot, I know, but—"

Diego interrupts her again. "Absolutely not! Forget it. Consider it a fraternal act of mercy. You've worked too hard to get where you are. So even if you're stupid enough to self-destruct, I'm not going to let you."

Carlos returns with another folding chair. He sets it down carefully, sits, and picks up his food. Maggie concentrates on her own plate, decimating its contents in steady bites.

"Do you want me to come back?" Carlos asks. "Did I walk into something?"

"Not at all," Maggie reassures him, a bit surprised the tension between her and Diego is so obvious. She turns her full attention to Carlos, engaging him with questions about his upbringing, his length of service in the force, local politics, and favorite foods, ignoring Diego's probing stare.

The afternoon passes, more or less in the usual fashion of these weekly dinners. Maggie argues sports with her dad, talks college applications with her oldest nephew and reality TV with her sister-in-law. She deflects questions from her aunts about when she'll be getting married. She dodges her cousin Sandy's gossip mongering about the Elliott case. She helps her mom clean up in the kitchen and happily accepts the care package of lasagna she knew would be ready for her.

She avoids Diego, an unfortunate turn of events as he's her favorite brother, but she's determined to duck another lecture. Besides, she no longer needs his help.

Carlos is going to run the photo for her on the down low. In return, she's letting him take her to dinner next week. She's actually looking forward to it; she'd enjoyed talking with him, and that makes her feel cleaner about the whole thing.

I'm sure I'll do worse once I'm undercover. It's just a meal.

Besides, the check will probably come up empty. And even in the unlikely event the software spits out a match, there's nothing to prove the girl in the footage is involved in the disappearance of the Elliotts.

Except that she showed up in their lives shortly before Betsy and Bear disappeared. She was careful to keep her face concealed when she suspected she might be on camera, angling her head and making judicious use of hoodies. Most intriguing in Maggie's opinion is that Roger Elliott couldn't identify the woman. He claimed to have no knowledge she'd been an employee of the family's, which was at odds with statements from other people in the building and with his prior statements about their staffing arrangements. He became riled at the mere suggestion that this woman might have worked for Betsy without his knowledge, displaying a hot flash of anger before recovering his usual charm and diffidently asserting that he "left the childcare up to Betsy."

Something off about his response. Something off about him. Maggie tingles just thinking about it.

GOLD STAR

———

Catherine,
London, England

The lilting chime of the doorbell echoes for the third time. I take a quick scan of the street. There's some foot traffic and a handful of cars, but no one's paying attention to this drab lady in her sensible shoes. If there's no answer in the next five minutes and I can confirm the place is empty, I may just break in. I've only been in London a few hours but I am burning bright.

I press the doorbell one more time. *This is it. Then I'm going to Plan B.*

"Yes?" floats a man's voice from the other side of the door. "Who is it?"

I hold my wallet up to his peephole so he can get a good look. Move it aside so he can see my face, deliberately softened with a tentative smile. "I'm here about your wife."

Peter Lombard cracks open the door of his London townhome. I once again marvel at the easy access granted by official-looking identification and a non-threatening appearance. The ID I'm flashing says I'm with the U.S. embassy in London. The photograph it sports matches my current look: cropped mousy brown hair, heavy, square-framed glasses. It identifies me as Marilyn Phelps.

A huge dog with a lolling tongue pokes his head out next to Peter, its cavernous black nostrils twitchy and wet. "Who's this?" I coo, surreptitiously slipping the monster a treat. I was expecting the dog of course; research is truly a girl's best friend. It was also in London years ago that I learned a doggie bribe is always a useful thing to have on hand (but that is a story for another time).

"That's Baxter," Lombard replies, keeping a tight grip on the dog's collar. "But if you're looking for my wife, she's not here. She went home to New York."

I know this too, although I instantly affect a look of mild, sympathetic surprise. "Who could blame her, after the ordeal you two went through in Hong Kong! And you, poor thing, had to go back to work, I assume? I hear how those City jobs are! Brutal, am I right?" I hold up a paper bag. "I brought bagels. Did you even know you could get a good bagel here? Aha! I thought not. Best kept secret in jolly old London town. Can I come in? Have a cup of coffee?"

Lombard's hesitation is written all over his careworn face. The man looks frayed to the edge of breaking with his bloodshot eyes, greasy hair, and white-rimmed lips, his handsome features knocked askew like a Cubist painting.

Lowering my voice to a confidential whisper I continue, "We just have a few follow-up questions regarding how you were treated over there in Hong Kong, particularly, and I hate to say it about a colleague, but how Francesca Leigh handled your situation. Some things have come to light . . . and, well, they're not inconsistent with prior allegations. . . ."

The door shifts open wider as Lombard's hunger for vindication plays nakedly across his face.

"Anyhoo, Mr. Lombard, as one citizen to another, you'd be doing us a solid. I mean, how our officials behave and are perceived abroad is crucial to all Americans. Just a few questions. What d'you say?"

Baxter anxiously stays at his master's ankles as Lombard ushers me into the kitchen and brews a pot of coffee. I let this ritual rule without speaking a word, knowing full well the universal ache to fill silence.

Seven minutes later we are situated at a hastily cleared corner of a kitchen island cluttered with take-out containers, beer bottles, unwashed cups, and unopened mail. Baxter settles on the floor near Lombard's feet and thumps his tail in a slow, mournful rhythm.

"He misses Eva." Lombard gestures to the dog. "I do too."

I ask him to tell me about the events in Hong Kong from the beginning, but I've barely finished my request before words spill from his mouth like flung confetti. His story would make little sense if I didn't know most of it already, particularly given the sections he omits, glosses over, or artfully reconstructs. Lombard happily nurses his grievances against Francesca Leigh, diving in with rigor to criticize her "lazy-ass attitude," "prune-faced innuendo," and "false platitudes."

Stephanie and Jake don't appear in Peter Lombard's effectively vague version of the truth, except as shadowy, possibly Canadian connections to some equally shadowy Triad members who mysteriously appeared to assist the Lombards, before all disappeared back into the mists. I wonder which one of my two operatives proposed that interpretation of their involvement for Lombard's narrative. *Gold star.*

With no comment other than the occasional encouraging exclamation of sympathy, shock, or shared outrage, I let Lombard rattle on. It's only when he begins to run out of steam that I ask if he still has the suitcase with the slashed lining. With renewed energy, he springs to his feet and fetches the bag from a hallway closet.

"I knew I should keep it," he says triumphantly. "Look!" He unzips the suitcase and points to the savaged interior. It doesn't occur to him that neither his suitcase's whereabouts nor its condition has anything to do with the alleged misconduct of legal attaché Francesca Leigh. I don't remind him of this fact.

Close examination reveals that Lombard is likely correct; something *was* hidden in the lining of this suitcase, an expensive Rimowa hard shell with a silky nylon interior. Despite the shredded lining, careful examination reveals that the original seams of the lining were carefully opened and then reclosed, an alteration almost invisible to the naked eye.

"Did the bag feel heavy to you?" I ask.

"It did, yes, but only when I thought about it after the fact. I've never had hard shell luggage before, you see, it's the first time we used this set and then, well, when we pulled it out and packed . . . that night was complicated."

"The luggage was new? When and where did you purchase it?"

"I have no idea what shop it came from. The guys at work were all talking about this brand and I sent my PA out one day at lunch. Look, you believe me, right? Because I don't know what to do. I think *my boss* is implicated, but in what I don't know. I'm afraid to go back to work. Fuck, I'm afraid to go outside. I would have gone home to New York too if it weren't for Baxter! But Eva was going to let him stay in the kennel until she decided if she was coming back here, and I figured if my marriage had a chance in hell I should take care of the dog while she takes a breath."

Lombard drums his fingers on the countertop and shoots a paranoid look out the kitchen window. "But that guy who attacked us in Hong Kong? For all I know he's in our backyard!" Baxter whines in response, a low, anxious growl from the back of his throat.

"Is this the man?" I present a photograph of the man Lombard last saw drugged unconscious by Jake's hand at the Star Ferry car park. Peter doesn't have to speak; his sharp recoil reveals his answer.

"It's all right, Mr. Lombard. You don't have to worry about this man anymore."

"Yeah? Why's that?" His skepticism is apparent.

"He was found dead yesterday in Hong Kong."

"How?"

"Did he die? He drowned. Accident apparently."

"Drowned?" Lombard's look of shock cycles through to a fascinating succession of emotions: Relief. Confusion. Calculation. Realization. Then the mask of stress and fear returns to pinch his features closed.

"That's great. Couldn't happen to a nicer guy," Lombard opines bitterly. "But I still don't know what I've got us involved in. Just because this asshole's dead doesn't mean someone else won't be right around the corner! And what about Eva? How can I protect my wife?"

"Would you like me to open an official investigation?"

"Yes! Can you do that? And I don't know, put men on her, or whatever it is you call it?"

Better me than anyone else. "I can, Mr. Lombard."

"Thank god! It's just—Forrest, he's been like a second father to me. I can't believe it," he continues mournfully. "But maybe Eva's right, maybe I was so busy worshipping the guy I couldn't see what was right in front of me. Like a fucking putz. And Derrick! I mean, I thought I *knew* these people! That I was part of something."

Lombard reaches down to stroke Baxter's head, and I'm grateful I don't have to meet the man's eyes. His words sting like salt on my already open wound; the wound I share with this perfect stranger. Holly can dazzle, crack open all your defenses and summon you to him like a sorcerer. I know it all too well.

I request and receive Lombard's permission to record our interview. Pose questions that mirror (and don't challenge) the sketchy narrative he's already presented. Collect information that will best allow me to quickly get protection on Eva Lombard in New York. Probe on the subjects of Forrest Holcomb and Derrick Cotter like a dentist scraping an infected tooth.

Lombard's twitchy eyes can't stay away from the photograph of his now dead assailant. I tuck it away as an act of mercy. I won't tell him the truth, so there is no point in provoking questions that will be answered only by lies.

The truth does have a delightful if dark resolve, a creamy cara-mel center of karmic justice for this man who cavalierly abducted a toddler from the arms of his mother in the middle of the street.

Alerted by Jake, Yuan's foot soldiers picked up all three of the men Jake and Stephanie left incapacitated but alive in the back of that white panel van. In his report, Jake was quietly proud the Lombards were safely out of the country and the threat to them neutralized without any loss of life. (Stephanie's report was con-siderably more boisterous, boasting about the success of the play she largely designed and spewing thrilled outrage about her bullet wound, luckily a clean shot that passed through the meat of her calf.) What neither of them know, and will never need to, is that little Ian Blake's grandmother plays mahjong with a group of el-derly women in the back of her antiques store on Hollywood Road. The longtime coterie of players includes my Internet café–owning friend Gracey and Yuan's aunt Lydia.

All three of the men that Jake was so proud to have left alive in the Star Ferry car park were painfully executed within hours of their "rescue."

You don't want to mess with the grandmas.

MATCH

Magali Guzman,
Hoboken, New Jersey

The restaurant is a superb choice, an Italian joint specializing in fresh seafood. Carlos is delightful, helping her off with her coat, pulling out her chair, soliciting her choice of still or flat water. He's dressed up for the occasion too; his button-down shirt strains appealingly against his muscled chest. But he proves he really knows the way to a girl's heart when he lifts a first glass of wine and announces, "I got a match for you."

Maggie can't believe it. "For real?"

He slides a folded sheaf of papers from the inside breast pocket of his sport jacket and hands it to her. Maggie scans it eagerly.

Finally a name for her phantom. *Stephanie Regaldo*. Arrests for prostitution, drug possession, vagrancy. Regaldo's most recent mug shot confirms she is indeed the girl in the Elliotts' security footage. But there's something different about her too. In the mug shot, her eyes seem vacant, her features riddled with the effects of addiction. In the security footage, she looks healthy, clean, aware, alert, *invested*.

Overactive imagination. Maggie chastises herself, realizing she's been so absorbed in scanning Regaldo's sheet that she's not even thanked Carlos. "I owe you," she says.

"I hope so," Carlos flirts. "And don't worry, not a word to Diego."

"You really do know how to make a girl feel special," Maggie says, smiling at him.

The rest of the date is perfectly fine as far as dates go. The salad is crisp and fresh, the seafood linguini exquisite, the conversation lively. Maggie confesses she has a rule against dating cops, but coyly reveals she's heard rules are made to be broken, and is delighted by the grin this elicits from Carlos.

As much as she genuinely enjoys herself, however, she can't wait to get home and in front of her computer. She likes Carlos enough to share a molten chocolate cake and a kiss outside her apartment building, but when she finally ducks inside it's with an audible sigh of relief.

Once situated, Maggie pores over Stephanie Regaldo's record a second time. She compares the mug shot to the image she's printed of the woman's face from the security footage and lays them side by side. She feels that tingle again. She's certain something *changed* for this girl.

Regaldo's last arrest was eighteen months ago. Where was she and what was she doing between her last encounter with the law and now? Maggie types "Stephanie Regaldo" into her search engine.

Maggie's looking for the near past but her search takes her deeper back. The story is a gruesome and tragic one. Sixteen-year-old Stephanie Regaldo lived with her construction worker father and older brother in New Jersey. Her parents had been divorced for three years. During the first two summers after the split, Stephanie and her brother had traveled together to visit their mother in Hawaii, where she had moved permanently. That summer, Stephanie's brother wanted to stay in Jersey with his friends as he was off to college in the fall, so Stephanie went to Hawaii alone.

She returned home to find the bloated, mutilated bodies of her father and brother, victims of brutal stabbings, a suspected home invasion gone terribly wrong, a crime that is still unsolved.

Following Stephanie's trail is easy for a while. Headlines after the murders. Then Stephanie moves to live with her mother and graduates high school in Kauai. Shortly after, barely eighteen, she has her first arrest for prostitution in New York City. The pattern that follows is a rotation of arrests and probations, missed court appearances and short-term incarcerations, court-mandated drug treatment and community service, only leading to more arrests. Then Stephanie seems to disappear off the face of the earth. Given the recidivism rates for drug-addicted prostitutes, this in itself is anomalous, but even odder is that there are no public records for her anywhere. If Maggie wasn't looking at a photo of Regaldo from just a few weeks ago, she would have guessed the girl was dead, and had been for a year and a half.

Stephanie Regaldo evaporated into thin air. Just like Betsy and Bear Elliott.

That can't be a coincidence.

BAGGAGE

———

Catherine,
London, England

My heart pounds as I enter the swanky reception area of Holcomb Investments. It's not meeting my Target that's making me nervous; I'm certain I can play Peter Lombard's personal assistant like a Fender bass guitar. No, it's the thrill of seeing Holly's name etched in thick gold letters on the doors, the heady proximity to the man himself. *A man who may yet betray me, who may already have done so.*

I ask the elegant receptionist for Peter Lombard's assistant, a woman with the stolid English name of Jane Brown. It turns out the appellation suits her: lank hair, brown eyes, pale eyebrows, thick ankles, no effort.

"I so hope you can help me," I launch in as Jane comes toward me with a cautiously polite expression on her face. "I work at the Rimowa branch over on New Bond Street and there's been a frightful toss up about some luggage that was supposed to be on hold being given to another customer." I fully embrace the role of oppressed London shopgirl with my tweed skirt and rayon blouse, flat shoes and practical tote, wispy ponytail and harried expression.

Jane Brown's face turns uninterested. "I'm sorry," she says flatly. "I hardly see how I can help."

"Didn't you purchase some luggage for your employer with us recently? Our records show his card was used. Where did you take the luggage after you bought it? Did you hand it over to him here at the office?"

"I authorized a purchase for him," Jane explains. "But I never actually saw the luggage, so I'm no help, I'm afraid. Another gentleman here at the firm was intending to go to your shop that day. He offered to sort out the set for me while he was there. But I believe he had it all sent directly to Mr. Lombard's residence. Don't your records tell you?"

"Do you mind if I ask who it was that was so kind as to offer to help you? Don't often see people helping each other out these days, do you?"

"What? Well, I did think it a bit odd of Mr. Cotter actually. . . ." A furrow creases between Jane's almost invisible eyebrows. "Is that all?" she asks, catching herself mid-sentence, smoothing her skirt.

"What was odd on your end exactly?" I let loose a nervous giggle. "I'm sorry, it's just that I'm trying to get a picture of what happened that day. Who might have been sold our missing luggage by mistake? I'm in a heap of trouble. Please help if you can."

Jane shifts a glance at the receptionist before leaning in. "I can't imagine my *odd* has anything to do with your *odd*, it's just that you know how it is in offices. That Mr. Cotter offered to do *anything* at all for Mr. Lombard. I've told Mr. L many times he should watch his back when it comes to that one."

Jane shuts down then, suddenly rendered awkward by the instinct she's overstepped some boundary she never knew was in front of her. "You're welcome to check directly with Mr. Cotter," she tells me crisply. "I can let his PA know you'd like to speak with him if you leave me your card."

It doesn't really matter if I speak to Derrick Cotter; in fact, I'd prefer it if I didn't. I want to stay invisible as I turn the kaleido-scope lens and watch all the colors of the truth swirl into place before my eyes.

I thank Jane Brown for her time and offer a twenty-five percent discount the next time she comes into the store.

TROLLING

Magali Guzman,
New York City

Maggie's been avoiding Diego for days. She continues this policy as she punches REJECT on her cellphone once again. She'd listened to one message her brother had left and that was enough for her to know that she doesn't want to listen to any more. At least until he cools down. If he ever cools down.

But it was worth incurring Diego's wrath. Instinct sent her searching and after many fruitless hours of trolling unsolved crime chat boards and online survivor support groups, Maggie found the one fluttering handkerchief that Stephanie Regaldo left behind when she fled her old life and became someone new.

The chat room Stephanie infrequently frequents is composed of the desperate, the crazy, the manipulative, and the compulsively sad. The majority of the visitors to the site, which serves partly as a support group and partly as a tip line, are survivors, the battered, lonely leavings of murdered families. The trolls and predators can't resist joining in, of course, raising false hopes in some cases, purporting to communicate with the dearly deceased (for a fee) in others.

Stephanie's pattern on the site is consistent with her arrest and other public records. She was a much more active visitor up until her last arrest, engaging with other members at least once a month, but she has only posted three times in the last year and a half. Each time it was to offer encouragement or ask a pointed question when a fellow survivor posted a lead about his or her own case.

Three days ago Maggie dangled a tasty morsel for Stephanie Regaldo. It was a fishing expedition, but Maggie likes to fish. It teaches patience; her dad taught her that.

She composed a carefully worded DM to Stephanie with just enough specific information about the Regaldo murders to make it sound legit. She made an offer to provide more details in person. She didn't make her appeal about money; she claimed a guilty conscience, that she'd been with the guy who'd done it back then and wanted to come clean now that she was finally free of him. Maggie carefully hinted at the perpetrator's abuse without laying it on too thick.

The insider details she'd been able to provide were thanks to Carlos, who'd done Maggie another favor. That favor is the reason for Diego's many outraged calls.

Whoops. Dios mío. *Busted. I owe Carlos at least one more zesty session before I cut him loose.* Maggie smiles thinking about their last zesty session, but UC school starts in a heartbeat, and she's leaving *everything* behind. Her imminent departure left her uncharacteristically unguarded with Carlos, and Maggie's ruefully grateful the relationship has a clock on it.

She logs on to the survivor chat site and starts to poke around. When she sees that her message has received a reply, Maggie feels it, that *tingle.*

Stephanie Regaldo has taken the bait. Agreed to a meeting.

Maggie's first instinct is to call Diego, share her process and her progress, bat around next steps while positing countless what-ifs. She glances at her cold phone and resists the temptation. Diego's family; he'll have to forgive her eventually, but until then she's on her own.

THE BENEFITS OF INVISIBILITY

———

Catherine,
London, England

All roads lead to Derrick Cotter, it appears, so I start to make a map. Hacking into his credit card and financial history, I discover Derrick has joint checking and savings accounts with his wife, an educational trust in place for his daughter, an investment portfolio with Holcomb Investments. Nothing staggering there.

His wife is a cosigner on all of Derrick's credit cards but one—a limitless Black Card that bills to a postal box. Interesting. Deeper digging turns up a cleverly concealed shell corporation with dubious purpose, its prime asset a nearly empty London bank account with a history of large payments wired to it from a bank in Hong Kong, and with subsequent wire transfers out to two other financial institutions, one in the Cayman Islands and the other in Sierra Leone.

London. Hong Kong. The Caymans. Sierra Leone. Four corners of a square. Four sides of a picture I can't yet see. Answers that only lead to more questions.

London makes sense. Derrick and Holly live here, after all. The Caymans too, as a universally acknowledged safe haven for dirty cash. But why Hong Kong? Why Sierra Leone?

Social media is the death of privacy and also its perversion, I reflect as I data-mine all of Derrick Cotter's. Incessant public posting makes it harder to hide or rewrite personal history. Virtual communication also allows for a false life or lives to be lived solely behind the anonymity of a screen. (Sadly for me, it also presents challenges to creating new identities out of nowhere when I need them. It's why I'm careful to protect and care for the stable I have, stories for another time.)

On the main, however, I find a lot of benefit to other people living their lives out loud. Today is no exception. Derrick Cotter's social and family life is well documented, and I've pieced together a fairly complete portrait of his existence. Point of pride on Cotter's feed goes to shots with Holly, of course, with Miranda Holcomb and Cotter's wife, Louise, often posed adoringly by their husbands' sides. Another frequent theme features pix of Cotter, Louise, and their young daughter cruising the Thames on a sleek riverboat. There are a significant number of photos of Cotter at various charity events where Holly is being honored. One or two where Cotter himself is the honoree.

A photo of Holly commands my attention, receiving an award for a significant donation to a charity that rescues endangered pygmy hippos from Sierra Leone. Holly looks good in his exquisitely tailored monkey suit; he always could rock eveningwear.

While Sierra Leone is apparently the home of pygmy hippopotami and mysterious bank accounts, I know little about the country (when you're largely self-taught there are bound to be gaps). It strikes me as interesting that Sierra Leone has come up twice all of a sudden. *Reticular activation*, it's called, when something hasn't been on your radar and suddenly it's everywhere you look. I love that there's a term for this phenomenon. But also believe it's a call from the universe to pay attention.

What else do I know about Sierra Leone besides pygmy hippos? For that matter, why pygmy hippos? It sounds like the kind of bullshit Holly makes fun of wife #4, Miranda, for, although I admit it gives me a pang that he does so with affection in his voice.

I research. I always do. I learn that Sierra Leone is also a hub for smuggling blood diamonds out of Africa. I break down the sides of the square again and again and only put the story together when I realize it isn't a square at all. Hong Kong is also a hub, used for washing bloody diamonds clean, shipping them to Mainland China to be cut, relabeled, and sold.

I track flight records and passenger manifests, bank payments and electronic correspondence. The picture gradually swims into focus.

The planes Holly dispatched to war zones must have been carrying more than endangered animals and altruism on their way back to England, counting on minimal screening of planes entering the country carrying adorable, defenseless animals rescued from explosive battlefields by daring young pilots. One beautiful thing about diamonds is their easy portability.

Tracking the money tells me the plot was initially financed out of Hong Kong, which explains a Triad tie. The recent transfers tell me that the operation began slowly and is getting more aggressive; the dates are closer together, the amounts larger.

With each revelation my heart sinks a little lower. I had blinded myself to Holly's true nature all along. Most damning is the reported arrest of a young woman last year in Hong Kong for diamond smuggling: caught bringing the gems in, arrested, and sentenced. My research reveals payments to her from Cotter's shell corporation. Staring at a news photograph of the girl's wide-eyed and terrified mug shot, I wonder: Was she a complicit part of their scheme or another innocent whose life has been shattered by their gluttonous pursuit of money?

I reopen the photo of Holly from the pygmy hippo benefit, the one where he looks so sharp in his tuxedo. I almost miss the next piece of the puzzle, and wouldn't have blamed myself if I had. It's no more than a look captured between two people, one that could have been explained away as a trick of the light or the camera angle's misleading distortion. The pair is not even in the foreground of the image; Holly has that distinction.

I push in on first one face and then the other, all the yearning and planning and smug complicity somehow caught in their locked eyes. A cold wave of foreboding washes over me. I have to click the image closed. A terrible secret threatens to erupt from within this frozen moment.

An easily accomplished siphon of Derrick's cellphone's Wi-Fi history reveals a base carelessness about erasing his digital finger-prints, one that allows me to track his routine. That Derrick logged into networks at his own flat, his daughter's school, and Holcomb Investments was not a surprise. The number of expensive London hotels populating his history was more unexpected.

Personally, I appreciate a high-end hotel. Growing up poor is partly why; the luxury of crisp sheets and thick, clean towels changed fresh every day is a delicious indulgence. The anonymity a hotel can provide is also attractive; it's easier to stay off the radar in a place perpetually populated by transients.

Hotels suit me for a variety of reasons. But why would Derrick Cotter, owner of a perfectly nice flat in Chelsea that he shares with his wife and little girl, and with access to a luxurious office in a tower in the City with every modern convenience, be spending quite so much time in London hotels? What needs are propelling Derrick's quest for anonymity and spotless linen? Could these neutral locations be where Holly and Derrick met their less "acceptable" business partners?

Tracking the dates of his room charges against Derrick's virtual calendar (also linked to his cellphone, *honestly, people just make it too damn easy to have their privacy exploited*), I am able to put together a pattern. As I dig deeper and the facts reveal themselves, I have to admit I am shocked. The secret that threatened to erupt from within that benefit photograph is confirmed.

Why do we hurt each other so? I wish I knew.

The latest winner in the Derrick Cotter hotel sweepstakes is an exclusive boutique establishment in Covent Garden. I settle into a club chair in the lobby bar, one that has an unobstructed view of the doors to the street as well as the front desk. When the spotty young waiter approaches, I order a gin and tonic (when in London, after all) and settle down to wait.

I'm relaxed as I sip my refreshingly tangy drink. By cloning Derrick's texts I know his planned rendezvous is not scheduled for another half an hour. My research has revealed whom it is he's meeting. I know they are meeting here.

They like to think they've been careful, with their judicious use of coded messages to communicate and the rotating cycle of hotels they've frequented, but really it's all playacting. Anyone who was looking could find them. Maybe on some level they want to be caught.

I don't have to stay here at the hotel. The cameras I installed in the rendezvous hotel room before their arrival are motion activated. It only took fifty quid to get a hotel staffer to reveal that Mr. Cotter had a favorite room and to provide access. I could sit in the comfort of my own hotel room down the street and watch the live feed if I could stomach it. I order another drink.

Derrick comes in and greets the desk clerk with familiarity. A key card slides across polished wood. Derrick requests that a bottle of champagne be sent up to the room.

I observe him with frank curiosity, certain he will take no notice of me. He hasn't seen me in years. But beyond that, clad as I am in drab layers of crinkled linen, with orthopedic shoes on my feet and a gray wig on my head, I might as well be invisible. Not only to Derrick, but also to most of the people who've passed me in this lobby. Apart from the spotty waiter, the single person to acknowledge me in the time I've sat here was an elderly woman with a walker whose eyes sought mine in commiseration of the indignities of aging.

Derrick's a little heavier than when I last saw him, his hair thinner. He's vain about his hair, I can tell; a few long strands are draped across an incipient bald spot. He's also adopted a cocky swagger that he displays in his amble to the elevators.

Miranda Holcomb arrives seventeen minutes after Derrick. I've never seen her in the flesh before and her appeal is readily apparent. Dewy pale skin with that perfect English rose flush on her high cheekbones. Curls of auburn hair escaping from a silk scarf loosely knotted around her head. Miranda saunters through the lobby with a sinuous, languorous grace that causes every man in the room to stare. And more than one woman. Miranda wields her sexual power like a club.

From what I've pieced together, Miranda and Derrick have been having an affair for over a year. *Sweet relief.*

It's not that I don't care Holly's been betrayed. I do. I feel his pain like my own. But if he's betrayed, he's not complicit. It's Derrick's hands that need a washing, after all.

I like to believe that Holly will be more hurt by Derrick's betrayal than by Miranda's, but I'm not just flattering myself that I hold his heart. The adulterous pair deceived Holly on a business level as well as a personal one, using the cover of his contacts and associations. Holly has no children; Holcomb Investments is his baby, Derrick his most trusted lieutenant.

I speculate about Miranda and Derrick's plan. They've amassed quite a tidy sum in the Caymans, although nowhere near Holly's immense fortune. Do they have a "magic number" they are trying to accumulate? What then?

In a sick way I can understand Derrick's motivation: a score that thoroughly humiliates the man to whom he owes everything. Dependence can be corrosive, rusting out gratitude and turning it hollow. But would Miranda actually walk away from Holly's billions and his social prominence? Endure the predictable scandal? The world that Holly moves in will inevitably pick sides, and Miranda and Derrick won't be on the winning end of that coin toss.

People do all sorts of idiotic things in the name of love, I remind myself. I'm not immune, try as hard as I might. It's why it's best for me to live the way I do, untethered, responsible for others only as I choose to be, and never out of need or desire. It may be lonely, but it's safe.

PERFECT

——

Magali Guzman,
New York City

Maggie reminds herself that since she created an avatar to interact on this site, whoever it is she's communicating with may have done exactly the same. This might explain why after an eager response to her first message from a person she believes to be Stephanie Regaldo, there has been considerable and frustrating negotiation about how and where to meet, including a number of postponements of scheduled appointments. Maggie sighs. The latest message is yet another delay.

She feels a presence over her shoulder and switches computer screens without missing a beat, hiding her chat room conversation from prying eyes. Swiveling around in her chair, she sees Karen staring at her expectantly. "I'm sorry," Maggie apologizes to her colleague. "I was a million miles away."

"Clearly. Listen, girl, I'm trying to plan your going-away party. Brennan's or McNeil's?"

"How can you even suggest Brennan's?" Maggie asks, laughing. "Not after the Christmas party!"

"McNeil's it is." Karen laughs back, before going on to debate the relative desirability of a Thursday versus a Friday night.

Planning the party makes Maggie's life as a UC feel tangibly and tantalizingly close. *Diego's right. Why risk everything I've worked so hard to achieve by chasing a shadow in the dark? What do I even expect to learn?*

Overactive imagination.

"Magali Guzman! I can't believe that didn't get a laugh."

Maggie startles when she realizes Karen is staring at her, with hands planted on her hips and an expression of faux outrage on her face. "What? I'm sorry. A lot on my mind," she apologizes.

Karen points discreetly at Ryan Johnson, lurking a few cubicles down. "I said, we should call it for McNeil's but tell *him* it's Brennan's."

Maggie rewards Karen with the roar of laughter her friend was seeking. But seeing Ryan takes Maggie back to the interviews they conducted together when working the Elliott case. Rachel Ferris's words float through Maggie's mind so loudly she's shocked Karen doesn't hear them: *"Anything that looks perfect is a lie."*

If "Stephanie Regaldo" ever does give Maggie a firm time and date, she may meet her, after all. She'll have to be careful, play her role with precision, just long enough to see if there is anything tangible linking this blue-collar Jersey girl with the tragic past to the disappearance of a wealthy Manhattan socialite and her son. Just long enough for Maggie to see if she tingles. This can be the end of it, depending on what she finds. Or she can turn it over to official channels. Maybe she'll find nothing. It's probably nothing.

Maggie wonders if Diego has ratted her out to their parents. He probably wouldn't say anything to their mother, but Dad is entirely possible.

Sometimes it's easier to ask forgiveness than permission. Maggie learned that from her dad too, although he applies the principle to such matters as eating the last slice of chocolate cake or impulsively splurging on a new barbecue. She's not entirely sure Dad would approve of her current interpretation, but the lure is impossible to resist.

After all, it's just one meeting.

WILD

Catherine,
London, England

For nostalgia's sake I picked the Mandarin Oriental hotel in Hyde Park for our rendezvous, even though I have no idea if the warm feelings I harbor for the hotel's counterpart in Paris are mirrored within Holly in any way. He's had a new wife, and probably other lovers too, since our limbs tangled in silky sheets back there in Paris. It's possible he doesn't remember the Mandarin at all.

He's expecting to meet an emissary dispatched by me with information that is "too sensitive" to relay except in a face-to-face meeting. The last half is true at least. And once I share what I know he'll be grateful I came in person.

I slide onto a barstool, aware of a few appraising and appreciative glances coming my way. My hair is loose and frames my face. My dress is clingy and dips suggestively into my cleavage. My shoes are patently absurd, sky-high stilettos with straps that snake up my calves. I haven't seen Holly in over two years and intend on making an impression. I order a Lone Apple, from the signature cocktail list. It seems appropriate.

Early so I could pick my position and assess the room before Holly's arrival, I have to bat away the overtures of a handful of overconfident men in bespoke suits as I wait. Holly's running late and my nerves rise. My pleasant memories of the Mandarin Oriental in Paris twist to less charming ones: a bruised Jake Burrows stumbling from the hotel, the resistance of the plunger as I stabbed a hypodermic needle into his neck, catching his body before he crashed to cold concrete. It was for Jake's benefit, but he's harbored some resentment ever since I came clean about the incident.

A hush falls when Holly enters the bar. This is a money crowd and Forrest Holcomb is made of money. No one is so gauche as to point at him or whisper. It is the *absence* of sound that demonstrates his status, the way conversation stops and even cutlery dare not clink. He pauses in front of a gold-etched glass panel, his features illuminated by a pool of light beaming from a copper fixture suspended overhead. His beard and hair are more silver than when I last saw him, his eyes a little more weary. But it's Holly, my Holly, my man.

Holly's appearance in the bar is assessed and digested. The patrons move on to fresh gossip. The buzz of conversation swells again. Holly's eyes scan the room with the possessive power of someone who could buy everyone in it if he so wanted.

When those evaluating eyes meet mine, I stay poised despite the flush of heat I immediately feel between my thighs. I cross one leg over the other and let Holly get a good long look.

He crosses to me in a few bold strides. Orders a drink from the bartender and kisses me on both cheeks. "There you are, luv," he says affectionately. "About time."

It doesn't take much to get him upstairs; a whispered invitation and we casually saunter to the elevator. His hand slides under my dress and up the back of my thigh to cup my ass. He moans when he realizes I'm not wearing underwear.

At last the door to the suite slams behind us, and we fall to the carpeted floor, urgent, panting, hungry, wild. The release when it comes is exquisite, a free fall from a great height, waves of pleasure rocking me across the universe and then back to the earth.

Later, curled together amid our strewn clothes and sharing a cigarette, I ask Holly about Peter Lombard.

"What about him? I told you. Good chap. A lot of promise. Could be the son I never had. Batty business what went on in Hong Kong, what? But, darling, what did you have to tell me in person?" Holly props himself up on one elbow and plucks the cigarette from my fingers.

I lay out my thought processes and research, presenting the information in a logical manner, asking Holly to let me finish the numerous times he tries to interrupt. I tell him my guess, that the shipment Lombard unknowingly brought into Hong Kong was a big score, maybe big enough for Derrick and Miranda to make a move if they're planning on one. I also share my supposition that Lombard was picked for the role by Derrick precisely because of Holly's affection for the younger man. If Peter succeeded in getting the diamonds into Hong Kong, it would be a win. If he got arrested and charged, it was a win of a different sort.

Holly pulls another cigarette from the pack and lights it with the burning ember of the butt we have going. He takes in a harsh inhale of smoke and plumes it out through his nose.

"Thank you," he says gravely, running a finger along my cheekbone. "It won't be forgotten."

"Of course."

He rises then, pulling on his trousers and shrugging into his soft cotton shirt. He steps into his shoes, leans over to kiss me deeply, and leaves without saying another word.

I can't blame Holly. I was the one who set our rules and boundaries. But as the door clicks closed behind him, my heart breaks all over again.

MAD WORLD

———

Magali Guzman,
New York City

Never has time ticked by so slowly. Stephanie Regaldo finally confirmed a meeting. All day long Maggie's been anticipating its cancellation, but with just ninety minutes until their appointed time it looks like they're good to go.

Never has Maggie been so conflicted. She lured this young woman with empty promises of new information about the murders of her family, a cruel trick if Maggie discovers there's no link between Stephanie and the Elliotts. That's guilt-inducing enough, but the many ignored calls from Diego add a whole extra layer of spice.

She checks the clock again. Go time. It's now or never, particularly with the unforgiving vagaries of the New York City transit system. Maggie shuts down her computer and pulls her handbag from a desk drawer, mentally rehearsing the role she's about to play. *Keep her talking. That's the objective. Find out all you can, but don't push so hard she's scared away. Establish sufficient trust to keep the channel open.*

Maggie has several different ideas about how to integrate the Elliotts into the conversation depending on what she encounters. She strategizes her options as she rides down the elevator and into the lobby of the Federal Building. She's so absorbed in her thoughts that she collides with Ryan Johnson, who's exiting the building just in front of her.

"Whoa, baby, you don't have to maul me, just ask nicely if you want to take a ride on my pole." Ryan smirks at her.

What a very consistent dick he is. "Thanks for the offer." Maggie sidesteps him. "But I've got better plans."

"What could be better than me?" Ryan blocks her way when she tries to pass. Gives her a sly grin. "And why am I the only one not getting a taste of your hot taco?"

Maggie dodges him again. *I do not have the time for this crap.* "Cut it, Johnson."

"Yeah, cut it, Johnson!"

Maggie turns her head to see Diego, red-faced and furious, arm cocked back like he's about to strike. She's seen her brother's temper enough times to know this is a critical moment.

"Who's this?" Ryan taunts. "The better plan you're spreading your legs for?"

Hearing those words, Maggie relinquishes any faint hope she might have had of stopping Diego's balled fist. It connects resoundingly with Johnson's square jaw. *Men! Hijos de las gran putas!*

Pedestrians scatter and yelp. Maggie can't deny the burst of satisfaction that erupts inside her, seeing Johnson's shocked face, but she grabs Diego by the elbow and hauls him down the street and around the corner. The crowd absorbs them into its flow until she gives her brother a solid, angry push. "What the fuck, Diego! I have to work with that asshole."

"Asshole is right. How long you been putting up with that shit?"

"Why does it matter? And anyway, I'm a big girl. I can handle my own business."

The need for confrontation hardens Diego's features. "Can you? Without, say, *using* Carlos for your business?"

"That's not fair. I like Carlos."

"Sure, as long as he can get you something you want. And for a case that was *shut down* as an embarrassment to your beloved Bureau? I've never been undercover but I know it's hard to keep your moral center if you're in deep. How are you going to manage that if you can't even keep your shit straight now? I'm disappointed in you, Magali, no lie."

Diego's words sting every bit as much as they are intended to. Maggie longs to bite back and spew some judgment of her own. *It's not like you're some kind of saint! And what have I done that's really so bad?*

Knowing she's about to secretly add another sin to the list of her offenses makes her choke back the venom. She considers explaining it all to Diego. His intentions are good. Even now he's only here because he's looking out for her. Maybe she can make him understand. She glances at her cell. If only she had the time!

"And now you can't stay off your *maldito* phone?" Diego glowers at her.

"I've got to go. I'm late for something important. But I promise you I'm not doing anything stupid."

"Yeah, well, your current track record indicates otherwise." Diego's ire still runs high; even the satisfaction of the hard connect with Johnson's jaw hasn't dulled his sharp edge.

"Get out of here. Take a run and a shower. Cool down. We'll talk tomorrow."

"If you answer my calls," he shoots back, rippling with attitude.

"I will. I promise." Maggie hurries off, her urgent steps melding into the familiar fast pulse of the city. She needs to get back into her groove after this double whammy of idiocy: Ryan (ordinary idiocy) and Diego (unordinary, extraordinary idiocy).

Partly her nerves jangle because she knows that Diego's right. Not only is she taking risks that go against her training in this pursuit, she's also brushing up hard against her personal moral lines. But she can't shake the faces of Betsy and little Bear Elliott. Or her conviction that *something* is up with Stephanie Regaldo. It may not be what Maggie expects, but she's embraced another of her dad's philosophies, that of entering every encounter with "high hopes, but no expectations."

Hell, no one may show up. Or someone may show up who's not the woman I'm looking for. Or Regaldo could show up but have no info about the Elliotts. It could all be a mega waste of time.

Maggie reminds herself to be wary and alert. It's also conceivable that Stephanie's been turned into a state's witness. Maybe she's working undercover for another agency. Perhaps as an informant of some kind? That could explain her sudden turnabout a year and a half ago. It could also lead to big trouble for Maggie depending on the circumstances.

Is she, Maggie the hunter, also being hunted?

Maggie dashes down the subway steps. She's got a long ride uptown. And despite all of her misgivings, she doesn't want to be late.

LOOSE ENDS

——

Catherine,
New York City

I had a heady time in London. I saw Holly three more times, each encounter more urgent than the last. We didn't talk much, and not at all about Derrick and Miranda. He told me he would handle it. I told him I would let him.

As I had a team on Eva Lombard, I knew she was returning to London the day before I was intending to depart. I parked myself across the street from the Lombards' townhouse and patiently watched until her arrival. She took a few minutes, visibly composing herself before ringing the doorbell, a choice I thought odd, perhaps intended to make a point to her husband: *I'm back, but we are not back to normal.*

Eva's reunion with Baxter was joyous: the woman on her knees, the dog's meaty paws on her shoulders, his huge tongue lavishing her with kisses. The couple's greeting was more stilted, Eva reluctantly pulling herself away from the dog and hesitating in the doorway to exchange a few sentences with her husband. I drove away as she crossed the threshold. I've since learned she's pregnant. I hope they work it out.

At least they are safe from any danger at the hands of Derrick Cotter. He drowned in a freak accident one day while out on the Thames in his riverboat. Tragically for the self-made billionaire and noted philanthropist Forrest Holcomb, his young wife perished just a week after his oldest friend. The examining physician ruled it an accidental overdose, but rumors of suicide swirled, generating additional sympathy for Holly. He always does know how to play to a crowd.

I confess that the news of the deaths thrilled me in my darkest heart. Are you shocked? It's a perverse reaction, I know, especially since I've dedicated my life to protecting others. But it feels good to knock Holly off his pedestal and into the muck with me. We are broken together, and aberrant as it may sound, that knowledge comforts me. I have to decide every day who I will choose to help and who I'll turn away. Aren't I sentencing *someone* to possible danger or death with every choice? Is that so different from choosing to eliminate two people so vile they could betray anyone and everyone, including their greatest benefactor?

My perception might be altered if I had a different lens on Holly; I'm honest enough to admit that, but I choose to find the spin that links us.

Remember, every storyteller twists his or her lens to suit an agenda. Or protect a heart.

Steve Harris told his particular story admirably. The scandal exploded across the media, sparking outrage, lawsuits, and Knox Pharmaceuticals' plummeting stock prices. It's always a good feeling to sit back and reflect on a job well done.

There are a few loose ends, of course. Where to place the Harrises, if they agree to go. Debriefs of both Jake and Stephanie. An appropriate "gift" to my friend Gracey in Hong Kong. A cleanup of any trails, digital or otherwise, that may have been left behind there.

I'm scheduled to meet with Jake at the Manhattan apartment he and his sister, Natalie, inherited after the murder of their father. He rarely uses it, but it's always a discreet place for us to talk and I have my own set of keys.

Stephanie has been more elusive, claiming "wicked jet lag," but

I suspect she may just be dodging my suggested plan to dye her hair red. She needs to learn how to take on a more diverse set of identities. A radical change might jolt her into understanding the art of taking on a character.

With the Harrises still in Mexico City, I need to return. I send Stephanie a nagging text. It strikes me that our exchange on this topic has been poignantly familial, as much as I can understand the concept of a family at all.

LINGER

Magali Guzman,
New York City

Maggie hurries up the subway stairs just as dusk throws its magical golden glow on the gritty gray streets. She hasn't been this far uptown in a long time, and never before to the meeting place suggested by her correspondent: the East 110th Street Playground, set in the northernmost reaches of Central Park across from the Harlem Meer.

Central Park has never figured largely for Maggie despite her living in Jersey her entire life, and she had no idea what the heck a Meer even was until this invitation. As the peaceful rush-encircled lake comes into view, she's transported back to the time of the city's original Dutch origins, just as Central Park designers Olmsted and Vaux intended.

The playground that is her destination blends into this bucolic environment, with swing sets flanked by leafy trees and a climbing structure that looks like a giant's discarded set of Lincoln Logs. Maggie knows the playground is one of the more recent park renovations, featuring the latest in playground design as part of the Central Park Conservancy's "Plan for Play" initiative. She'd at least had the sense to do a little research and study a map before she hauled herself up here.

She slows her pace, letting her eyes sweep rapidly over the assortment of people in the park. Given the hour, it's sparsely populated, a few children linger noisily in the sandbox or on swings, their caretakers gather sippy cups and plastic snack containers as they prepare to corral their young charges home.

No one stands out to her as a likely candidate, the mere height of the women in her view eliminating them by dwarfing Stephanie Regaldo's small size (five feet and one inch, according to her arrest records).

Maggie runs through the information she has, parsing known fact and suspected fiction. She reminds herself once again that she is probably on a fool's errand. As the time agreed to for their appointment comes and goes and dusk's burnt umber descends upon the park, it seems more and more likely that is the case.

GONE

Catherine,
New York City

Dusk is my favorite part of the day. It's the changeling quality of the light during that hour, as well as the reassurance that I've survived another day. Even if the night ahead is still in question.

I watch from a ridge above the playground as the woman I've identified as Special Agent Magali Guzman of the Federal Bureau of Investigation takes up a position, her eyes as sharply searching as my own. I let her wait. Manipulation of anticipation and expectation is a reliable way of keeping situations under my control.

Guzman's body deflates. I see defeat in the set of her shoulders. She checks the time for the hundredth time since I've been observing her. She shifts to gather her bag as if she intends to leave. It's time for me to move.

I circle around so I come up to Guzman from behind.

"Don't turn around," I warn softly.

I'm disguised, of course, with a curly blond wig and a body belt that adds thirty pounds to my gut and changes my gait. Nonetheless, why take chances if I don't have to?

"Okay," she replies instantly. "Are you Stephanie Regaldo?"

"Who's looking for her?"

"Like I said, I have information about the murders of your father and brother."

"Bullshit," I snarl. "I know who you are, Special Agent Magali Guzman, FBI. What do you really want?"

There's a long silence. I let it build.

"Okay," Guzman finally replies. "I'm looking for a missing woman and child. Betsy and Bear Elliott."

She turns her head, the desire to see my reaction to this disclosure burning fiercely in her eyes. My curly blond locks surprise her; she squints at my face, trying to peer past them.

"I said don't turn around." I keep my voice low and menacing. Guzman obediently twists her head away from me and holds her hands up in the universal gesture of surrender. I go on the attack. "Have you no shame, attempting to exploit the most tender and vulnerable wound that woman has to carry?"

"Who are you and why do you care?" Guzman retorts.

She's got spunk; I'll give her that.

"I believe Stephanie Regaldo is involved in the disappearance of a woman and her son," the agent continues. "I think I'm within rights to tell a lie if it means they can be located."

"Betsy and Bear Elliott are entirely safe," I assure her. "Now listen to me, because I am going to say this only once. You've heard about the Knox Pharmaceuticals scandal?"

Guzman nods.

"Start here," I say, tucking a flash drive into her palm. "You'll see that Roger Elliott dumped a ton of their stock just before it broke. Elliott's also responsible for channeling the money that was used to pay for murdering a Knox employee, Leslie Virgenes."

Maggie Guzman turns again, unable to hide her shocked dismay at this revelation.

"Turn around! And leave Betsy and Bear in peace. After an argument in Italy last year that got ugly, Betsy tried to leave Roger. He threatened to kill her and their boy if she ever tried again. Betsy's tip saved the life of the other key witness in the Knox case. Now that Elliott will be exposed, he will be even more vicious."

I let silence fall again.

"His money can buy a long reach," I murmur in her ear. "Don't add any more odds in his favor."

I back away from Guzman slowly, my sneaker-clad feet padding soundlessly on the playground's springy flooring. I keep watch on her as trees and the falling darkness swallow me up.

She finally senses my departure and spins, her eyes desperately searching for me in the shadows.

But it's as if I was never there.

Acknowledgments

I loved writing this novel. I know that part of the mythology of the writer requires us to be tortured, battling the blank page with fevered angst, and while I did have my moments of doubt and struggle in this process, for the most part writing this book was a joy. I attribute that joy to the support I had around me.

Kate Miciak, my amazing editor, knows how much I rely on her support and guidance because I tell her all the time, but I would like to acknowledge her again here. I am also grateful for the support of the entire team at Ballantine/Random House: Kara Welsh, Kim Hovey, Sharon Propson, Allison Schuster, Quinne Rogers, Loren Noveck, Denise Cronin and her team, and the many others with whom I don't interact, but who are involved in the process. I'd also like to thank my excellent reps Emma Sweeney, Darryl Taja, Marcy Morris, Andrew Howard, Ian Greenstein, Katie McCaffrey, and Lynn Fimberg.

I am very grateful to David Sebastiani, who generously provided background and technical support about the FBI and became a friend along the way. I also have to thank fellow author Tom Avitabile, who read an early unfinished draft and was both enormously kind and helpful in providing inspiration that allowed me to take the novel to the next level. I'd also like to acknowledge Hannah

Phenicie for being a valuable early reader and an especially solid human being, and Richard Geddes for letting me ruthlessly pick his brain about Hong Kong.

A deep and heartfelt thanks to all of my readers. To the Burial Society street team and Facebook discussion group: You are all amazing and I thank you for your support. I also have to give a shout-out to my original super fan Cathy Shouse; I will never forget our weekend of icy rain and spirited conversation in Indy.

My personal team, the friends and family who always have my back, you know who you are, but I'd like to acknowledge you here anyway. My kids, Raphaela and Xander, you amaze me constantly. Keep it up. May only love and peace envelop you always, along with Gary Hakman, Ed Sadowsky, Jonathan Sadowsky, Laura Steinberg, Ivan Sadowsky, Julia Sadowsky, Richard Sadowsky, Mary Clancy, Eric Sadowsky, Katherine Sadowsky, Suzanne Sadowsky, Heather Richardson, Sadie Carter, Josh Carter, Jacob Carter, Arielle Hakman, Daniel Hakman, Darius Margalith, Janet Cooke, Sean Smith, Ralph Hakman, Barbara Zerulik, Debbie Hakman, Robin Sax, Kingsley Smith, Laina Cohn, Michelle Raimo, Deb Aquila, Betsy Stahl ("Betsy Elliott" is for you), Debbie Liebling, Analia Rey, Katrina Kudlick, Tarek Bishara, Matthew Mizel, Sukee Chew, Brenda Goodman, Robin Swicord, Wendy Leitman, Felicia Henderson, Lisa Kislak, Shandiz Zandi, Ruth Vitale, Jeff Stanzler, Kathy Boluch, Linda Bower, Debbie Huffman, and Judy Bloom. Alexandra Seros, Andrew Wood, Jan Oxenberg, Cathleen Young, Nicole Yorkin, Rebecca Asoulin, Sue Ann Fishkin, my wonderful community of USC students, both current and former, and all the women of the Woolfpack. I am indeed blessed.

I would also like to acknowledge Hedgebrook, where I began this draft while co-teaching the screenwriters lab. That place is magic.

ABOUT THE AUTHOR

NINA SADOWSKY has written numerous original screenplays and adaptations for such companies as The Walt Disney Company, Working Title Films, and Lifetime Television. She was the executive producer of *The Wedding Planner,* has produced many other films, and was president of Meg Ryan's Prufrock Pictures. Sadowsky is the program director for NYU Los Angeles, a Global Programs initiative that provides an experiential learning environment for students preparing for careers in the entertainment and media industries. This is her third novel, following *Just Fall* and *The Burial Society*. She is at work on her next novel.

ninarsadowsky.com
Facebook.com/nina.sadowsky
Twitter: @sadowsky_nina
Instagram: @ninasadowsky

ABOUT THE TYPE

This book was set in Sabon, a typeface designed by the well-known German typographer Jan Tschichold (1902–74). Sabon's design is based upon the original letter forms of sixteenth-century French type designer Claude Garamond and was created specifically to be used for three sources: foundry type for hand composition, Linotype, and Monotype. Tschichold named his typeface for the famous Frankfurt typefounder Jacques Sabon (c. 1520–80).